D0879767

B E S T
LESBIAN
EROTICA
2005

B E S T
LESBIAN
EROTICA
2005

Series Editor

Tristan Taormino

**Selected and
Introduced by**

Felice Newman

CLEIS
PRESS

Copyright © 2005 by Tristan Taormino. Introduction © 2005 by Felice Newman.

All rights reserved. Except for brief passages quoted in newspaper, magazine, radio, or television reviews, no part of this book may be reproduced in any form or by any means, electronic or mechanical, including photocopying, recording, or information storage or retrieval system, without permission in writing from the publisher.

Published in the United States by Cleis Press Inc.,
P.O. Box 14697, San Francisco, California 94114.
Printed in the United States.
Cover design: Scott Idleman
Cover photograph: Celesta Danger
Text design: Frank Wiedemann
Cleis logo art: Juana Alicia
First Edition.
10 9 8 7 6 5 4 3 2 1

"Frozen" © 2003 by Andrea Dale first appeared in *Dyke the Halls* edited by Cecilia Tan (Circlet Press, 2003); "Envy" © 2004 by Teresa Lamai first appeared online at www.erotica-readers.com (March 2004); "My Debut as a Slut" © 2004 by Jean Roberta first appeared online at www.sliptongue.com.

TABLE OF CONTENTS

Foreword
Tristan Taormino

I wrote my first piece of lesbian erotica in 1992 accidentally. I was a junior in college and had just come off a crazy summer in Los Angeles where I did a stint as a go-go dancer at a lesbian bar. It was full of skimpy outfits, hot butches, and dyke drama. I wanted to capture the intensity of the experience, the exhibitionism, the power exchanges. I wanted to convey how the story was written in and on my body. Sexual desire and awakening lay in every blue sequin of the narrator's bra, in every sweaty encounter, yet I didn't start out to write erotica *per se*. But there were fingers shoved in pussies, cocks strapped on, and shuddering orgasms...so it became erotica. After I graduated, I worked on the piece and submitted it to *On Our Backs*, where it was rejected. I kept writing. A year later, the story was accepted by Lesléa Newman for an anthology, and in 1995 it was first published in *The Femme Mystique*.

That year, my friend Michael Thomas Ford, a fellow writer, and I had sent a joint book proposal to Cleis Press for an annual his-n-hers anthology series called *Best Gay Erotica* and *Best Lesbian Erotica*. Our idea was to collect the top erotic writing of the year culled from self-published zines, open mikes, and the libidinous minds of a growing network of writers whose sexually explicit work deserved a bigger audience. Store bookshelves held plenty of gay male smut, we argued, although most of it was not very well written, edited, or marketed. Its lesbian counterpart was harder to find, with a few notable exceptions. Naiad Press romance novels featured little explicit sex except for the novels of Robbi Sommers. Boston-based Alyson Books published a couple of anthologies with unfortunate titles like *Bushfire* and *Afterglow* (my apologies to whoever named them; they just didn't sound like they had hot sex waiting between the pages). Alyson also published the groundbreaking erotica of Pat Califia. There had to be other Pat Califias out there in the queer universe, and I was determined to find them. Susie Bright had just published *Best American Erotica*. Susie kicked major ass with the *Herotica* series and the then-new *Best American Erotica* series, but I could find no by-dykes-for-dykes-about-dykes equivalent. I wanted to put together a book of sharply written (literary even!), well-edited, intelligent, sexy stories unafraid to be sold with a dirty cover and to embrace its smutty self out loud and proud, a book that refused to be relegated to the top (unreachable) shelf, the bottom (out of sight) shelf, or only the shelves of adult bookstores.

Cleis Press publisher Frédérique Delacoste invited us to lunch to discuss our idea. When Mike and I scheduled a trip to the Bay Area and confirmed our meeting, we didn't realize that "lunch" meant we'd be sitting in her living room chatting over homemade food. Ever the gracious host, she fed us fabulous breads and cheeses, a vegetable pâté, and a huge salad. With her sparkling eyes and French accent, she was warm and inviting, but I knew then she was a shrewd businesswoman. She hadn't come as far as she had based on bad decisions. She offered us dessert—the tiniest piece of some of the richest, most delicious chocolate I've ever tasted—and then told us the projects were a go.

Putting together the very first collection proved to be quite a struggle. Although lesbian erotica was in its infancy as a genre, everyone seemed to already have a clear idea of what it was, and how their work wasn't it. I coaxed, coddled, and convinced until I got a group of amazing stories. *Best Lesbian Erotica 1996* came out in January, with a stunning photo on the cover: no well-lit piece of fruit with vulvic implications or mysterious hand on murky body part, but instead a shot by dyke photographer Phyllis Christopher of the real-life lesbian couple Shar Rednour and Jackie Strano unmistakably having sex.

It's been a decade since this series debuted, and cover dykes Shar and Jackie are still together and, in my humble opinion, hotter than ever. But their union remains one of the few elements of that first book that is the same as it was. *Best Lesbian Erotica* has evolved amidst a backdrop of huge changes in the dyke world: the relaunch of *On Our Backs,* a new dyke sex and porn revolution, the coming out of celebrities and public figures, and unprecedented mainstream media inclusion and visibility—to mention just a few.

With each year, the number of submissions I receive for the series increases, as does the quality and creativity of the writing. The sheer volume of lesbian erotica—in magazines, in books, and on the Web—has increased tenfold. A genre that was once fringe and underground not only has found its way into major bookstore chains but has its own section; in addition, lesbian erotica has spawned writing classes, warrants reviews in literary journals, and has been recognized by the LGBT community as a vital, valuable contribution to queer literature. We even have our own category at the Lambda Literary Awards, the significance of which cannot be overstated. I believe these forms of recognition have given people permission to write what they want without fear of being pigeonholed or branded a lightweight or hack because they write erotica, and have even made it possible for some writers to concentrate on sexually explicit writing and publish widely.

It's not just the numbers and the acknowledgments that have grown. I believe that the very notion of what constitutes erotic writing has expanded as well; for over the years, in addition to short stories, *Best Lesbian Erotica* has featured novel excerpts, poetry, and performance art texts in an eclectic range of subject matter. The different themes that emerge each year are fascinating. In 1996, many of the stories had a dark, dreamy, other-worldly quality, as if lesbian desire existed in an alternative universe (sometimes it sort of does). By the time of the 1999 collection, I could see how butch/femme, an iconic dynamic in dyke relationships, was thriving, in all its complexity and glory. By 2002 I was struck by how powerful emotions—adoration, longing, love, obsession, revenge— fueled the year's best stories. This year, I felt overwhelmed (in a good way) by the number of submissions I received that featured cocksucking as a central plot point. (Felice Newman, this year's judge, believes initiation stories, her personal favorite, topped the list of erotic scenarios.)

I believe that all the submissions I receive *do* reflect lesbian sex in America and that lesbian erotica *does* take the pulse of what is making our cunts wet and our hearts beat a little faster. I also think that the relationship between sex and sex writing is symbiotic: Our writing has changed as a reflection of our sex lives' evolving, and our sex lives have shifted because of the proliferation of sex writing.

Undeniably, the writers behind the stories—their experiences, their writing, their courage, their vision—form the backbone of this series. They make it layered, insightful, seductive, inspiring. They make the whole thing worth doing and reading. Over the years, this series has showcased the writing of literary legends like Dorothy Allison, Pat Califia, Chrystos, Cheryl Clarke, Cherríe Moraga, Joan Nestle, and Carol Queen. It has given voice to writers who've gone on to their own successes, writers like Lucy Jane Bledsoe, T Cooper, Alison Smith, Elizabeth Stark, and Terry Wolverton. It has spawned a new generation of erotica writers, each with their own growing body of work, including Rachel Kramer Bussel, Skian McGuire, Peggy Munson, and Alison Tyler. Several writers published in this series have gone on to write their own books, become professors, transition from female to male, become parents, get married, and it's exciting to watch their careers and life-changes from afar.

I would like to pay tribute to three very special contributors. Nancy Stockwell, whose story "Lucky Girls" appeared in *Best Lesbian Erotica 1996,* died of complications from a double-lung transplant in 1999. In 2001, Susan Rosenberg (a contributor to *Best Lesbian Erotica 1999*) was released from prison—where she was incarcerated for sixteen years—after her sentence was commuted by President Bill Clinton. Heather Lewis—who was guest judge of the first anthology, a contributor to the 1997 edition, and my friend and mentor—took her own life in 2002. I dedicate this book to Heather, who helped me get this series off the ground, and whose talent, generosity, wit, and candor I will miss forever.

Editing this collection has brought me into contact with some of the most talented, eccentric, mesmerizing, challenging people I will ever know. It has been even more rewarding to meet in person the scribes behind the stories. When I travel to do a reading and get to greet people in the flesh, I find it tremendously exciting. I sometimes also get the scoop on the back story of the story I selected for the book. It's fascinating whenever I find out that a story I love is all completely true, or totally made up. It's always unexpected, the way it goes, which

I think points to the fierce complexities of our sexual realities and the sheer depth of our collective erotic imagination. Wherever these tales come from, they are built on our erotic truths, real or imagined. These are the stories of what keeps us up at night, what drives us, what haunts us, what turns us on, what connects us to our bodies and to each other.

Tristan Taormino
New York City
September 2004

Introduction
Felice Newman

I live to make your clit hard. I want to make you need to beat off. I'll be happy when you feel your cunt pulse with blood, your asshole pucker.

I want you to call your girl in the middle of the afternoon and tell her things that make her squirm in her pantyhose. I want you to crouch low behind your computer screen and post a personal ad on LesbiaNation, Lesbotronic, ClassicDykes, LeatherDyke, Technodyke, Strap-on.org, one finger ready on a function key to clear the screen, another gently stroking the seam in the crotch of your jeans.

I want you to think about sex when you get up in the morning and when you go home at night. I want you to be startled by the smell of your own heat rising from your crotch. I want the taste of butch cock on your tongue. I want *girlsex* flashing in your brain like neon in the elevator, subway, traffic jam, sidewalk crowded with people hurrying away from their jobs.

I want you suddenly to remember that you have a body, to swim in the juice of your erotic need until your workaday skin sloughs off and all that's left of you is your pulpy hot blood-engorged self.

I don't want you to forget for a minute that *sex* is why you call yourself *lesbian queer bisexual.*

I want you to know that you are alive.

Ten years ago, when Tristan Taormino proposed the idea of an annual "best" lesbian erotica series, she invited writers to expand the definition of what could be considered "sex writing" or "erotica," or, for that matter, "lesbian." "Send me the stuff everyone else won't touch," she said, smut too hard-core to print in a book and literary fiction that doesn't read like your typical erotica story.

> *I had been reading some hot, fierce, sexy fiction and poetry in small publications and homemade zines; I was impressed with the erotically-charged work of new writers I had heard at literary events and open mics in New York City. Because of the carnal content of their work, these writers weren't being published in mainstream books and magazines. There was an entire body of work waiting to be tapped into that was not only arousing but also made you think.*

She chose judges who themselves were literary and cultural icons: Heather Lewis, Jewelle Gomez, Jennifer Levin, Chrystos, Joan Nestle, Patrick Califia, Amber Hollibaugh, Cheryl Clarke, and Michelle Tea. She invited a generation of writers to open up the genre of girl-meets-girl erotica to stories of "lust, memory, obsession, attraction, anticipation, longing, love, hate, transgression."

The permission that gave writers and readers cannot be overstated.

Lesbian sex, which had been lurking on the fringes of lesbian literature, no longer had to be sanitized to fit the formula of lesbian fiction. Love indeed had conquered all, including our sex writing, which often masqueraded as romance, with the "good parts" floating above the grit and sweat of our lives. Even books explicitly intended as erotica, books filled with clit-thrumming sex stories, were packaged softly. To sell lesbian sex as sex was just too blatant.

Best Lesbian Erotica gave us permission to get real. It was not always pretty, the protagonist did not always get the girl (who may or may not actually have *been* a girl), and the plot did not always neatly conclude with a hyperbolic spray of girl cum. These stories did not give their allegiance to the three-act-play predictability of the genre.

Tristan gathered the best lesbian sex writing and the widest range of sexual experience, and if you don't think that has given you the means to expand your own sexual horizons, think again. In the introduction to *Best Lesbian Erotica 1996,* she identified a few conventions of lesbian erotic stories that had already become standards:

> *The is-she-or-isn't-she-a-dyke narrative of wonder and seduction. The one-night-stand-who-became-the-girlfriend tale. The "butchflip" story of unexpected role reversals. The very existence of such conventions suggests that there is a recognizable (dare I say) canon of lesbian erotic writing with identifiable authors, publishers, and even themes.*

Five years later, in introducing *Best of the Best Lesbian Erotica,* she previewed the forty-four stories she had chosen as the cream-of-the-cream of the more than 140 stories published by then:

...war stories, ghost stories, initiation stories,
and one night stand stories. Stories full of knife-
wielding tops, cocksucking femmes, basketball-
bouncing butches, greedy bottoms, budding porn
stars, naughty nuns, Jewish newlyweds, hungry
boydykes, and courageous FtMs. They are players
in dark fairy tales, femme-on-femme fantasies,
transgressive tales, and personal ad encounters.
This all takes place in movie theaters, bubble
baths, gym locker rooms, S/M play parties, gay
male sex clubs, hotel rooms, and martial arts
dojos. As they rub up against one another, these
erotic pieces boldly contemplate, demonstrate,
and celebrate the complexity, uniqueness—the
muff diving mélange of lesbian sexuality.

Today our sexual options, both in print and in the sheets, continue to grow wider and wider.

Long before I got to live the kind of sex life I wanted for myself, I wrote a story about it. I know a lot of writers who can say that—even Patrick Califia wrote "Jesse," the classic lesbian S/M story, years before ever wielding (or yielding to) a whip. Before that, I read every piece of lesbian erotica I could get my hands on and a prodigious quantity of both gay and straight porn in which I crossed gender to get off.

What we have now in lesbian erotica makes us rich.

The credit for *Best Lesbian Erotica* goes to Tristan, who reads and reads and reads, writes about sex in print and online, shoots sex TV shows and porn films, crisscrosses the country teaching workshops and giving lectures, brews storms in academe, and sets women's eyes afire with lust and possibility. Tristan is dedicated to good-fucks-for-all and has the energy to back it up.

At Cleis Press we are so proud of Tristan Taormino and *Best Lesbian Erotica*, each year the most intelligent and provocative lesbian erotica anthology available—and now winner of the Lambda Literary Award two years running. From the beginning, we took a stand: Lesbian erotica, we believed, should combine high-quality writing and hot sex; it should be subtle and searing; it should be complicated in ways that provoke us to look at ourselves. With Tristan, we have held to that standard, publishing more than a hundred writers in a partnership we hope will continue for decades more.

As publisher of the *Best Lesbian Erotica* series, I am the editorial voyeur to hundreds of imaginary and thinly veiled (or unveiled) acts of sex. What I want is the knowledge of your pleasure. I want you to read stories that describe the sex you are having now and the sex you have always wished for. I want the stories you read to sharpen your need for more sex, different sex, the sex you've never admitted you think of alone in the dark when your hand snakes down your belly. I want your desire to become irresistible, like a force of nature pushing you beyond reason. I'll settle for no less than torment. Why? Because I want your need to become inescapable. When a detail or image or scenario from one of these stories lodges in your brain, I want it to feel like a hot poker forcing you to action. Go ahead. Unburden yourself from *if only* and *what if*.... Go get it.

And I want to imagine you doing it. Why? Because that's *my* thing.

You don't think I do this out of altruism, do you? You're my kink. Now do it for me.

Oh, yeah. Just like that.

Felice Newman
San Francisco
September 2004

How I Do It
Jack Perilous

Here's how I do it: on the corner of the desk. On the corners of the sink, table, kitchen counter. It started with my rocking horse, when I was three. When I sat back, leaned forward, butterflied my proto-ballerina legs, I felt something I didn't know women had to work for. For a while I did it everywhere, then after I was shamed (for that, for sucking my thumb till the age of eight, for glasses, for being Jewish, for whatever), just on the bathroom sink, door locked. At nine, I learned from a child development book what it was I was doing. Masturbating. Having orgasms. It was normal, like fleeting feelings of homosexual attraction. At twelve, I imagined my best friend watching me do it. I imagined watching her do it, too. I imagined her kissing my back and neck as I fucked myself. Now it's the desk in my Brooklyn bedroom, the one my girlfriend got in parts for free. Leaning forward, legs butterflying, hands clutching—sometimes I let myself balance on my clit. I imagine my girlfriend sucking my cock with her pink-lipped mouth. To be honest, it takes me less than two minutes to come.

Here's how I have sex: with her. With her, not her with

me. I work on her ten, twenty, forty minutes, till my hands are soaking, her blond-skinned tits and pink nipples rubbing against mine. I make her say, "Please let me come," and I make her come. When she screams, that's it. I hold her head back by the hair and watch. Her clit shakes and she soaks me, her torso convulses. Her face is just gorgeous. I come along with her. "Thanks," she says. I kiss her whole long body, her hot smooth skin, touch her tits. She swings her legs over the side of the bed, and I straddle her left knee as I once straddled that rocking horse, as I straddle the desk when she's not there, and she tells me the story of how I first captured and fucked her—a cops-and-robbers, cock-and-pussy story—and I stare at her tits, her wide-open mouth, and the dark hair that peeks out as I pull down her panties; I scissor my legs, rub my butch clit all over her girl knee, and come on her like a fucking dirty old perv, an explosion in ninety seconds flat.

Two Girls in a Basement
Cheryl B.

We were what you would have called mall chicks, typical Jersey girls with painted-on stonewashed jeans, tiny fringed T-shirts stretched tight across our tits, and long hair that invited petting. Our nails were perfectly painted rectangles that extended way past the tips of our fingers, shining like new linoleum.

The summer of 1989, I graduated from high school and although I didn't plan on it, I was about to figure out I was a lesbian. That summer I moved out of my tiny childhood bedroom and into my parents' basement. I didn't know what I wanted to do with my life and I couldn't afford to live on my own. But I couldn't stand to hear their fighting anymore. So I bought a soundproof door at the Home Center where I worked as a head cashier and had my ex-boyfriend Guido (yes, that was really his name) install it for me. That way I could think, figure things out.

As he worked, I stood below him on the stairs and inspected my acrylic nails, which in my memory of that day were done in a bright purple with alternating white and gold stripes. Occasionally I handed Guido a tool from a big orange box he'd brought with him or gave him a rag to wipe up the sweat that had gathered on the hairs that poked out from underneath his tank top mingling with his gold chains.

When he was finished with the door Guido pulled it closed and we were alone on the stairs leading down to my new "apartment." He had done a good job and I told him so with a hug and a peck on the cheek.

Guido pulled me toward him and put his hand on my ass. "How's about a little candy, Lina?" he asked as he squeezed my left buttcheek. Guido was five years older than me and we'd been dating since I was sixteen. My parents wanted me to marry him because he was a plumber and "you always need a plumber."

I looked down and saw the bulge in Guido's pants growing. I could feel his eyes burning hopefully on the top of my head. He wanted a blow job. I can't say I wasn't slightly tempted. Guido, for all his Guido-ness, was a good-looking guy and during our relationship he got a blow job every day, sometimes more than one.

Normally, I would happily get on my knees for him, mouth hungry, eyes wide. Not so much out of lust for Guido. I don't think I was ever even in love with him, but I just liked doing things with my mouth.

But that night was different. That night was Girls Night In, something I'd read about in a magazine, probably *Cosmo*, where as a show of your female independence you're supposed to hang out with your girlfriends, leaving the guys to themselves...or something like that. Besides, Guido and I had broken up more than a month ago, and rumor had it that he was seeing Christie, who was a total bitch, not to mention a complete slut. He could get her to blow him.

"I don't think Christie would appreciate that too much," I teased him playfully, pushing him away from me. But really I wanted him to leave, because I had to get ready for my guests.

Actually it was only one guest, Tammy, since most of the girls I invited already had plans with their boyfriends, and one actually said her boyfriend wouldn't let her come. So much for female independence.

"Where'd you hear about Christie?"

"Oh, you know, around," I said looking at my watch.

"You got something better to do tonight?"

"Yeah, you know I told you I was going to have the girls over."

"Oh, yeah, the women's lib thing."

"No. It's just like a sleepover."

"That's kind of hot, all you girls snuggled in together," Guido said dreamily.

"You sicko," I said. Why wouldn't he just leave. "Oh you, get out of here," I said, punching him playfully. I opened the door that led up into the kitchen. My parents were fighting. Dad sat at the table in a dirty T-shirt, his tiny boom box in his hands, trying to find his favorite country music station. Mom was over by the sink, angrily scrubbing a pot.

"Can't we listen to normal music for once?" my mother complained, in her North Jersey accent. "Instead of that cowboy shit?" She was actually annoyed at my father's crush on Naomi Judd.

"Oh shut up, will ya?" my father retorted. He then looked at me. "You been playing with this radio?"

I shook my head. "Why would I touch your stupid radio?"

My mother turned around, ready to either start in again with my father or put me down. Then she noticed Guido and she changed her tone. "Oh hello, Guido," she cooed, coming over to him. My mother really liked Guido.

"Hello, Mrs. Gennaro," he said, leaning in to give my mother a kiss. "Hey, Mr. G.," he said to my father, who barely looked up from the radio to acknowledge him.

"I see you put the door up for Lina. She's so ashamed of

her parents, she wants a separation. It's like the Berlin wall," my mother said.

My father found his country station at last. "All right!" he said, "Hey Guido, ever hear of The Judds? They're having a live concert on the radio tonight."

My mother spoke over him. "Are you staying for dinner, Guido?" This could pose a problem. Guido really liked my mother's cooking. Maybe *they* should get together.

Tammy would be over in less than an hour and I needed to get ready. Before Guido could answer I said, "Oh no, he's on his way out. He's a very busy guy," and led him to the front door.

I turned my cheek as he leaned in to kiss me on his way out.

He looked at me, pointing his finger. "Don't be turning into some dyke on me." And then he added in all seriousness, "Don't drop the soap."

"Have a good night, Guido," my mother called from the kitchen as I closed the door on him.

Tammy was a new friend I met a few months ago in aerobics class. Turns out we both pretended to have cramps one day and wound up together in the locker room of Living Well Lady sneaking cigarettes by the window.

I noticed a gold bracelet she wore around her slender wrist: a cut-out heart covered in tiny diamonds on a thin rope chain. It sparkled in the light coming in from the window and reflected off the tiles in the bathroom.

"I like your bracelet," I said.

"Thanks," she answered, taking another drag off her cigarette.

"Can I see?" I held out my hand and she lifted her wrist. I fingered the diamonds, touching the soft skin on either side of the bracelet. "Nice," I said, and for some reason I didn't let go of her hand right away. Suddenly I was confused. I wasn't sure if I was appraising the bracelet or the skin on the underside of her arm.

"Got it from the boyfriend," she said, taking her wrist back and inspecting the bracelet herself, "for Valentine's day."

"Cool," I said, taking a final drag off my cigarette before stubbing it out on the windowsill. As I did this, I snuck a look at her and noticed for the first time that her silver leotard had a cut-out midsection. Her stomach was a combination of firm and curvy. I wanted to touch the skin in the center. It had a beautiful, bronze sheen, the perfect tan. I was filled with a strange combination of jealousy and attraction and I totally lost myself in the gaze. I continued to watch her. Her lips when closed were a glossy, pink bow. When she opened her mouth to take another drag off her cigarette, her teeth were like perfect white Chiclets, her tongue wet and red.

"So you got a boyfriend?" she asked. I quickly stopped checking out her tongue and shook my head.

"No. I mean yes, his name is Guido," I said, embarrassed although I didn't know why.

She smiled. "Yeah, I know what you mean. Sometimes I think it would be good to be single again too."

I smiled shyly at her and we became friends. Over the next few weeks we shopped together, modeling clothes for each other in the dressing room of Macy's. Tried on high heels together at the mall and helped each other into lingerie at Victoria's Secret. At one point while I was buttoning her into a black lace bustier, her blonde hair brushed against my hands and I had the urge to slip my hands around her waist, push her against the wall, and rub myself all over her. Instead, I dropped my hands to my sides. But I swear there was this bizarre sexual energy flowing between us. I think she felt it too because we could hardly look at each other the rest of the day.

Now she was due to come over in, like, twenty minutes!

And my basement room was a mess! And I barely had my makeup done! And I hated all my clothes! Tammy usually wore short skirts. So I decided to wear tight jeans as a contrast. I put on my push-up bra and pulled a cut-off Bon Jovi T-shirt out of my drawer. I splashed a little perfume on my wrist, smudged some blue eyeliner on my lids, and gave my long, dark hair a once-over with a generous spray of Aqua Net. I turned off the overhead lights and flicked on a few old table lamps. I took my favorite tape out and placed it by the stereo. I poured some Doritos into a bowl. Put out a few Diet Cokes and took a long sip from a bottle of Jack Daniels, then threw it under one of the cushions on the couch. I wasn't much of a drinker but I thought I could use a little booster. I slipped my feet into a pair of heels I'd bought with Tammy one day. They were her favorites: pointy toed with a four-inch spiked heel in a midnight blue that matched the blue in my T-shirt. Tammy said they made me look like a porn star. And sitting there waiting for her on my parents' old couch, I felt like the sexiest woman on earth.

At this point, I have to make a confession: The Girls Night In thing was only a front. I put the invitations out there, knowing the other girls would decline. I just wanted Tammy to myself.

I heard the doorbell ring upstairs. She was right on time. I'd already instructed my mother to let her in. And I could hear Tammy's heels on the floor above following my mother down the hall to my basement door. I was so nervous, I was shaking. I stood at the bottom of the steps and could see the doorknob turning, hear my mother's voice burrowing its way through insulated steel, repeating the "Berlin wall" line. As the door opened the light from the kitchen shone down the stairs, and I could hear The Judds droning from my father's radio in the background.

Tammy stood at the top of the stairs in a pink skirt so

short I could see her baby-blue panties. Her hair was big and blond and wild. She made her way down the stairs in her fuchsia spiked heels. My mother stayed on in the doorway as I regarded Tammy coming toward me.

"I've never heard of this, two beautiful girls hanging out in a smelly basement when you could be out on dates," my mother said. "I don't know where you kids came from."

Tammy reached the bottom of the stairs.

"You look great," I said.

"So do you, Lina," she replied. I could tell by the way she looked at me that we were there for the same reason.

"I swear, if I had your figure I'd be out playing the field. I wouldn't be sitting in some basement full of my parents' old furniture," my mother continued from the top of the steps.

"Thanks, Ma," I said as I made my way up the stairs to lock the door.

"Remember, you're only young once," she continued as I closed the door and locked it.

By the time I got down the stairs, Tammy was already sitting on the couch, one long leg tucked under her while the other stretched out across the couch. She was taking a sip from a Diet Coke and fingering the dingy material on the couch.

"Sorry about the furniture. It's kind of crappy," I apologized.

"I think it's so cool you did this. It's like you have your own little place. I'm still sleeping in my little room in my parents' house. There are still unicorns stenciled on the walls!"

I crossed the room and stood in front of her sprawled leg on the couch. I expected her to move the leg for me to sit down but when she didn't, I sort of slid in underneath it, placing her fuchsia heel on my lap. Suddenly I felt like a guy, or like I was the guy or was playing the guy's role or something. I needed a drink. I reached under the couch cushion where I'd stashed the Jack Daniels and pulled out the bottle, taking a long sip. I offered the bottle to Tammy even though she doesn't really drink much either. She took a bigger sip than me.

I tried to make small talk. "So, have you seen the new clothes at The Limited?"

I realized I'd begun running my hand up her leg. Her skin was unbelievably smooth. I wondered what she used—whether she shaved or waxed or….

Tammy reached forward, pushing me back on the couch. She straddled me, grinding her hips into me, and kissed me in a way that I could only describe as "with abandon" as if she wanted to swallow me whole. It really knocked my socks off. But I was not to be outdone. I pushed her off me and got her flat on the couch. I reached my hand up her shirt, felt the lace of her bra, and I swear—I soaked my panties right there on the spot. I could feel the wetness in the confines of my tight jeans.

"Ohhhh," I moaned. I reached down and kissed Tammy, mashing my mouth into hers. I worked my hands around her back to unsnap her bra and to my amazement did it on my first try! Tammy quickly pulled off her tiny shirt, which I noticed was airbrushed "Jersey Girls Best in the World!" We both looked at the shirt and began giggling.

"I guess I picked the right shirt," Tammy laughed.

She had picked the right shirt and the right skirt and the right panties, which to my surprise I quickly pulled off so I could feel between her legs. Tammy pulled her skirt up farther—at this point it was practically a belt—and spread her legs for me. I don't know if there is such a thing as a moment in which you "turn gay" but if there is, it was that moment looking down at Tammy. It sounds cheesy, like something from a bad porn film, but the thought of my hands, with their long, purple nails, grazing her neatly shaved pussy is something that to this day still turns me on. I can still feel her heat and the wetness and the uncontrollable excitement let loose in my body. I was a baby femme-top and I didn't even know it.

We kissed and rubbed some more, got my pants off, sucked each other's nipples, then she fingered me, her hot pink nails making a circle around my clit. Somehow I wound up kneeling in front of her on the floor. And I buried my face in her, at first poking around with my tongue, trying to figure out what to do. She ran her hands through my hair and moaned, spreading her legs farther apart, moving her pussy closer and closer to me. And I just went for it, licking her in tiny circles, then long laps, then little flickerings on her clit until I felt her stiffen, then shake and moan. And I swear, as she came I felt the earth move, the room spin. She pushed my head away from her.

"Please stop, I'm gonna fall apart," she laughed, falling back on the couch and closing her legs.

I sat down next to her and we both began giggling.

"It's a good thing I got the soundproof door," I said.

"I'm sorry, was I loud? My boyfriend says I'm loud."

I could feel myself frowning. "Let's not talk about him now."

We sat there, my head on her shoulder, and, amazingly, I began to drift off.

"Hold on there," Tammy said, touching my face. "It's your turn."

"Oh, really?" I said.

"Oh, yeah," she said, getting down on her knees.

"Wait," I said. "I forgot the music."

I got up and crossed the room to the stereo, and in true Jersey Girl form picked up my Led Zeppelin 4 tape, popped it in the player, and pressed repeat.

Our Women Know What to Do
Madeleine Oh

"Is it too much to ask?"

Lying warm and replete after lovemaking, my body still weak from climaxing, I couldn't refuse Ahmet. "No. It's just...."

"Just what?" Ahmet asked, his breath warm against my face.

I couldn't say, "Too weird, too kinky." To a Turk, to a Muslim, it was a reasonable request. A cultural requirement, if I had any hope of fitting into his world. "I'm just not sure I can go to the beauty parlor and ask if they'll do my pussy when they wax my legs."

"Of course not!" His chest fluttered under my hand as he chuckled, a low and sexy sound that had the power to make me wet even when I still ached from the last time. "That is not how our women do it."

"How *do* your women do it?" I leaned up on one elbow, my fingers smoothing the soft pelt on his chest, and grinned.

"Woman!" He growled, rolling me on my back. "They show respect to their men and obey without question."

Yeah, right! I knew his sister, Leyla. She was my age, a

journalist, resolutely single, and as self-assured a woman as I'd ever known. But since he now lay on top of me, I chose not to belabor that point, or rather, I belabored his nipples with my fingers. Besides, curiosity got the better of me. "How *do* your women wax their pubes?"

He raised a dark, beautiful eyebrow. "How should I know? Women know that. I'll call Leyla."

That would be a conversation worth overhearing. I'm close to my brother, but discussing pubic hair removal? I think not.

It wasn't so with Ahmet and Leyla.

He called me the next day at work. "Leyla will expect you Thursday, after lunch." My day off and he knew it. "She will show you what to do, with her cousin Yildiz." Yildiz and who else? I'd never though of depilation as a social event, but what the hell—life had certainly been different since I'd taken a Turk to my bed. Ahmet was not your average midwesterner.

"Do I need to bring anything?" Towels? Razor blades? Baby oil? A covered dish?

In the pause, I imagined him raising his head and clicking his tongue, a sexy crease shaping between his eyebrows. "How should I know?" His voiced eased a little. "You will be there? She's making preparations."

"I'll be there." I hung up, scared. What had I agreed to?

On Thursday Leyla greeted me with a hug and offered mint tea in curved glasses. Cousin Yildiz smiled shyly as she handed me rose-flavored wafers and sesame cookies. I nibbled cookies and sipped the fragrant tea, my cold, nervous hands cupping the warm glass.

"Ahmet..." I began. Someone had to broach the reason for my visit in the middle of the afternoon.

Leyla dismissed her brother with a shrug. "What does he know?" Her dark eyes met mine, a suggestive smile curving her full mouth. I grinned back. So much for respect and obedience.

Leyla refilled my glass as Yildiz slipped out of the room.

A few minutes later I heard water running overhead. "Your bath," Leyla said, "to help you relax and soften your skin. The first time can be worrying." She put her hand on mine and gave a reassuring squeeze. "Trust me, I have done this since I was fifteen."

I took her word for that as my fingers meshed with hers. "I suppose so. This is very new to me."

"New can be very, very satisfying." Leyla stood up; I followed. We were joined at the palm and sort of rose together. "Come on."

A dark cloth hung over the bathroom window, leaving the room in twilight. Perfumed candles flickered in shallow brass cups, adding warmth to the already steamy bathroom. Scented bubbles came to the rim of the tub.

"Beautiful!" I said, and meant it. I wasn't sure what to say next. I didn't need to worry: Leyla was running the show.

"Get in and soak while we prepare." Leyla wrapped her arms around me. "Don't look so worried. We will take good care of you." She kissed me and swept out the door.

My fingers shook as I unbuttoned my blouse and unzipped my skirt. I was nervous as a virgin. Which, I supposed, was exactly what I was. I eased into the too-warm water and leaned back, chin in the bubbles, inhaling the strong scent of lavender and roses and trying to forget what was coming next. I lay there for ages, languid in the heat and the steam, more than content to spend the afternoon in the tub. In fact, the more I thought about it, I wasn't sure I really *wanted* a bald pussy, not even for Ahmet—although it was perhaps a small price for the best sex I'd ever had.

Either way, I was too relaxed to do much but stand up when Leyla appeared at the door holding a towel the size of a small sheet. If I'd felt lethargic before, I was positively boneless after Leyla's warm hands patted every inch of my skin. I barely had energy to pull the terry robe around me. Was it nervousness that made me trip on the rug by the bedroom door? Leyla caught me and helped me lie down on the king-sized bed.

The curtains were drawn, shutting out the afternoon and the world beyond this warm, sequestered room. More scented candles flickered around the room. Out of the corner of my eye I saw Yildiz stirring a small pot.

"Almost ready," she said. "Just let it cool a little."

"What is it?"

"Honey, beeswax, and lemon," she replied.

Was I nuts to lie here while a woman I'd never met before spread boiled-up honey on my pussy? Leyla's hands eased along the soft skin inside my thighs, spreading my legs. I'd never felt this vulnerable, or this relaxed.

"Lift up your hips." Leyla slid a pillow under the small of my back, tilting my hips upward. Before I quite came to terms with that, her hands closed over my ankles and set my feet flat on the bed. My legs spread, my pussy exposed, a tremor of apprehension skittered through me. What next?

"It's okay," Leyla soothed, her hand still lightly holding my ankle. "You're fine."

I wasn't. I was scared. I shut my eyes and wondered if it would hurt as much as leg waxing. It had to, and I was nuts—no matter how much confidence Ahmet had in women knowing what to do.

Leyla sensed my growing fear. "Don't worry." She settled behind me on the bed. "Yildiz does this for me. She is experienced." Leyla moved nearer, propping my head and shoulders against her chest. Reassured by her words and her closeness, I relaxed and looked straight down between my spread legs as Yildiz pulled up a small table and set the white enamel pan on a tiled trivet.

I watched, dry-mouthed and fascinated, as she clipped my curls with a small pair of scissors. Her fingers were cool and confident and I shivered. I'd been touched before, by lovers, doctors, nurses, but never with such gentleness and ease. I relaxed against Leyla's breasts and watched the younger woman between my legs. As she trimmed, Yildiz caught the clippings until her cupped hand was full of golden-brown curls.

"Your hair is the color of orange blossom honey," she said, admiring the heap of curls in her cupped hand before dropping them in a wastebasket.

I was halfway there—or was I? So far it had been easy, if embarrassing. It couldn't all be this painless. I tried to focus on the perfume of candles and beeswax as Yildiz smoothed rose-scented talc on my cropped pussy. Her touch soothed. It wasn't exactly a caress, more an encouragement.

"Now this will feel warm." She was right. Warm, pleasant, almost relaxing. It took only seconds for her to spread the golden paste on the left side of my pussy, and not much longer to take a strip of cotton fabric, gently press the heel of her hand into my crotch, and with a deft twist of her wrist, pull.

I let out a yowl like a crazed animal. My body arched off the bed in pain. I'd have been airborne if Leyla hadn't held my shoulders as Yildiz pressed her warm palm hard into my crotch.

I shivered, shuddered, and muttered a few choice epithets.

"That bit's over. It'll ease quickly," Leyla promised. Even as she spoke, the pain eased. Yildiz continued the pressure, now rocking her hand back and forth. Somehow the movement did ease the pain to a dull sting.

"You might have warned me," I said, relaxing as the sting slackened into an ache.

"It's not so bad, is it?" Yildiz asked, her hand still pulsing my gently throbbing skin.

"Not now," I admitted. A minute ago it hurt; now, under the ache, a strange pleasure stirred.

"It's just a few seconds," Yildiz said. She eased the pressure of her hand and gently rubbed her fingertips over my tingling skin. "That came away beautifully. Your skin is so fine and soft." She looked up and smiled, her dark eyes gleaming. "Rest a minute and I'll get the other side."

"I don't mind waiting." Heck, I wouldn't mind quitting now. Maybe Ahmet would like the halfway look.

"Not too long"—Leyla's hands rested over my collarbones like a warm caress—"or the mixture will cool. Then it sticks and hurts."

As if that first bit hadn't! "Let's get it done then." What had I said?

Yildiz repeated the spread, press, yank. This time I was ready and didn't yell to scare the pigeons off the roof. I managed with just a stifled groan and a slow shudder that set my breasts wobbling and my stomach quivering. I was more than ready for Yildiz to press hard on my throbbing flesh, and welcomed Leyla's soothing massage, kneading and stroking my shoulders and chest, her fingers stopping just short of my breasts.

"Let me see," I said as Yildiz slowed her rubbing and the pain eased. I'd had my eyes squeezed shut most of the time, but now a strange fascination had me wanting to look. I was almost bare. Reddened, still tender skin showed on both sides of my slit. A swatch of hair still decorated the top of my pussy and I felt rather than saw the thinner hair between my buttcheeks. "Are you taking it all off?"

"Oh, yes!" Leyla said, her breath warm in my ear. "We do everything."

I leaned back against her, her breasts flattening against my back as Yildiz spread gook across the top of my pussy.

"This may be harder," Yildiz said, setting down the thin brass spatula she used for spreading the warm paste. Harder? I almost croaked. The other two procedures hadn't exactly been fun. "Here." She took my hands, placing one on each side of the cooling paste. "Pull the skin tight."

I pulled for all I was worth and held my breath for luck. A

rip, a flash of pain, and my fingers relaxed as Yildiz eased the throbbing with her hands. I exhaled; the worst had to be over. I closed my eyes and breathed in as Leyla and Yildiz soothed my discomfort with knowing hands.

Leyla's hands now were on my breasts. Her gentle touch on my hard nipples had me wanting more. I blinked a minute. Was I nuts? Wanting a woman, even if she was a good friend, caressing my breasts? I gave up. Why not? Leyla was my friend, and a woman I hardly knew had her hands and fingers all over my pussy.

Yildiz plumped up the pillow I'd flattened with my shifting around before her hands spread my legs wider, smoothing my now bare pussy as if admiring her handiwork—or was it my body? I looked down, amazed at the sight of naked pink skin where I'd worn curls since puberty, mesmerized at the sight of golden brown fingers stroking my flushed skin.

Leyla eased back on the bed until I was almost lying flat, my head in her lap, my hips tilted above my head. Talk about exposed! But I was getting accustomed to soft female fingers on private parts. I even welcomed Yildiz's gentle stroking.

Her hands moved away and I braced, ready for the soft touch of her warm concoction and the sudden rip of pain. "Oh, dear." Yildiz tutted her tongue and I heard the pan clink down on the stove. "It's too cold. Let me warm it at little. You don't want it sticking to your skin."

She was right about that! Not that I minded lying there, my cheek against the soft fabric of Leyla's skirt, her hands on my shoulders, fingertips skimming my breasts. I felt groggy, inhaling the warm air redolent of roses and women. Was this what it had been like in the harems? Heady scents, heated rooms, and women preparing their bodies for sex?

"Steady now." Leyla's hands closed over the tops of my breasts and held me as I felt the warmth of Yildiz's concoction between my thighs and waited for the tug. Was I getting used to it, or was this part of me less sensitive? I still welcomed Yildiz's touch as her hand pressed away the ache, her fingers close to my slit and her breath warm on my thigh. The other side she took care of with equal efficiency, her fingers lingering. I realized I was getting wet. Had to be all the skin contact or...I no longer cared.

They had me on my belly now, lying diagonally across the bed, my head in Leyla's lap. I could smell her through her skirt. Or was that me? Or both of us? Was I getting turned on despite the pain and awkwardness? Was she? And what of it? I didn't *do* sex with women—or hadn't. I hadn't had my pussy denuded before, either.

I had that and plenty more to think about, but Leyla was placing my hands in position to spread my buttcheeks. Talk about embarrassing! "Is this necessary?" I asked. "Pussy" didn't include this part of me, in my opinion. Seemed it was vital, though, I held myself open. Waiting. I knew what to expect by now. Why was I getting my knickers in a twist? Especially since I wasn't wearing any. Wearing anything, for that matter. I was naked, prone and holding my bottom open for Yildiz to slather me up. Which she did with confidence and efficiency.

This time it hurt more than before. Why? Embarrassment? Shame at having another woman see my most private place? I'll never know what sent the hot tears running and soaking Leyla's skirt. I sobbed and sniffed. "I'm sorry. I don't know what came over me."

Leyla wiped away my tears with the pad of her finger. "I understand," she said, and kissed me.

What was so special about that? We were friends. She'd kissed me scores of times. But not like this. A gentle brush of her lips and I felt whole, renewed—and horny as hell. My pussy still hummed, my ass throbbed, my breasts ached, and my cunt was wet and wanting. Leyla smiled as she lifted her mouth from mine. I smiled back.

Without a word, Leyla rolled me on my back and stretched out beside me, a hand on my breast, her lips in my hair. This was nutty, crazy, and absolutely wonderful. As Leyla's lips met mine, I sighed and opened my mouth. Her fingers strummed my nipples, rippling arousal right through me. I quit thinking, abandoned myself over to sensation, and kissed her back. I forgot there was another woman in the room, until I felt Yildiz's fingers, spreading sweet oil on my pussy and between my thighs. It seemed only natural that those same fingers entered me, stretching and filling me as I groaned and raised my hips to bring her deeper. A mouth closed on one breast, fingers on another, and my entire body began the slow spiral climb. Between Leyla's teasing and Yildiz's touch, I was sighing and whimpering.

What was I doing? Feeling wonderful! Climbing! Wanting! Yildiz bent between my legs. The soft, damp touch of her tongue on my wet clit wrung a moan from me. I shuddered. My jaw wobbled. My stomach quivered. My knees shook. Yildiz touched me again, a soft, impudent dart of her tongue. I felt it through to my core. I groaned louder, my whole body arching off the bed. That soft tongue stabbed me once more. That was all I needed. I took off, yelling in the quiet room, leaping over the moon, soaring into the heavens, and landing like a boneless mass in the middle of the big bed.

Panting, gasping with satisfaction, I opened my eyes and met Yildiz's grin. "Incredible!" I managed to gasp out.

"Worth it?" Leyla asked in my ear.

Was she kidding! "Ahmet said you knew what to do."

They both laughed, high, lighthearted peals of female joy. "My brother," Leyla said with a slow, secretive smile, "doesn't know as much as he thinks he does."

She was right, but so was Ahmet. These women did know what to do.

Roulette
Shannon Cummings

Women got there earlier than the crowds at the nearby South of Market bars. Straight from work, proudly displaying the sweat of a day's work on their clothes. Tidying up would have been a sign of vanity, of femininity. A glob of pomade to grease the hair back was all the eveningwear they needed.

There was an unspoken rule that you couldn't park your bike in front of the club if it was smaller than someone's who had already arrived. Think your ride is better than someone else's, you better be prepared to defend it. The only exception was of course if you had a high femme riding bitch.

If you arrived late, you had to park your bike a few blocks away and hope you could get to the club without being roughed up by the neighborhood crew. A few trucks lined the alley out front. No one messed with you if you had a truck. It was assumed it was for work and was therefore off limits. Jobs were scarce, so if you could earn a living without losing your edge you were never ridiculed.

Lou had gone there on many occasions, sometimes returning home via the emergency room after bottles had been broken or blades pulled. Fights often started over motorcycles or the call of a pool shot. Or someone talking about how some stone had cracked.

The worst fight had happened after one girl had underestimated the locker room talk and bravado of both her lovers. While trading tales over whiskey, they realized just how much they had in common and ended up in a brawl. The next day they both called her to say they had defended her honor. But it was their own they were fighting for. One got a cut just above her eye; nearly blinded her, the doctor had said. The other's hand was sliced along the life-line, or was is it the love-line?, when she grabbed the blade swinging at her. She lost the use of her thumb and earned three months' disability leave from her machinists union. Women practiced their swaggers and rubbed their imaginary beards during pauses in conversation. It was a club for women with a rule of "no girls allowed." I was dying to go.

For six months, I had been crashing at Lou's place. I had run out on my last lover and showed up on her doorstep. I had taken over closet space and control of the tape deck, had started four kitchen fires, and had run up a long distance phone bill to my sister out east. Lou regularly threatened to kick me out but I would always coo to her until she got into bed so she could get to work on forgiving me. She was a good fuck and I was determined to stay. Sometimes when she was at work I would hustle some money at the pool hall to get by, pay a phone bill, or buy something sexy to wear so she wouldn't notice I had trashed her apartment. And her life. She was the first lover I ever had who knew a compliment should be taken as a request for more. I steadily stroked her ego and she let me stay.

"Dress sexy," Lou tells me. "We are going out."

I dress hurriedly and return for her approval. She looks me over, undoes another button on my blouse, and leans in to trace her tongue over the now exposed lace of my bra. "Tonight I'm taking you to the bar." She grabs her cigarettes, sighs into her nearly empty wallet, and slides both of them into her pockets.

"Who's going to be there?" I ask her, trying not to sound overtly curious.

"It will be crowded. Nanc will be there too. Just be on your best behavior."

Nanc, Lou's best friend and sometimes enemy. We had spoken on the phone a few times.

"Lou there?"

"No."

"She leave you all alone?"

"Yeah, she's out. I'll tell her you're looking for her."

"No, I mean, if you're alone, why don't I just come on over. We can wait for her together."

"I don't think that's the best idea. She'll be home soon."

"She says you're real pretty. Why don't I come over so I can tell her what I think of you."

"Maybe...some other time. I'll tell her you called."

"Ah, come on, she's been talking about how you're a wild one, that you can't ever get enough. You're probably rubbing your clit raw right now. I'll just come over and help you out. Why don't I just come over there and introduce myself to your...."

"Ummm.... I should really go. Bye."

We hadn't met but I had replayed her words in my head enough to recognize her voice anywhere. The best sex is always in your head, and Nanc had a knack for climbing into mine.

Lou parks the truck near the bar's entrance and comes around to open my door and look me over. "Who do you love?" she asks, brushing my hair back.

This well-rehearsed mantra to sooth her fragile ego spills

forth: "I love you, Lou, you know that. Only you. You know you are the only one who can keep me happy."

"Is that right?" She smiles a bit and pushes me against the side of the truck to kiss me and then she pulls back, seems to be waiting for more. It is not the cock but the compliment that is the way to a butch's heart.

So I continue. "You know you are my love. You turn me on more than anyone else ever could. How many times have I told you so? I'm not going anywhere. Don't you worry, baby."

Lou looks me square in the eyes and says, "No matter what happens tonight, you just remember that."

With her arm around my waist, we head down the damp back street. I can see the bikes in silhouette and the shape of a crowd of burly women hanging in the doorway of the bar. There is a whistle or two as we approach, then smiles and nods to Lou as she ushers me inside. The room is dim but everywhere I can see the dark huskiness of the most handsome women. There are squeaks of leather as people turn and a hand brushes my leg now and then in an almost accidental way. Now I fully understand why femmes need a chaperone here.

I like my women tough. The rougher edged and bigger, the better. I like to watch them get restless, their tough exteriors trembling under thick denim when they talk to me. I regularly call them *sir* to make them think they are passing. I admire those who don't correct me—it is a compliment. All a good butch really needs is a femme to appreciate her.

I have taken to making myself the most appreciative femme in the city. I can appreciate the fuck out of just about any butch I come across. And it is the fucking that I am really after. The trick is to find the soft spot in the hard women and tickle it until they hike my skirt up to see if my pussy is as sweet as my words. Their little way of thanking me.

Shy butches on their barstools want to be told that I can tell they are thinking deep thoughts. One drink later we are in their cars and they are thanking me as deeply as their broad-fingered hands can in such close confines.

A cropped-haired mechanic who has been tinkering on a bike that has been parked, unusable, for months on the lawn wants me to tell her what a fine ride it's going to be. Wants to hear me ask if I can sit on it for a minute, have me hitch my skirt up and place my oops-I-forgot-to-wear-panties-cunt down on the seat, lean forward so my clit slides along the leather to reach the handle bars. "I bet you can make her purr," I say, feigning revving the engine. A minute later, the shop table has been cleared off and she paws me with grease-stained fingernails while her buddies go out for lunch.

Lou had been hard and secretive and didn't fall for any of my usual ploys. Her soft spot was hard to find. Two weeks after moving in with her, I discovered a hidden stash of books. A few worn-out trashy straight novels, an instructional manual called *The Erotic Woman,* and a thoroughly uninteresting not-very-well-illustrated version of the Kama Sutra. To stay with Lou I would need to find a spot I could tease her with that could last months. Ordaining her as the best lover I have ever had was a way to keep my side of the bed vacant and to prevent her from changing the locks. She was good, so it wasn't a matter of faking it with her, as much as playing down every other encounter I had ever had. She knew I played around, but all seemed to be forgiven when I whined about how frustrated I was and how I couldn't wait to come home to be with her. She let the indiscretions go and grew increasingly interested in the fumbling details of lovers I auditioned. Lately we'd been arguing almost every day, and my stories had gone up a notch to counter her complaints. Now, not only was no one even close to her in bed, but no one else could even make me wet. Lou, who had been jamming my things into a duffle bag, stopped what she was doing when I revealed this to her. With almost a sense of pity she seemed to feel obliged to let me stay. I always carried clean panties in my pocket, which I could slip on before I came home to convince her of the lie she so wanted to believe.

We stop to get drinks before heading to the table that Lou's friends have staked out. Nanc speaks to Lou but keeps her eyes on mine, watching me scan the crowd. "Ah, so you finally let her out of the house." They laugh, giving each other a one-shoulder butch hug/pat.

The floor is already sticky with spilled beer. Lou's friends make room for us at the table and I listen to the group discuss work. How the assholes at the plant are reducing overtime, how so-and-so at the cycle shop has some thingy and such part doodad. I can't follow the conversation and don't care. I sip my beer, bouncing my ankle, trying to catch eye contact in a crowd used to avoiding it. Conversations in the room grow louder and women set their beers down so hard in anger or humor that the tables are slick from the sloshing over.

Lou gets up to go fetch more drinks and Nanc slides into her chair. "So, what d'ya think of our little bar?" She moves my hair off my shoulder, giving it a little tug. She leans in to me, one hand on my knee. In her familiar voice, she whispers the gossip of those sitting around the table. "Jess—been single for over a year, a pity she can't find a nice femme like Lou obviously has." I lean into her slightly so her mouth grazes my ear as she speaks. "And see Ron there? She passes at work. Takes shots too, when she can get her hands on a dose. Did you know testosterone raises sex drive?" She laughs alcohol-moist breath into my neck, saying she'd bet I already knew that.

Lou interrupts us, shoves Nanc back to her own seat, and pulls me out of mine.

"C'mon, let's go."

"Lou, man, we're just talking. Geez, half the time you want her to find a new man. I was just testing the waters." Nanc punctuates this with a sizzle sound.

"We're just going outside for a smoke. We'll be back."

She leads me out of the bar, squeezing the pinkies on both my hands in her fist as she pushes our way through the crowd.

Lou ignores me when we get outside even when I kiss her throat and try to jam my hands into her pockets. She has rolled us a joint she didn't want to share with her friends and we lean against the wall in silence trying to hang in the shadows. She feeds me drags between her long puffs.

Three women leaving the bar pause as they catch the scent and come over to ask directions to some other bar in an obvious ploy to get offered a hit. Lou vaguely gives them the information they want, and when they linger, she hands them the tight-rolled cig and they chat as they pass it around.

Lou introduces herself. Then she introduces me as the insatiable curse who couldn't be left alone for a minute without trying to make a pass at her best friend. Lou laughs it off and says that even if her friend had taken me into some back corner and tried to rustle up some lust, I would just have come crawling back to her.

Lou tells them that last week I went to the bathroom between pool-shots and convinced someone to feel me up. How after the woman was unsuccessful at using her fingers to arouse anything more in me than a need to pee, I came storming out, saying I'd have to use a pool cue if I wanted to get off. She tells them how she caught me crawling back into her bed with chalky hands and a blue smudge on my nose.

She complains that I am always picking up girls and going home with them, just to end up horny and frustrated and then have to steal cab money or hop a late-night bus back to her place. Like an alley cat who keeps wandering back in the window whenever you shut him out. With this, she let out a meow-moan and they laugh as if they know what it's like. It is the first time I have heard her retell these tall tales and I can see her eyes sparkle with butch pride. I see how much of herself is tied to this reality I've been weaving for her.

"Baby, tell them how no one can turn you on like I can."

I raise my eyebrows a bit and nod.

"Shit, if you can do it, you can have her." Lou says seriously as she sends the tiny butt around for one last pull from each of them.

The three step back. They look at my boots, the sheer black stockings of my thigh, the skirt that has been inching its way up as I shift from one foot to the other. "I bet I can make the bitch wet," one mumbles to another, meaning for Lou to overhear.

Lou warns them that many women have tried, even a couple of men, with no effect. But if they are willing to give it a shot, they would be doing her a favor. She drops the roach to the ground and grinds it into the sidewalk with the heel of her boot, saying she would be glad to get rid of me so she could get some sleep for a change. She tells them that I've jacked up her phone bill and owe her money. So, for $50 they can have three minutes to get a chance to make me wet. Three minutes of kissing. Lou tells them that she doesn't give a shit, throw in some tit- and ass-grabbing too if they want. She lays out the terms: They can't touch my pussy and I have to keep my hands behind my back. But most importantly, if they make me wet, they have to promise to keep me away from her.

The thought of her handing me over to these women, these biker chicks with their huge hands and rough talk and their cocky attitudes, has me on the verge of coming already. I am not sure if Lou is setting this up to be rid of me once and for all or if she wants me to prove my devotion to her in some grand Russian roulette gamble based on a lie I've been tickling her with for months. I am still wondering this when the most boisterous one of the group steps up to the bet. She watches Lou as if she is afraid it might end up being a joke worth fighting over and pulls her wallet out of her back pocket. Fifty dollars, surely an entire day's pay if she is one of those lucky enough to have a full-time job. She holds it out, as if daring Lou to take it.

Lou tells her that we need to make sure I am dry, to judge fairly. She reaches up under my skirt and with the sleeve of her shirt wipes my pussy off with a rough stroke. She turns back to the three, takes the money, and announces, "Whenever you're ready."

I can feel Lou's presence behind me. My pussy is already pulsing. I clamp down in an attempt to keep any moisture inside.

Bulldagger number one steps toward me. She chooses the direct route, kissing me confidently, open-mouthed, with her tongue darting deep into my throat. Her hands are on my shoulders, pulling me in, bending my neck back. This eager suitor smells of leather, whiskey, and motorcycle grease—a scent so bewitching I could be Pied Piper down the street with it. I hold my breath as she strangles me with her mouth. I just let her go at it, barely kissing back, resisting the urge to correct her faulty style with a few quick nips of my teeth to her tongue. I try to force my mind to wander from the situation. I try to think dry thoughts. I will win the bet for Lou and make her proud.

The three minutes are up and I have not so much as sighed. No groan. No pelvis seeking hers. No melting into her.

Lou turns to me. "Anything, honey?" she asks.

I shake my head "no" and lick the taste of whiskey off my lips.

Lou sighs and says that it's never as easy as it looks.

Number one steps back, tries to laugh it off, saying I am an uptight, frigid bitch, a fucking ice queen. She starts to walk off but her friends stop her.

The second dyke fumbles with her wallet and hands over the cash for her chance at the challenge. She apparently thinks that if the hard teeth-clanking kiss didn't work, perhaps I am a soft femme who needs seduction. She has three minutes. She kneels at my boots, and I avert my gaze to avoid the pull of her green eyes staring up at me. She licks the rim where the leather meets my calves, runs her tongue on the underside of my knee, and slides her hands slowly up my inner thighs. Lou stops her just as her fingers disappear under my skirt. She is stopped just before I make the decision that calloused hands and warm breath are worth bending my knees for, moving myself down to cease the agonizingly slow pace. She is stopped just before I drop my cunt down to meet her palm. Temptation number two moves her hands to softly cup each breast. I stand still, knees braced so as not to lose my balance. My hands search behind me for Lou—she takes both of my pinkies into her fist and gives them an encouraging squeeze. If I can pull this off, I know it will be the best compliment I have ever paid her.

Lou tells her that her time is up. I shrug, act unimpressed.

The two who have tried, chide the third into an attempt, telling her it was a good three minutes whether they won me or not. Razz her about how all night she's been lookin' for a femmey girl and here is one standing on the street just waiting.

The third bulldagger wants to know how we are measuring. She wants to see for herself if I am wet, wants proof. Lou reaches under my skirt and runs her fingers under the elastic of my underwear—quick, unceremonious, careful not to rub my clit. Her fingers barely skim the surface, but I gulp a breath of air at the long-awaited touch and they seem sure that she's penetrated me. She takes her hand out from under my skirt, grabs number three's hand, and rubs the definitely dry fingers along her thick wrist.

Lou holds out her hand for the money and bulldagger number three hesitates slightly before lifting her wrist to her nose. Just the faintest scent of pussy assures her that she wasn't tricked. She reaches into her pocket and pulls out some crumpled bills.

Lou resumes her position behind me, taking hold of my pinkies. I take a deep breath, trying to figure number three out so I can prepare myself. She is slow, strong, suspicious. Lou clicks her tongue, worried. We are so close to winning this cruel game that I couldn't bear to lose now. Couldn't bear to disappoint her. I imagine the ways she will thank me for this public gesture of appreciation.

Number three steps forward, trying to read my face for clues as she considers the best approach. She leans heavily into my body, wrapping her arms around me. Pushes her bulk into me. Our legs are interwoven and she pulls my hips into her thigh. She starts in on a brain-fucking whisper. "Oh you smell like sex just like I knew you would. I've been looking for a hot little woman like you. I want you so fuckin' bad right now. I can feel your cunt heat on my leg, burnin' a hole right through my jeans. I can practically feel it swelling. It's making me so fucking horny just thinking about how slick and sweet you're getting for me. I already know how I am gonna fuck you." She hugs me into her and presses me harder down onto her thigh. I struggle to tilt my hips up so as not to catch the fullness of her leg rubbing my cunt. Lou's fist closes down harder around my pinkies, tugging me back enough to relieve the pressure building on my clit.

The bulldagger pulls me hard against her chest, breathing on my neck. "That round sexy ass of yours has been drivin' me crazy since I first saw you. I am getting so worked up I don't think I could stop even if you wanted me too." She clamps a hand down on my asscheek and pulls my cunt up to meet the slow swivel of her hips.

Lou puts her fingertips lightly on my back to steady me and I rest back into her hand. Allow her to ease me back and rescue me from this impending arousal. "When I get you home," she goes on, "I'll give you the fuck you've been looking for. I'm gonna work your hard little clit—just pull it right into my mouth and lick your sweet juices. Then I'll open you up with my fingers, just slide in and out. Swirl my hand into you until you beg me to fuck you harder. Beg me to fuck you deeper until you come."

I think of throwing the bet and wrapping my legs around her, opening my mouth to hers. My cunt is tired from being clamped down for so long and I have lost track of my inhales and exhales, my breath starting to sound like whimpering.

"I know how to satisfy a cat-in-heat femme like you. You won't be stumbling home at night. You'll be flat-out exhausted from all our fucking."

I wonder what Lou would do, wonder what proof would be requested after this test, wonder what I could get away with. My pinkies are locked in Lou's fist and she twists them, bending them back into a stinging stretch, clearing my head.

The three minutes is up and Lou makes sure contestant number three has backed away before she pushes me back up to hold my own weight. I am lightheaded and keep hold of Lou's hand, looking down.

"Sorry," Lou says. "Like I told you, she isn't as easy as she looks." Lou takes my waist and turns to escort me inside, but number three grabs her arm and yanks her back so she can look straight at me. I know this look, the look of having found the soft spot and waiting for the tickle to take hold.

The bulldaggers start throwing insults and accusations at us. Number three in particular thinks she's won. She continues to talk to me, starting in the now-familiar whisper ringing in my ears, but each phrase rising in pitch of anger. "I know I made you wet. I know you're just dying to grind that sweet cunt into me. Let's finish this up and get out of here. Tell them how wet I made you. Didn't I make you wet? Huh, bitch?"

I try to ignore her voice, her words.

Lou tells her to shut up for a minute and we can prove it to her.

In a gesture too quick for me to stop, Lou pushes me back against the brick wall and yanks my skirt up. I take a deep breath and keep my pussy lips clamped together as tightly as I can. Lou pulls my panties down to mid thigh in front of these three bulldaggers whose wallets have just been emptied. Three bulldaggers with wounded machismo can see that I am not glistening.

Lou takes number three's hand and folds it into hers as she would a child's, leaving two fingers out and the rest curled into a fist. Lou guides her hand from one pale thigh, over my pussy lips, to the other. Three bulldaggers who are feeling quite underappreciated hear her announce it. Dry.

"I don't fuckin' believe it. She must be fuckin' frigid. Whatever. Keep her, man. You deserve the bitch." They saunter off, play-punching each other and grabbing their imaginary cocks.

They round the corner and Lou turns to me, looking me in the eye for the first time in almost a half-hour. She smiles and tells me she is quite proud, tells me she guesses its okay if I stick around for a while longer.

We go back into the bar and sit down at the table. I excuse myself and head toward the bathroom. "Nice hip-check," I say as I pass by Nanc at the pinball machine. She follows me, leaving an unplayed ball, and locks the door behind us. After a quick slick finger-fuck that she has been promising me for weeks, Nanc leaves to resume her game and I pull my clean panties out of my pocket, wrapping the damp ones in a paper towel and throwing them in the trash. I return to the table to sit on Lou's lap, whispering to her how I much I love her, that she is the only one who can keep me happy, how she is the only one who knows how to turn me on.

Envy

Teresa Lamai

The moment I saw Aracelli, I decided I hated her.

I was nineteen. For a year, I had been scrambling in the back rows of class and rehearsal at American Ballet. She appeared one sweltering May afternoon, a new student, serene, frail, with skin that gleamed like melted caramel and indigo hair so glossy it seemed always wet. A reverent space cleared for her at the head of the class, her very first day. Fresh from the Kirov school, she was flawless, an amber figurine come to life.

A stab of envy made my spine twist. My tongue swelled hard against my teeth as if I'd swallowed something too sweet. She smiled at me and I looked away.

When she and I were paired for the final allegro of class, grand jetés across the floor, my eyes stung. I was convinced our teacher had paired us on a cruel whim. I looked like a pudgy, red-haired gnome next to her smoky opulence; her sweat-slick skin glistened with copper and turquoise lights.

I decided to pleasantly ignore her, but that only lasted a week.

"You know, Kim, the thing I like most about this place is the friendliness."

It was the first time I'd heard her voice. It trailed up my neck like a silk scarf. I turned to where she sat in a perfect split, leaning forward on her elbows, smirking up at me. Her dark breasts swelled between her arms. Her damp, pink-covered legs writhed gently into the grimy floor.

We were the last ones in the studio after a distinctly miserable class. As soon as the pianist had begun playing for the warm-up that morning—just a quiet sarabande to nudge us out of stillness—Miss Greta, our teacher, had opened her bright red mouth and let forth a stream of outraged, piercing shrieks. Where her critiques lacked clarity, they had more than enough volume. Some students responded by spreading the hate around; gaunt girls gathered in the corners between exercises, watching as the others danced and sharing elaborate pantomimes of disgust. I resolutely ignored them but couldn't escape their whispers, *she—she—*, like spit landing on my back.

I gazed at Aracelli for a moment after she spoke, almost convinced that she was playing with me. She drew her coltish legs into herself, resting her cheek on her knees. She blinked slowly. Her deep voice surprised me; it sounded pained and rough.

"Everyone's so well-adjusted, and kind." Her velvety eyes were wide and grave, but her mouth twitched.

A delighted laugh burst from my chest, startling me. I looked up at the ceiling, letting it shake along my spine.

"Yeah." My raucous voice echoed down the corridor. "This is the one place I just say, 'fuck it,' and be myself."

"You know it! Just let it all fucking hang out." She was rocking with laughter now, her throat flushed. When her cheeks rose, her eyes narrowed and glittered, black as onyx. Her smile was fresh with kindness and a bite of wicked humor. Irresistibly subversive.

The empty studio seemed to hum uncertainly around us, as if unused to the sound of laughter.

She rose to her feet, slow and indolent. I tried not to let my smile fade as she stood, still smirking, shifting her weight into one hip. So perfect. My throat ached. Her tapered legs were taut and sleek, her waist slender as a sapling. The twin swells of her breasts were high and full, nuzzling each other playfully when she moved.

She moved toward me, chin lowered, a half-tame gazelle. Her lashes curled toward her temples. I reminded myself that I disliked her.

"I get the feeling that we're not supposed to be friends. That's, like, against the rules here, isn't it?" She spoke more quietly than she needed to. I had never seen such a beautiful face so close to mine. Her cheekbones glinted like burnished gold.

When she was near enough to take my hand, she started whispering, a lazy purr. "How about we become friends anyway, and bust this joint wide open?" She squeezed my wrist and grinned. Her crowded teeth gave her a sly, feral look.

I couldn't help licking my lips before I spoke. I blushed, knowing it made me look clumsy and weird.

"All right, we can shake on it." I tried to regain some composure with a tinny laugh.

My laugh turned into a gasp when she kissed my cheek, swiftly. Her cool ear brushed my temple. I closed my eyes as she kissed one cheek, then the other, again and again. Her breath was sugary, her lips light as petals.

My hands twitched at my sides. Panic filled me; it seemed wrong to be this close to something so exquisite. I felt like a careless child about to smudge and drool over a priceless jeweled statue.

She kissed my forehead, my eyelids. Her scent filled my head. She wore some brisk expensive perfume, light as white wine, but underneath it her heated skin gave off the scent of cloying swamp flowers and moss. I rested my shaking hands on her shoulders and lifted my chin toward her glowing face.

We both moaned when our lips met. My awkwardness fell away like an old dead skin, and the flesh underneath was painfully alive, hissing with a low current. She drew my mouth into hers, gentle then gently deep, as if she were tasting a new fruit. I let my palms graze over her face. My eyes squeezed shut as I felt her delicate temples, her tiny chin, her trembling arteries. I never wanted to stop kissing her; it was like gulping spring water.

Her palms glided over my ass, cradling it, lifting it lightly. I cried out. My pulse thudded in my stomach, heat pooled between my legs until I felt my clit struggling fitfully against my tights, a tiny captured bird.

When I caught the tip of her tongue and sucked on it, she growled. She lifted one leg and wrapped it tight around my waist. Our breasts pushed together, play-fighting for room. She clutched the back of my skull, sinking her nails in deep. Bobby pins clattered to the floor.

Footsteps rang in the corridor, sharp and purposeful.

I started, covering my breasts as if I were naked. I stared at Aracelli and was shocked to find her smirking again, sinking her teeth into the plump flesh of her lower lip. Her smile was steady and unsettling. She reached between my legs, resting her hand over my swollen mound, trailing her elegant fingers one after the other in an unhurried beckoning. My legs shook. Her other hand slid under my palm to my breast. She brushed my nipple with her thumb, then turned away, just as the footsteps rounded the corner.

"What is this?" Miss Greta always wore a smart checked suit and a fox stole, no matter how hot the weather. Her eyes widened at Aracelli and me as we stood, side by side, squeaking with strangled laughter.

She was inhaling deeply, preparing to raise her voice, when I grabbed Aracelli's hand and pulled her through the door. Miss Greta's blistering stare followed us down the hallway. We burst into the dressing room, screaming and giggling, breathless as if we had fallen into icy water.

We spent the rest of the sweltering afternoon in my dank closet of a room. Some violent, insatiable spirit took hold of us completely. We struggled, slick with sweat and saliva, grunting, sliding from the bed to my narrow, stained rug. Aracelli dug her nails into my ass when she came, wailing inconsolably, her back arched and still until she finally broke into furious thrashing. Her fists slammed into the wall beside me.

When sleep finally took us, it was mercifully swift and heavy. We lay unconscious, fists still wrapped in each other's hair, bodies twisted tight and covered in tiny red scratches like kitten bites.

Three weeks passed. Aracelli spent every evening in my room, her long dark body stretched beside mine.

"You know, Kim, when I first saw you, I thought you were so fucking beautiful I couldn't stand it." She laughed.

I loved to close my eyes and let her voice glide over me like heated oil. My wind chimes rang softly out on the fire escape. Broadway's traffic roared far below, a distant surf. I felt her lift partly and rest on one elbow. I lay still.

After her first orgasm, Aracelli was always transformed, losing her slit-eyed smirk and becoming winsome as a cat. She trailed one strand of her hair over my collarbone. With my eyes closed, I felt her shape shimmering beside me.

Her voice stirred the hair on my temples. "I couldn't take my eyes off you, you were just so tiny and delicious. Your vanilla-cream skin, all downy and velvety like you were covered in powdered sugar. Your mouth, like a little candy rosebud. Mmm."

She kissed me and I opened my eyes. Her hair cascaded slowly, swaths of heavy black silk over her shoulders. She looked contented and wild. With the dusk, the corners of my room were retreating into dull blue shadows. She gave off a soft crimson glow in the darkness like a banked fire.

She kept talking, her eyes moving up and down my body, her fingertips trailing across my stomach and combing through the damp, matted curls over my sex.

"You know, Kim, I first thought that I hated you, isn't that funny? But it wasn't hate, really—more that I wanted so desperately to be you, or just be close to you, all the time."

Her fingernails were like polished opals, scratching over my pale nipples. She smiled down at me when I shuddered.

"Maybe envy," she murmured, resting her lips on my forehead, "is that fine edge between hate and love."

I bit my lip. We burst out laughing at the same time.

"Come here." I lifted myself up, straining to see her face.

I gripped her shoulders, shifting down until my mouth was at her tight, salty breasts. My tongue moved restlessly, anxious as if it could never get enough of her skin. I rolled her onto her back, trailing kisses down her flat, muscled belly. I lifted her ass in my palms so that I could keep watching her face as I closed my mouth over her slippery cunt. Her hips started to writhe but I held them tight, my fingers sinking into her flesh. My forearms shook with the effort.

I kept my eyes fixed on hers as I turned my head sideways. I let my tongue glide. Her pelvis pitched up when I found her clit. Still holding her, I lapped at it, persistent and gentle, until her spine coiled and her fists clenched in the sweat-soaked sheets.

I didn't stop until she had come two more times. Aracelli was never more beautiful than when she lost control, her eyelids fluttering, her mouth working soundlessly, tendons shifting in her long throat.

Afterward, I rested my cheek on her stomach. She filled her palms with my hair, lazily drawing out tendrils and spreading them all around my head.

"Kim, are you sleeping?"

"Mmm, no." I woke up and kissed her navel.

"Let's form an unholy alliance. Let's work together this summer and go further than anyone else."

Our strategy quickly took shape. I would teach her all of American Ballet's repertoire, the uniquely angular, neoclassical style that she found so new and awkward. She would help me with my desperately weak technique. We felt we'd cracked a code, combining our strengths, each the other's secret weapon.

Gossip spread that the summer workshop performance would feature *Jewels* this year. Recruiters from every major company would be invited, ready to give contracts to the most outstanding students. We decided that I would be cast as Emerald, and she as Diamond, and absolutely nothing else would do. We had five weeks before auditions would be held.

We sneaked into the studio on Sundays, pleading with the maintenance guys until they let us have a key. I had a bootleg videotape of *Jewels* and we learned all the choreography, every phrase, from beginning to end. No matter what they threw at us in the audition, we would be ready.

One hazy Sunday, a week before the auditions, we watched each other run through each of the variations twice. Music echoed brashly, rushing to the ceiling. Aracelli finished the Diamond coda, then fell into a cartwheel, squealing with glee. She stood panting, radiant, sweat streaming down her neck. Her eyes were dilated and inhumanly black.

"Fabulous. The best one I've seen." I slouched against the mirror, applauding weakly, drumming my heels into the floor.

She peeled her leotard down and leaned to work her tights off her legs. She was still panting when she lifted her arms into her flowered red sundress. I watched her flushed body disappear under a billow of rayon. By the time she shook her sweaty head free, I was standing and struggling with my leotard straps.

"No way, Kim. You need to do those sixteen fouettés again. Seriously."

I glared. My legs were numb. "I did that phrase, like, five times today."

"No," she almost shouted. I took a step away from her. I'd never seen her like this. Small blue veins writhed in her temples.

"Aracelli, what the fuck. I did—"

"You did twelve fouettés and then, like, four half-assed turns to get through the rest of the music. Do you think no one will notice?" Her voice was so shrill my ears hummed.

She looked down. "Kim." She swallowed, turned her head sharply. Her voice became deadly quiet. "If you want to just have fun, to just chill out and dance like a corps dancer.... Then why am I wasting my fucking time with you?"

Her last words were a strangled, half-whispered scream. Her balled fist smacked into her thigh. I flinched at the impact.

I turned away, feeling my eyes darting about. The room still rang with her shrieks.

"All right. Go sit down and turn on the music." My voice wavered.

"Don't fake it this time—"

"FOR CHRIST'S SAKE, I HEARD YOU!" I yelled it as loud as I could. Anything to drown out her voice. My nails dug crescents into my palms.

The music blared again, just as I turned and saw Aracelli's blank, stricken face. She leaned her back to the mirror and sank into a squat. Her lower lip shook, her eyes filled.

I ran to my mark.

When I finished dancing, she was sitting with tears streaming down her cheeks.

I turned off the tape. She was sucking her breath between her teeth, squeaking and trembling. Her eyes followed me.

I lay back on the gritty floor, trying to fill my lungs again. I wiped the sweat off my face with my forearms.

She gulped twice before she could speak. "I'm so sorry, Kim."

"Yeah."

"I don't know what happens to me sometimes, it's like I just become this monster. I hate myself when it happens. I try, I try to control it."

I turned away from her, resting on my side. I felt I could fall asleep. The blood throbbed back into my feet and the pain made me wince.

"You think I'm a bitch, Kim, don't you?"

"Sure."

I cringed, expecting her to freak out again. Instead she was silent. When I finally rolled to face her, she was covering her face with her dress, hunched over, utterly still.

I saw my reflection just past her, pale and sweat-drenched, purple shadows under my pained eyes. Half my hair had come loose.

When I stood, stars sparked orange and silver in front of my eyes. I reached down and squeezed her shoulders. She started, staring up at me. Her face was streaked with tears and sweat. I pulled her to her feet.

She rested her forehead on mine. I cradled her skull in my palms.

She was whispering now. "Do you ever feel, like, numb and raw, like your skin's been all scabbed over?"

She glanced at me, swallowed, then kept speaking.

"Like it's all been fried, like someone poured battery acid

all over it, and then it just grew back all thick, with no nerves, no feeling."

"Okay, okay, Aracelli. Shh." I spread my hands over her burning head. I hardly knew what I was saying, I just heard deep, soothing sounds coming from my chest.

"I'm sorry, Kim. It's hard to remember that other people get hurt, feel pain, that I need to act a certain way or else you'll just...."

"Shh, baby." Before I could say more she squirmed into my arms.

When our mouths met, searing lust rose up in my stomach. The room went dim around me. I bit at her mouth, her shaking neck. I pulled out her bobby pins and twisted her hair in my fingers, grabbing thick handfuls and pulling until she jerked with the pain.

We stumbled into the stool and I turned her around, pulling the straps of her dress off her shoulders. It rippled to the floor. I ran my hands along the gleaming topaz curve of her back.

My boldness made me shake. I had no idea what I intended to do. She was panting. I gently guided her, leaning her forward until her elbows rested on the stool's seat. Her hair nearly reached the floor, a heavy gleaming curtain.

"Oh god, you're so beautiful, Aracelli."

I kissed her downy spine. I wanted to bite her. Goosebumps rose along her arms. My nails left soft pale furrows on the twin swells of her ass. Her moan was low and deep.

I dropped to my knees and lifted one of her bare feet, setting it up on a side rung. The sight of her naked cunt was like an electric shock to my breastbone. My breath stopped as I ran my palms up her thighs. Her labia pouted obscenely, engorged and vulnerable. Her black curls glistened. Her scent was stronger and sweeter than I'd ever known it, rich as spiced honey.

When I touched two fingers lightly to her anus, her fluted inner lips unfurled at me, dark as plums. She bucked.

"Don't move." I rested my thumb under her clit, letting my tongue glide down one side of her labia. Her curls tickled my cheek. She sobbed and jerked, twisting toward my mouth.

"Shh, just feel it." Her hair moved under my breath.

She kept twisting. I stood and swatted her ass once, playfully. She squealed. I rested my hands on her thighs, massaging, feeling her heat radiate up through my arms. Her ribs heaved.

"You felt that too, didn't you?" I tried not to let my voice tremble. "Don't make me smack it harder."

I knelt again. Still kneading her flesh, I watched her labia contract and spread, a thick-petaled flower. When I saw her inner thighs shining, slick and golden, I couldn't resist anymore. My eyes stung with tears.

I leaned in, my tongue tracing lightly over her mound, my fingers covering her clit in tender circles. The smell of her made me lightheaded and I moaned when she finally lifted her head, her back perfectly straight, writhing furiously and shrieking. Her cunt pulsed in my mouth. She shook for a long time afterward, slow delicious aftershocks, turning her head from side to side and cooing softly to herself.

I eased her off the stool. We stretched out on the cool, dusty floor, cradling each other. Our breath became quieter as the room darkened.

We went to Aracelli's place the next night. She shared a West Village loft with her aunt, an art teacher at Cooper Union.

Aracelli had been inviting me there all summer, but I kept finding excuses to stay away. It wasn't that I hated the Village; it was glorious. The neighborhood was vibrant, endlessly complex, like a chaotic masterpiece of performance art that was just about to reveal its central theme. Each new block had something fascinating: flame-colored murals and steel statues, tiny stores packed with books, scents of lilies and fresh bread, snatches of mournful clarinet and Creole laughter. Art here was serious; there was an unspoken imperative to create constantly, to produce something that would appall and transport and devastate. To be the absolute best in your field.

I felt it should have inspired me but instead it made me numb with anxiety, wanting to curl up and hide.

"Kim, are you okay?" Aracelli was staring at me. Her face was gritty with dust. "You're all pale."

"It's just...." I rested my palm on my forehead. The crowd surged around us, bristling with energy as the sky darkened. "It's just so hot. The air's so heavy."

"It's cooler upstairs. Come on, we're here." It was an old art-deco building, gleaming in the last rays of the sun as if it were gold-plated.

Aracelli's dress puffed and floated around her legs as she bounded up the stairwell. "She's away. We get it all to ourselves. Hurry up!"

I reached the top floor in time to see her poppy-red figure disappear down the murky corridor. Muffled shouting came from the other rooms.

I sucked in my breath when I followed her through the doorway. The loft's whitewashed walls were draped with pastel silk prints and grainy, obscure photos. Half-formed statues, made of found objects and spray-painted silver, perched along the moldings like deranged household gods. A patched satin sofa was the only furniture; the rest of the front room was covered in faded, multicolored carpets and velour cushions.

I was speechless as I walked over to the window. The old-fashioned shutters opened over Washington Park. The sky was deepening to teal, with a haze of rusty brown and scarlet still glowing at the horizon. The park was a nest of tangled green shadows and flaring lights, filled with music and screams.

"I know, I know. I love it." Aracelli grabbed me from behind, clasping her arms tight around my waist and rubbing her breasts into my back. Her thin dress was already gossamer with sweat.

She raked her fingers through my hair. I shook it from my eyes. Her tender fingers found the back of my neck and I moaned.

"Kim, you look like one of those old paintings of angels." She kissed my throat. "In your little blue dress, your hair all over the place."

I sighed, leaning my head back on her thin shoulder. She ran her index fingers along my arms, from my shoulders to my wrists and back again, light as moth wings. My sex throbbed as if she were already cuddling it in her palm.

When she spoke again, her voice was hoarse. "Oh, Kim, I want to tie you somewhere and just fuck you and fuck you and fuck you until you're screaming for me to stop."

The wide darkness outside seemed to suck at me. My head spun. I tried to back away from the window but Aracelli gripped my neck and bit my ear. Her hips pressed mine into the window's ledge. I pressed my palms into the rough frame, bracing.

"Screaming and screaming until I gag you." Her nails in my throat made me whimper. "I'd gag you and make you come the way you've always needed to, come so hard you'd forget everything."

She knelt. I was already wet, panting when she pulled my panties to my knees. She tilted my hips back and just rested her languorous tongue on my still-folded cunt, soft and maddening. The darkening streets swam before my eyes.

When she finally fed me her strong fingers, one after another, my broken cries were sucked into the heavy, humid wind.

We woke late the next morning, strewn flat across her aunt's futon. We hadn't eaten anything the day before and we were weak with hunger. We clanged down the staircase and burst out to the sparkling clear day.

We started with our usual coffee and one biscotto each, just to check out a dark, stylish café. We added more pastries, growing even more famished as we ate. The second breakfast turned into lunch. We finished with an armful of chocolate bars, giggling madly on a sun-warmed stone bench in the Chinese garden, sucking the last melted bits from the foil. I couldn't remember when I'd eaten so much. My blood was so full of sugar that the world seemed painfully bright.

With my shoulder leaning on Aracelli's I looked out over the slow-moving crowd and realized suddenly it was all laughably easy. Absolutely anything was possible. I let myself tumble down and rested my head on her lap. I didn't care who saw us. Above me, she closed her eyes and lifted her sharp chin into the sunlight. Tendrils of wisteria and honeysuckle hung low, shaking vivid petals into the breeze.

We sat that way until the sun sank behind the trees.

"Come on, we shouldn't wait too long." Aracelli's voice had a leaden ring as we descended into the deserted subway station. She tugged me into the women's bathroom. Filthy shadows pooled in the corners.

"Wait for what?" I felt like I was drunk.

She knelt in an open stall, leaning over the toilet, her left arm working frantically at her mouth until her back spasmed. The smell made me retch and I stepped back.

She coughed only once and stood up, pressing a tissue into her lips. Her skin seemed to be dusted with ashes. I gulped, sucking in air around my tongue, willing my stomach to stop clenching on itself.

"What," she barked. But I still couldn't speak. She glared, her eyes dull as charcoal.

"I'm sorry." I turned away. "I don't do that. I—I don't think it's healthy."

"You don't...."

"I just, you know, diet."

"You diet!" I didn't need to see her face. Her laughter was strangely loud. "Well, Kim, no wonder...."

I faced her now. My ears rang and the miserable room went dim.

She yelled in earnest. "Don't give me that bullshit, Kim. What, you're just going to let all that sit on your stomach?" Her voice ricocheted over the tiles. "With auditions in six days? Jesus Christ, you're going to gain, like, five pounds."

I flinched, blinking. Panic flooded my mind. I felt my skirt already growing tighter around my thighs.

I knelt where she had been and looked at my hands. "I don't know how," I murmured.

Her voice was gentle, almost sweet. "Here." She crouched close beside me, holding out her long, bronze palm. "Use two fingers, hard, on the back of your throat."

I tried. It just tickled. I hadn't thrown up since I was five. My eyes became wet.

"Press really hard, on the part where your throat becomes soft." Her voice was brittle with impatience now. "Christ, either do it or not."

I reached further back, gingerly, breathing in little gasps, until I found the spot that made me gag. Before I could pull my hand away, Aracelli grabbed my wrist and shoved it toward the back of my head.

She stood up as I finished.

I couldn't stop sobbing afterward. My temples throbbed and my insides felt as though they'd been soldered into a black, smoking mess. I felt her standing over me and thought she would leave in disgust. Instead she knelt and wound her cool, slim arms around my neck, pulling until I fell back into her, holding my damp head under her chin. Her skin smelled like baby powder and vanilla lipgloss. She trailed her slender fingers through my hair.

"Kim, what did you expect?" Her voice was very quiet.

I was usually the first one at the studios in the morning, so I was surprised to hear voices in the cool, clean hallways that Wednesday as I arrived. A group of girls already huddled near the office doors. I made my way through them, slowly. I tried to listen for gossip, but there were only quick whispers, full of hissing rage.

A sheet was hung at the top of the bulletin board. Summer Workshop Performance Cast List.

Before I could read further, my shoulders tingled. I turned around. Aracelli gave me her mildest doe-eyed smile.

"What the hell, did you see this?" I pointed toward the board. "Auditions are this coming Saturday, aren't they? This must be a mistake."

"Well, they asked a few of us to audition for the principal roles last week. Everyone else will be the corps."

"They asked—" I pressed my hands to my temples. My stomach squirmed, turning ice cold. I realized my mouth was open and I shut it quickly.

"Don't get mad at *me*, Kim." Aracelli's tone was perfect; affectionate and reasonable. "Am I supposed to insist that they audition everybody?"

I laid my palms on my burning cheeks. A few girls were staring at us.

"Kim, a good solid corps dancer is so immensely valuable to a company."

I closed my eyes and felt her arm slip around my shoulders, hugging tight before she disappeared into the murmuring crowd.

Una
Andrea Miller

The first time I ever really talked to Una, she was sitting at a café terrace, sipping iced mochaccino. "Hey, honey," she said, as I passed by. "I like the way you walk; can I film you from behind?" I finally put it together, then, that all those cute waitresses I'd been scoping out over beers were actually one woman: Una. The thing is, she always looked so different. Sometimes she'd have on a wallet chain and a wife beater, and at other times sequins and stilettos. And everything changed with the clothes, even the way she put a drink down, even the way she walked. Swagger to hip swing, if you know what I mean.

Una had the latter going on right now and she was prancing circles around me, shoving bikinis and thongs into a suitcase for a road trip—a slow drive down the East Coast to the dyke event of the year in South Beach, Miami. I, on the other hand, was staying home for a spring that smelled like dog shit and mildew because I couldn't take the time off work from my glamorous job at a used bookstore specializing in porn and romance novels.

Corey and Mel, Una's travel companions, were waiting for her in the living room. Una had recently met them at the bar and she wanted us to be couple friends, but there were problems with that. They usually pretended I didn't exist and, although always inseparable, they were only a couple every second day. Today they seemed very much in love—their tongues down each other's throats.

By the time Una put on her shoes, I was pretty depressed. Missing her already, I desperately wanted a few minutes alone with her, but that was impossible. "Film us saying good-bye," she said, thrusting her camcorder at Mel. Kissing me hard.

The door clicked shut and I spent an hour smoking cigarettes and trying to call friends who weren't home. Then I decided to start watching the videos Una kept in the bedroom. I'd seen many of them before and I had certain favorites, but I hadn't a clue how to find them on my own. Although the tapes were neatly labeled and lined up on the shelves, there were more than two hundred of them and the labels were cryptic—usually one or two words that barely connected to the content. So I just chose that first tape because it was at eye level. I popped it in, turned down the lights, and crawled into bed.

At first there was only a muffled sound and an image of a floor, with table legs in the background. Then, suddenly, Una filled up the screen, cowboy hat tilted to one side, chaps framing her cunt. She was kneeling on the ground, flashing her crooked smile, and working oil over her tits. Tits that were the size of plums and that were now glossy like them, too.

When Una had pinched her nipples into pointed stones, she slid a hand down her ribs and between her legs. She brushed her fingers over the clipped fur then, licking them, used the slick of her saliva to rub her clit. My own cunt creaming at the sight.

Una reached for the lube and squeezed it into her hands

and over her snatch—even let it trickle to her asshole. Then she picked up a long, black dildo and stroked it until every ridge of it glistened. She rested the flat dildo base on the floor, squatted over its cock head, and lowered down. The mouth of her pussy swallowing.

With one hand behind her, propping her up, the other resumed rubbing her clit. And she really got into it, just bounced up and down on that dick until she suddenly stopped. Pulled out and repositioned. This time to have her asshole hovering over the head. I winced then because Una still owned that dildo. I'd had its thickness in my cunt a few times and I couldn't imagine it anally. But jerking off, Una pressed into the tip. And as she got closer to climax, she couldn't help grinding down, impaling herself.

Most of the videos on the shelf were like that—Una getting off solo somewhere in some kind of glam outfit. She used the videos for foreplay, although I knew she also watched them on her own 'cause I'd caught her a few times. Jacking off to her own recorded moans.

Una usually filmed herself, but sometimes she got someone else to do it and for the past year that someone else had been me. Filming her still made my pussy drip every time. Yet as titillating as it was, it also frustrated me.

Sometimes I just wished we could have normal sex—you know, in bed with the lights out—because with Una, if it wasn't the camera, then it was watching the action in a mirror or doing it in public, in danger of getting caught. And it seemed like she only ever paid attention to my pussy for the effect of it—how she looked sporting the strap-on, or how her tongue looked curling to my clit. I guess I'd started thinking that way the night we fucked behind an Italian restaurant.

All I could smell was pizza and all I could hear were the cooks chopping and talking in their singsong way. But I was licking Una's snatch and the rub of it on my tongue was making me juicy. Suddenly she shuddered, grabbing the back of my neck. And just as suddenly, some guy named Tony opened the back door, ending our game. So I was still all creamy and pent up when we got home and I wanted nothing more than to have Una fuck me with that dildo of hers. I saddled up to her and whispered my proposition in her ear, but she just snorted. "Honey," she said, "butch is no deeper on you than your baseball cap. You don't even play ball."

I didn't exactly identify as butch, but what she said hurt because it was intended to and because it made me worry. Made me worry I wasn't what she wanted and that she might find something tastier at the bar.

I desperately wanted to hear Una's husky nighttime voice and her firecracker laugh—sudden and loud. But when I came home with takeout five days after her departure, there was still nothing on the answering machine. Still no call from Una. Disappointed and driven to vice, I cracked open a beer and popped in another video. But this tape didn't feature Una jacking off, and the pizza cheese felt suddenly gummy in my mouth.

Una was on her hands and knees, wearing a schoolgirl uniform—knee socks and a kilt that was riding up her ass—and Karen, her ex-girlfriend, was looming above her with a paddle in hand. "Next time," she said, her voice all sugar and metal, "you're gonna do what Daddy tells you to."

Karen leaned down and pulled up Una's skirt, exposing white little girl panties that matched creamy white thighs. She ran the paddle over the bare skin, over the cotton, and Una quivered as those first few soft smacks came down. Got harder. Knocking the wind out of my jealousy. I was getting wet for the scene, for Una and even for Karen. I'd never met her before, but on the screen she had a voice like chocolate and movements that were both fluid and crisp. I liked the way the line of her cropped hair met her neck and I liked her golden skin.

Karen paused, slid the edge of the paddle between Una's legs, tracing her slit. Then, with careful fingers, she pulled down her panties and fondled her tight globes. Una leaned into the touch and Karen smirked, the muscles in her forearms twitching.

"You want Daddy's cock inside you, baby? You want Daddy to make you cum?"

"Oh, yes," Una panted, now out-and-out grinding her snatch into Karen's hand. "Make me cum, Daddy. Please make me cum."

"Are you forgetting Daddy hasn't finished punishing you yet?"

"Oh, Daddy, my pussy's so wet. Please, I'll be good," Una begged. But Karen took her hand away and grabbed her by the hair. Shoved her glazed fingers in her mouth. Watched Una lick them.

"You're like a bitch in heat," Karen sneered. Then she brought the paddle down again—this time hard and fast. Noisy smacks louder than the phone ringing.

Although it was too late when I finally realized I had a call, I fumbled for the remote anyway. Pressed Stop. "Fuck," I said under my breath, thinking it might have been Una. I picked up the receiver and heard a string of short beeps indicating a message. I plugged in the code and there, indeed, was her voice. "Hey, Kitty," she said. "Guess you're not home. I'll call back later."

"Fuck," I said again—already wondering what Una meant by "later." After all, when she'd left she'd said she would call "soon," and "soon" had ended up being five days. I shuffled to the kitchen for another beer. Then back in the bedroom, I lit a smoke, turned the volume down, and pressed Play.

The screen filled with Karen's crotch and I realized two things: a third party was filming, pressing Zoom, and Karen was packing. Jeans bulging. Slowly, she undid her belt and fly, and I heard the sound of leather pulling tight, metal clicking cold. A lurid purple cock bursting out. Karen's fingers slipped off screen, coming back with lube—lube she dribbled on the head, squirted on the shaft. Then she choked that dick like she really could milk it. Her hands strong, her nails blunt. But Una was whining in the background, wanting some.

Karen took a seat on a hard wooden chair, her legs cocked open. "Come here, baby," she said. "Come get your treat."

Una skipped over and said please just like she was told to. With sugar on top. With a cherry. Then she got down on her knees and sucked her Daddy off. Flicked her eyes up to his face as she licked the shaft. And flicked her eyes up to the camera as she stretched her little mouth around the head. But (midswallow) I had had enough and hit stop.

I missed Una and I just couldn't wait until "later." I picked up the phone, pressed *69, and wrote the hotel's number down inside an empty pack of smokes. I guess I knew, though, that calling her was a dumb idea because I stabbed the buttons dialing fast, my heart pounding. Four rings. Nothing. Then, on five, Corey picked up—Una in the background shrieking and laughing. "Hi," I said. "This is Terry. Can I talk to Una, please?"

"Uh, she's busy right now. Is there a message?"

I let my hatred seep through the line; let it leave a pause. I hated Corey and Mel. Hated their mannerisms and little twin outfits. Tidy cargo pants and baby T's. "No, no message," I finally said, hanging up.

After that I thought about going out to shoot some pool, but instead I just stared at the cracked ceiling, the clothes on the floor, the lone limp plant. Five minutes passed. Ten minutes. Twenty. Then, the phone still silent, I decided to watch another video. A different one—a normal one—one starring only Una.

I popped out the Daddy tape and slid it back into its place on the shelf between two other tapes, one labeled "muzzle" and another unlabeled. I pulled out the unlabeled one, but I didn't wonder why it lacked a name or think about how hard it felt against my fingers. I just put it in the machine and pressed Play.

Una's face—immediately the entire picture—glowed pale against a severe black wig. Her lips, painted blood red, were slightly parted for a sly glint of teeth. And her eyes, rimmed in black, were heavy with iridescent green lids. She winked and the camera traveled to nipples poking out from behind a curtain of faux hair. Traveled to countable ribs and a navel jewel. Shaved slit and thigh-high boots. The very same boots that, three weeks earlier, Una had pranced home in and tried on with different panties. That made this video three weeks old. Tops.

I tried to gloss over the terrible gut feeling I suddenly had. Tried to hit Stop. But it was like I was mesmerized. Charmed by a snake—movement, skin, bone, muscle—at once beautiful and repulsive. I kept watching. Watched a hand creep to Una's cunt. Not her hand, or mine. Not her finger moving in and out. Not my fingers: two, three, four, fist. Rather, Corey's. Corey and Una sliding against each other—grinding sweat and juice into my bed. The bed I was in now—blankets tangling my legs, tears falling into my pillow. Everything growing wet.

And it only got worse; the camera suddenly cutting to twin outfits but not cargo pants or baby T's this time. Just flashes of thumb rings, harnesses, and one-eyed snakes. Corey and Mel were standing with Una between them and she was jacking them off—two lube-slippery fistfuls. Stuffing dicks in her mouth one at a time, sliding her fingers under harnesses.

Then Mel got flat on her back and Una straddled her—cock pressing into snatch. I heard the two of them panting, the bed frame thumping against the wall, the springs groaning. And I watched the camera pan from Una's bouncing tits to her swollen cunt, then zero in on her ass. Mel and Corey each had ahold of a cheek and they were spreading her open as Corey lubed the pucker and slowly slid in her cock. Making the trio look like some kind of perverse boot sandwich—spike heels digging into my mattress.

I started to sob then, hating how Corey had taken Una by the hips and hating how Mel's eyes were closed into tight pleasure-slits. But, both her holes now stuffed, Una was getting louder and the veins in her neck were bulging. She was getting close—and strangely, so was I. My pussy was pure slick and I was grinding into my hand.

So this is life with Una, I thought, crying and quivering until I came, until we came together—juice on the sheets. The two of us so much louder than the phone ringing.

Sno Ball's Chance in Hell
Renee Rivera

I know I said that I wanted to go to hell for just a little while. I didn't know it would be one long pajama party and that I'd be lying around in pink fuzzy mules watching *Grease*, *Grease II*, and all the Gidget films over and over while the devil girls eat Hostess Sno Balls and give each other manicures and pedicures.

I thought it would be big burly butch devils with thick-veined hands and cocks the size of baseball bats splitting me open in a night that would never end. I thought I'd be Vanessa Del Rio in *The Devil in Miss Jones,* and instead I'm getting just sick and tired of listening to those devil girls' dull chatter and—good god—I hate Hostess Sno Balls!

I ask the devil girls what they do for fun around here, "Don't you ever get a shipment of cute little butch boys in to pinch and bite and fuck silly and generally terrorize until they break down and sob? You know what crybabies butches are...." I manage a grin of conspiratorial encouragement but the devil girls just look back blankly. The first one asks without turning her gaze from the big-screen TV,

"Isn't *Grease II* just your favorite movie?" The next devil girl leans in, sympathetically offering the tiny red vial of polish and one of those electric-blue foam toe spacers, "Why don't you try Ruby Rum Punch on your toes this time?" And then the only other one who was even paying attention says, "Here—have another Sno Ball." If I have another Sno Ball I am going to vomit.

When I thought of myself here, the devil butches encircled me on cloven hooves, no two alike. The one who hoists me hard against her chest, feet off the ground, at the edge of the dark pit, is a great strapping brute of a butch devil wearing nothing over her ruddy skin and muscular limbs but the black cock, thicker than my forearm and just as long, traced with thick raised veins and lashed around her hips and through her legs with one long length of rough-cast chain. Above that, pressing against my back, she wears a leather breastplate buckled around her ribs and over her broad shoulders with two stud-traced star-shaped cutouts, one over each enormous brown nipple, leaving the erect flesh free to press against my back like two strong thumbs. Her horns are sawn short to match her short dark crew cut.

The small one who skitters up to start wrapping my naked body in cool soothing chain is as wiry as the first one lifting me is meaty, and her horns corkscrew to points through slicked-back greasy hair curling behind filthy protruding ears. As the little butch bends, coiling a loop around each of my thighs and pulling roughly outward, I can see a small piglike tail poking out of her bare bony buttocks. The crowd of butch devils watching from the other side of the pit are a jumble of snorts, hoots, stink, broad bellies hanging over leather- and cock-strapped loins, heads and crotches shaved to coarse stubble, chins with goaty twists of hair, and everywhere wet grins, grasping hands, and bobbing cocks, as they jostle and poke each other in anticipation.

I'm jolted from my reverie of remembered fantasies by the devil girls.

"I know! Let's crank call our exes!" the head devil girl says, shaking her short red curls. The credits are rolling on *Grease II* and absolutely everyone's toes glitter with Ruby Rum Punch. The devil girl grabs the big red Princess phone from the floor where it sits almost engulfed by the white shag carpet. She thrusts the phone into the hands of another devil girl lying on the carpet belly down kicking her drying toes in the air, and snatches the copy of *Us* magazine out of her hands, provoking a squawk from the busty blond devil girl.

"You can call my ex, and I'll call yours," the red-headed devil girl says. "I'll dial." All the other devil girls crowd around.

Boy, I've been here too long—even the devil girls are starting to look good. For a moment I consider just diving face first into the abundant cleavage of the busty blond devil girl holding the phone, the other one having just finished dialing the number.

"Hey, baby," the blond started in a breathy husky voice. "Oh baby, I just had to call, I can't stop thinking about the other night, and how you..." she trailed off and after a pause, "What are you doing?" Another pause, "I'm just waiting for you.... Anything you want.... Yeah baby, of course I remember...." All the devil girls are covering their mouths with their hands, and burying their faces in each other's shoulders or laps to keep from laughing out loud. The one on the phone is gesturing to show she's got the poor dumb butch on the hook. "Oh, don't you worry your sweet little head about that, baby, your girlfriend doesn't need to know about that." The devil girls are turning red and rolling around on the carpet now with the effort of keeping silent. "Oh baby, I need you, I'm just waiting for you.... You remember where to find me. I'll be here waiting for you, baby. Don't keep me waiting." The blond devil girl hangs up and all the others burst out squealing and laughing and tumbling over each other on the rug. "Omigod, that dumb butch," the blond gasps out between chortles. "She thought I was her trick from last Saturday night. Boy, is she going to get a surprise when she gets to that girl's house." All the devil girls cackle all over again, and then they all start demanding the phone to get in on the fun.

Back in my fantasy the devil butches have got me all locked into my chain harness, and I'm hooked, like a hay bale going into a hay loft, onto another chain hanging from the dark cavernous ceiling. The big butch holds me out over the pit so I can feel the blast of hot air rising up out of it, and I can see the glow of molten lava far below.

"That's where you're goin' when we get tired of you—so have fun up here while it lasts." I spin there on the hook, feeling the chains dig deeper into my inner thighs and tighten across my hipbones. The butch devil's incongruously cool blue eyes look right through me, and then past me to the gaggle of panting devil boys on the other side of the pit. "Hey boys," the big butch calls across the pit, "ain't this a tasty one?" The big butch's hands are all over me, spinning me back to face across the pit, but holding me from swinging over. Her huge hands are cracked and lined with dirt and end in long yellow split nails. Raised veins crawl like worms up the back of her hand and along the curve of her muscular forearm. Callused and dirt-dark palms drag hard across my bare chest, one hand grabbing the chains crossed there, while the other reaches down to pinch a handful of skin in the softest part of my inner thigh, pulling that leg open. "Yeah, all that's for you, boys," the big butch devil calls across the pit to the gibbering mob on the other side. "Have fun, boys!" And then I'm swinging over the pit—to the mob—hot air searing my crotch as I soar across. The blast of sweat, onions, tar, and ammonia overwhelms my senses before I even make contact, but then I'm up inside the cloud of odor, clutching hands, and cocks poking in from every angle, jammed up against my buttocks, my belly, looking for purchase. The devil boys grab and pinch at each other, as much as at me, as they fight for the prime spot between my legs.

The devil girls have tired of their games on the phone. After an hour of fun, things have quickly deteriorated into scratching and hair pulling, and more than one devil girl is sporting long red marks on a cheek, or breast, or buttock, from another devil girl's long Ruby Rum Punch nails. But now things have calmed down and the red-headed devil girl has popped another Gidget film into the VCR and squealed, "Oh, this is my absolute favorite!" and flopped belly down in front of the TV on the shag rug, her short marabou-trimmed robe flipping up to show bright-red panties. As soon as the titles roll the other devil girls quiet right down. One drops the phone back on a kidney-shaped end table, and then they are all riveted in front of the TV again.

My thoughts stray back to the devil boys and the pit, reentering my fantasy midswing. Rough hands are wrapped around my hips from behind as one of the bigger butch devils, who has fought all comers to take her place, is thrusting her huge cock in my cunt and it feels like it will just split me apart. From the front another pair of hands wraps around my ears to entwine at the back of my skull, and I'm pulled down into the mass of flesh and stink to find myself facing another huge shaft, with several more pressing against my cheeks. Facing the choice between one and three, I dive on the nearest cock, taking as much of it into my mouth and throat as I can, while the hands behind my head pull me down even harder. Hands and thighs and arms and cocks are pinching and rubbing and pulling at me over every inch of my exposed flesh.

I've no idea how much time has passed when suddenly the bodies part, pulling out and away from my battered and abraded body, and I swing free over the pit again, with the melting heat blasting up onto my raw skin. The butch devils are grinning and punching each other, and a couple are fumbling with the stiff leather straps around their hips, and moving their cocks aside to reveal thick mats of hair, or shaven mounds with huge swollen clits. I have just a moment to wonder what the hell they're up to when the first one lets go with a glittering golden stream arching to hit my right thigh as I slowly spin over the pit. Suspended as I am in the rising tower of heat, the liquid feels cool even as it stings my raw reddened skin. One devil boy after another starts to piss, onto my body or down into the pit, and I can hear the hiss and sizzle on the rocks below. The cloud of ammonia vapor envelops me and I see it rise off my dripping skin. I hear a metallic rattle and then I'm falling through the piss steam cloud and down into fiery oblivion.

I sigh, though not loud enough to attract the devil girls' attention, and pick at a half-eaten Sno Ball that's in danger of being ground into the carpet. Who would've thought it would be so boring in hell? One devil girl gets up and picks her way through the prone bodies on the carpet on her way to the bathroom. The movie has grown quiet and I hear a couple of snores, and then a cheery tinkle through the open bathroom door. Hell is not all I had hoped it would be.

Sound Check
Scarlett French

"And...cut," exclaimed my director. "Nice work, Juliet. Perfect first take. We'll have a short break before we do the vox pops. Back here in twenty minutes."

George, our sound operator, leaned his boom against a wall and drifted toward the gate for a cigarette, his headphones dangling around his neck. I took a drink from my water bottle and started toward the main dance floor at the other end of the complex. We'd been shooting solid for an hour—intros, outros, pieces to camera, interviews with revelers. I loved being a TV presenter but I needed a break. Presenting for the biggest queer dance party of the year would bring a lot of kudos for me in the community, but it was a story I would have preferred to be part of, rather than covering.

My crew were great guys: Dave was director and camera op, a difficult balance at times. George was sound op and purveyor of stylish clothes. Every time I saw him he was impeccably dressed in tartan trousers and black turtlenecks, or in some other offbeat and eclectic combination. Both Dave and George were straight, but they were sensitive to queer issues and didn't do that suppressed cringe common to straight men around gay men. They were both freelancers, but I used them for every story because they were reliable and appropriate and we'd built a good rapport. George had hit on me once, and I must confess there was a bit of a spark between us. But it was never going to happen—I wasn't interested in men in that way even if I fantasized about it occasionally. It was one of those erotic thoughts that just wouldn't work in the flesh.

I was feeling pumped, full of adrenaline and the enjoyment of being looked at by hungry eyes as I strode past a seating area full of bulldykes, heading toward the far dance floor to look for my girlfriend. I was wearing a black halter neck and very tight black nylon trousers that went up my crack and rubbed my clit as I walked. I knew they hugged my tight little arse and they shone a little in the light, accentuating its peachlike curves. I felt myself being watched and I relished every step, all the while feeling a building heat in my cunt as I thought about my beautiful girlfriend and felt the rubbing of the trouser seam on my hardening nub.

I reached the dance floor and took the stairs up to the balcony overlooking the DJ. I leaned my elbows on the rail and looked into the pulsating crowd searching for my girl. It took only a minute. There she was, right in the middle of the floor where she said she'd be, caressed by the music, moving with a deep primal rhythm. My soft butch sexy bitch, grounded and grinding, under the strobing colored lights. She was magnificent. I wanted her. I always wanted her. Our hunger for each other hadn't waned since the day we'd met outside a bar in the rain. Outside a bar in the pelting spring rain, waiting for cabs. I keep our meeting story gritty by the detail that no soft-focus lens could capture—her nipples visibly hard and rosy through her sopping white T-shirt and, minutes later, my eager tongue flickering over them, sucking them into my mouth through the wet cotton. That's what it was like with us: hot, urgent.

Always. My mouth watered watching her and I felt my pussy lurching with want, the crotch of my thong saturated.

At that moment she looked up and I caught her eye. I knew she was horny, too. She smiled that languid smile of hers and gestured for me to meet her by the open door. I made my way downstairs to her, grateful for the fresh air from the cooling October night.

"I've got fifteen minutes," I said, running my hand down her strong, sweaty back.

"Come with me, baby." She grabbed my hand and led me quickly down the dim, club-lit corridor leading to the restrooms. A couple of gay boys passed us and cooed, "Love the show!" I smiled thank you and we both walked faster, searching out a quiet corner. My girl used to bartend in this complex and knew every nook and cranny. She pulled me down a blind corridor that stopped with a single locked door and pushed me firmly against the wall. We were alone in the humid dark, the music from the next room muffled-loud and bass-y. I felt her breath on my neck, raising the tiny hairs in anticipation.

"You're all hot, baby. Why is that?" She touched my cheek. "You need to step outdoors?" She slid her hand over my clit and squeezed, just a little. Not enough. I let out a soft moan. "Or you need something else?" She squeezed again, dragging her fingers firmly back and forth over my aching cunt. I twitched, a spasm of pleasure running through my swollen clit.

"We don't have long, baby. What am I going to do with you in ten minutes?"

"Fuck me." I looked straight into her eyes, challenging her. "Fuck me!" I hissed, desperate for her cock. I hadn't felt her crotch but I was sure she was packing tonight. She had that raw air about her when she was harnessed up in public.

"Oh, that's what you'd like, isn't it? That's what you want.

But you get a lot of what you want so maybe you'll just have to wait for it. Maybe tomorrow, baby."

She undid the faux mountaineering clip at the top of my trousers and unzipped me all the way down. She shoved her hand, roughly, inside my underwear and I was ready for her—hot, swollen, and slick with juice. Her middle finger found my straining clit easily and stroked me right there, right on my hard little nub, over and over; rubbing, circling, pushing her finger back toward my cunt, teasing me. I was breathing hard, rasping, unconcerned that we might be discovered. That just made it hotter.

And then her finger slipped into my wet cunt. I caught my breath.

"Oh baby, you feel so good," she whispered in my ear. I clenched my muscles around her finger and she shuddered. "All right, baby, if that's what you want, that's what you get. You want me to fuck you? Huh? Is that what you want?"

I nodded, coyly. I wouldn't show triumph. She always gave me what I wanted but sometimes she made me wait if I was too presumptuous. It was a game we played, a game with a delicate balance. Her finger slid in and out of my pussy, causing the most delicious, desperate pleasure. But I wanted more of her. I wanted her cock. The cock she bought for me. The cock she knew would fit me good, just that little bit too big. The kind of cock I'd have to be dripping for.

She slid my tight nylon trousers down to my ankles. My oversized platform boots wouldn't allow me to remove them. I had no choice but to squat down a little, parting my legs from the knees, my feet firmly held together. I heard her zipper coming down and watched with panting need as her jeans dropped to her ankles and her boxers quickly followed. I could have begged, could have broken my rule about begging, but she saw it in my eyes and that was enough for her. She pinned me to the wall and slammed her dick into me. Hard, up to the hilt. A deep cry escaped me as I felt the length of her desire filling me. She was never this quick, but I couldn't wait any longer and she knew it. She always read me with precision.

"Is this what you wanted, baby?" Her voice was gravelly in my ear. She thrust into me again, hard. "Is it? My stiff dick inside you? That's what you've been needing all day, isn't it, baby?" She thrust into me again and again as she spoke, her cock slick with my juice as she plumbed my depths, driving it into and out of me with dizzying, rhythmic perfection. Every time she thrust into me, the harness slammed into my clit, nudging upward, rubbing it bottom up just the way I liked it. I could make only small movements to meet her thrusts; she had me pinned to the wall and I was trapped by my trousers, bunched and tight around my ankles. I felt a pinch in my back and slithered my hand around to smooth the back of my halter neck. I felt a wire, a long thin wire running the length of my back.

At that moment I realized that my radio mike was still on, attached to the back of my trousers on the floor around my ankles. The tiny microphone was still clipped to my bra and it was live. Through the fog of my cunt-driven brain I realized with a jolt that George could be listening. If any noise had been loud enough he would have heard it, even with his headphones around his neck. I couldn't stop us, though, couldn't bear to break the moment to reach down and find the off switch on the radio mike pack. As my girl's dick thrust into me again with force, a delicious thought ran through my mind: Maybe he was getting off on this, too. That's kinda cool, spreading the fun around. I wasn't interested in touching him but the thought of him touching himself while me and my girl fucked made me hornier, wetter, hungrier. My cunt started to clutch and grab, milking my girl's cock.

I felt taken over by her, by my own desire, and by the thought of a voyeur. I was panting like a dog, hard, fast, and guttural. She was grunting from deep in her guts as she fucked me hard and it was this that finished me off. My orgasm rocketed out of my body like a Guy Fawkes display. I cried out as I bucked and twisted on her shaft. She collapsed against me for a moment to feel my spasms before slowly and gently pulling out of me. We looked at each other for a moment, with a mixture of love and satiety.

"Fuck, twenty minutes! I only had twenty minutes. I must be late!" I pulled my trousers up, zipped and clipped, and kissed her squarely on her hot mouth as she slipped her cock back inside her trousers.

"Come and find me when you're finished, baby. I'll be dancing." She turned to walk away, then turned back. "By the way, your mike's on." She smirked at me and began sauntering back toward the dance floor. She knew! She knew and she didn't say anything. It made me want her all over again. Our chemistry was explosive, but even if I'd been reveling rather than working there would have been no more, not just yet. She liked to build it up, she liked to tease herself. She'd take one slowly built up orgasm for every four of mine. That was the way she liked it. I watched her sexy ass moving as she walked away from me, then I broke into a run to reach the end of the complex.

Half an hour had passed. I reached our meeting point and looked first at Dave. At least my panting could be attributed to the running.

"You're late," said Dave, slightly annoyed. "Ten minutes late. Time is money, y'know, especially for camera crew."

"I'm sorry, Dave. There was a long line at the bar."

"Well, I'll let it go this time. I got time for an extra beer, and George got a couple of smokes. You look a little flushed. You ought to have rested."

"Nah, I had a quick dance, Dave. It keeps me hyped."

"All right, let's get set up for vox pops."

I looked at George. For someone who'd spent half an hour smoking by a gate on a cool evening, he was looking pretty warm and relaxed. His hair also seemed a little sweaty on the ends, like he'd recently been in a hot, enclosed space. I looked at his headphones. They were around his neck as before, but I could see beads of sweat on the earpieces, glistening in the lights from the event complex. I smiled at the thought, hoping he'd had a good time on me.

Blue Suede Shoes
Kristina Wright

The invitation to my best friend's thirtieth birthday party had said, "Come as your idol." So, there I was in Caroline's living room, dressed in a skin-tight white dress that flowed around me like a cloud and flaunted my ample cleavage, sweating under a blond wig and more makeup than I'd ever worn in my life.

"Hey, girl, you look incredible!" Caroline screeched from across the room. She was dolled up in some sort of belly dancer's costume that winked and sparkled with every move she made. I had a huge crush on Caroline once upon a time. Her being straight didn't much matter to me. I valued her friendship too much to make a play for her even if she had liked girls.

"Let me guess—Cher, circa 1975?" I asked.

She laughed and her costumed twinkled. Caroline's cleavage made me look like a boy and I grinned appreciatively. A girl can look, can't she?

"No, Mata Hari."

I arched a perfectly sculpted brow. "Odd choice of idol material."

"She knew how to handle men." Did I mention Caroline was going through a bad breakup? I kept telling her she needed to give up men, but she wouldn't listen. Instead, she kept trading one jerk for another. Speaking of which, I watched Caroline practically swoon as a James Dean look-alike sauntered by with a boyish smirk.

"Good point. Now, could you point me in the direction of the beverage table?" I fanned myself. "I'm dying in this crowd."

Caroline pushed me toward the dining room where two guys wearing Jordan jerseys were tapping a keg.

"Thanks," I called over my shoulder as Caroline sashayed off toward Jimmy Dean.

I grabbed a plastic cup and thrust it toward the Jordan twins. "Fill 'er up," I said.

Jordan #1 filled my cup while Jordan #2 eyed my dress, his gaze hovering around my tits. I waved him away. "You're not my type, Mikey."

"How about me, darlin'?"

I turned toward the husky voice and fell in love. The brunette wasn't wearing a wig and her jet-black hair was slicked back in a sexy pompadour. She'd painted sideburns on her sculpted cheeks, but the full lips and smoky eyes weren't fakes. The leather jacket and black pants fit her like a second skin, and the guitar slung over her shoulder looked like a beloved friend rather than a prop.

"I'd play in your band anytime," I said with a grin and a swish of my skirt.

She smirked. "I'm looking for groupies, not band members, sweetheart."

Caroline came up behind me and whirled me around. "You've got to meet this chick," she said, gesturing at a cowgirl in chaps.

"Whoa, horsey," I said. "Who is she?"

"Annie Oakley." Caroline steered me across the room and I lost track of my leather babe.

Annie turned out to be a bit confused about what she liked, so I wandered away after the third mention of her ex-husband's dick. I had a cup of spiked punch in one hand and a plate of seven-layer bean dip in the other hand when I literally bumped into my new wet dream.

"Hey!" She swung the guitar away from me in one smooth gesture as punch went flying. "Nice move, Norma Jean."

I blushed to the roots of my blond wig. "Oh god, I'm sorry." I dabbed at her leather jacket with the corner of a napkin and got an amused grin for my efforts.

"Easy, dollface. It'll clean. My shoes, on the other hand...."

Her voice trailed off as we both looked downward. She was black leather head to toe, but her shoes...oh, her shoes! Blue suede leather with square toes and chunky heels. They were shoes with an attitude to match their owner, only now they were splotchy in places from my punch.

"Maybe if you take them off we can use some club soda on them." I rolled my eyes. "Oh god, I just channeled my mother!"

Her laugh was whiskey sexy. "She'd be so proud." She tucked a finger in the halter top of my dress and tugged. "C'mon, I don't care if you're Marilyn or Martha, if you're going to feel me up, let's do it in private."

I didn't think I could get any redder as she led me off to Caroline's bedroom. I followed her into the master bath, feeling like I was in some sort of surreal suburban dream in which the studly rock star invades the housewife's bedroom. Only I was no suburban housewife and my rock star was no stud.

She lifted the guitar strap off her shoulder and propped the guitar against the door. Then she stripped off her leather jacket, revealing a black T-shirt that showed almost as much cleavage as my white dress did. "My shirt is soaked," she said, but there was no anger in her voice. If anything, she sounded amused.

"I'm sorry." I wasn't quite sure why she wanted me in here and I was doing my damnedest not to stare at her chest.

She didn't help matters by pulling the shirt off and standing there topless. Her tits were small and pert with nipples almost as dark as her hair. She grinned at my stunned expression.

"Am I offending your delicate sensibilities?"

I found my voice and said, "Hardly."

"Good." She ran some water in the sink and tossed the shirt in.

I leaned against the counter as she sat on the edge of the tub and tugged her shoes off. "What's your name?" I asked, desperately needing to distract myself from her perky tits.

"Call me El," she said, dropping the shoes on the floor.

"You're kidding."

She arched a jet-black brow. "I never kid."

Whoever she was, she was getting to me. The vee of my halter was soaked with sweat and I was starting to think it wouldn't be a bad idea to get undressed myself.

El stood up and drained the water from the sink. She wrung her shirt out and hung it over the edge of the tub. "I think it survived. I'm not so sure about my blue suede shoes, though."

"I'll buy you a new pair."

"They're vintage. You can't replace them," she said.

Despite her mild tone, I felt my temper spike. "Well, what the hell do you want me to do, then?"

"Wanna be my groupie?"

I couldn't help it, her unaffected smirk made me laugh. "Is that a fair exchange? They're one-of-a-kind, after all. They look expensive."

She took two steps forward and hooked her fingers in the vee of my halter. "And you look like a good fuck."

"It's the dress," I said breezily, though I felt anything but breezy.

"Take it off and we'll find out."

My smile faltered. It wasn't that I didn't want to fuck her, it wasn't even that I hadn't had my share of party quickies before. I just wasn't sure I was ready to rock-n-roll in Caroline's bathroom, with the suburbs waiting just outside the door.

"Cat got your tongue?" she asked, her callused finger caressing my cleavage. "I know you're not Sandra Dee. Caroline told me a little about you, and she said you'd love me."

If she was trying to convince me with her husky drawl, she was going about it all wrong. "I've gotten a little more...selective in my old age," I said.

She pouted, her bottom lip full and sexy without a trace of lipstick. "I'm hurt."

"You'll get over it." I was starting to relax and enjoy this. "I'm sure you'll find your next groupie right outside the door."

"But I want *you*," she murmured, her hand caressing my tits through the silky white fabric. She tugged at a nipple when it hardened under her touch. "And I think you want me."

I licked my heavily lipsticked lips. "Who, me? Play with a bad-boy rocker like you?"

She smirked, a little more confident now. "Yeah, babe. C'mon, take off this dress and show me your tits."

I laughed, but it was to cover my nervousness. Did I really want to get it on in Caroline's bathroom with a woman who had jelled her hair into a ducktail?

Yeah, actually, I did.

I reached behind my neck to untie the halter of my dress. It fell, revealing those plastic shells that are supposed to lift and support the breasts without covering the nipples.

"Yummy," El said. She reached out and yanked the shells off my tits.

"Damn!" I shrieked. "That hurt!"

El leaned forward and kissed my open mouth hard, until I forgot the pain in my tits. She didn't touch me with any other part of her body, and it was both strange and erotic as hell to feel only her mouth and tongue.

Finally, she braced her hands on my hips and pulled me closer. I moaned in her mouth as she tugged my dress down so that it pooled around my feet. She leaned back to look at me in my thigh-high stockings and white heels and whistled softly. "Whoa, babe. Sexy."

I couldn't blush any brighter. "Thanks."

She braced one hand on my hip and leaned forward, running her tongue across my bottom lip. "You up for this?"

It sounded like a challenge. I hadn't exactly come to this party expecting to be picked up by an Elvis impersonator, but it beat the hell out of munching on bean dip and mini quiches.

By way of answer, I leaned into her, which pressed out bodies together from chest to hips. Her nipples were as hard as mine and I rubbed against her like a cat. She moaned and it echoed off the bathroom walls, or maybe that was me echoing her. A few minutes of bump and grind combined with the heat of our bodies had us both slick with sweat. She sat on the toilet lid and pulled me down so that I straddled her leather-clad thigh. The heat of her body through her leather pants made my pussy tingle in anticipation.

"You are the hottest thing I've seen in a long time," she whispered against my neck as her hands teased and tormented my nipples. "A boy like me could fall hard."

She shifted me higher up so that my cunt was in close contact with her crotch. Close enough so that I could tell she was packing. Just the thought of what she might be able to do to me with what she was carrying around in her pants was enough to make me moan.

She reached between my thighs and slid a long, callused finger inside me. "Naughty girl. You're supposed to wear panties."

"Easy access," I panted, and they were the last words I said for a while as she finger-fucked me to a delicious orgasm. I bit down hard on her shoulder to keep from screaming out loud and alerting Caroline and the rest of the mini-driving, car-pooling folks drinking punch and eating pinwheels just beyond the bathroom door.

"Little wild child, aren't you?" El asked, withdrawing her fingers from my dripping cunt. "You hardly made me work for it at all."

I shifted against her, driving my crotch tight up against her package so that she gasped. "But I still might make you work for it," I murmured.

"Like to see you try."

Now, the thing about me is this: Don't challenge me, because I'll leave you in a whimpering, quivering puddle when I'm done with you.

"Oh, you really shouldn't have said that," I whispered, slipping from her lap to my knees. "You're going to regret it."

I was pleased to see the self-satisfied smirk fade. What was left was an expression of anticipation and hunger.

I unzipped her pants, which was no small feat given that they were practically painted on and she was packing a dick. The dick wasn't a strap-on, so I pushed it out of the way as I dragged the pants down her hips, with her raising her ass to help me.

"Elvis doesn't wear underwear either," I said, tossing her pants aside.

The sneer was back. "Bad boys never do."

"Let's see just how bad you are." I didn't give her a chance to respond. I spread her legs as far as I could, holding her open before me. Nothing on the buffet table in Caroline's dining room had looked so good.

"Pretty," I whispered. I inhaled her musky, arousing scent. "God, you're soaked."

"Don't admire it, eat it," she rasped when I made no move toward her.

"Patience, El."

She made to close her thighs and I wouldn't let her. I pushed back until she was splayed even wider and she winced. "Not so fast, boy."

I kissed the inside of her thigh and felt her jump. I smiled and did the same to the other thigh. This time, expecting it, she didn't move. Still, I could feel the tension in her muscles, the quiver of anticipation and need. It made me feel powerful, in control. If she hadn't already gotten me off, I might have been as needy as she was. As it was, my desire was a soft hum beneath my skin, a quickening in my pulse that was palpable but not yet desperate. Not yet.

I parted her cunt with my thumbs, baring her moist pink flesh to me. She was beautiful and savage all at once, and I could barely restrain myself from devouring her and bringing her off as quickly as she'd finished me.

"So beautiful," I breathed, no more than an inch from her. "You smell like heaven."

"And I taste like ambrosia, so eat me."

I had to laugh at her fierce tone, so demanding and harsh despite the fact I was in control. She hadn't learned yet, but she would.

I teased her with a promise, a quick lick from bottom to top, lingering only momentarily on her luscious, engorged clit before drawing back to look up at her. "We should probably get out of here before someone interrupts us," I said.

"Okay." I knew she would call my bluff.

I released her tender flesh and started to stand, but she instantly had her hands on my shoulders, drawing me back down, holding me in place.

"No way, no fucking way." Her fingers dug into my shoulders. "Don't leave me like this."

I arched a delicately sculpted brow, imaging how I must look to her—a blonde bombshell on her knees, smiling innocently and angelically. No wonder she was gritting her teeth and scowling at me.

"What do you want?" I whispered, my fingers stroking the lips of her cunt so softly she shivered. "What do you need?"

"Your mouth," she whispered. "I need your mouth on me."

"Ask nicely." I don't know where the bitch attitude was coming from, but she inspired me to push harder.

"Oh god, please," she said, her hands urging me between the legs she spread willingly. "Please."

I wanted to wait longer, tease her, make her beg for it, but her voice, so husky and rough, made my pulse jump. Without warning, my need was suddenly as desperate as hers.

With a sigh, I buried my face in her crotch, sucking and licking her like a hungry animal. She clamped her thighs around my shoulders, anchoring me to her as if she feared I would stop again. I ran my tongue over her clit and down to the wet, open hole of her cunt, drawing her juice onto my tongue before circling her clit once more. She moaned and clutched at my head, the pins of the wig digging into my scalp.

I jerked back, yanking the wig off with a flurry of pins scattering across the bathroom tile. She stared at me, panting, as my brown hair cascaded down around my shoulders.

"I like that even better," she said, attempting to pull me back to her.

I fumbled around for the dildo she'd been packing, drawing it up between her legs. It wasn't particularly long, but it was thick and velvety soft. I teased her open cunt with it, rubbing the head against her clit before sliding it down and easing it into her ever so gently.

"Oh man, damn," she groaned as I pushed into her. "Fuck me."

"So hot, so needy, and still so bossy," I teased. I withdrew the dildo and rubbed it over her cunt without penetrating her again, spreading her juices over her lips and inner thighs.

"C'mon," she begged. "Don't be such a cunt tease."

"Stop telling me what to do," I said. But I didn't make her wait long. With one swift motion, I pushed the dildo into her up to the hilt, attacking her clit with my mouth at the same time.

She groaned from the multiple sensations, arching her back until she was bent nearly backward over the toilet, one leg hooked over my shoulder, the other braced high on the wall. I fucked her hard and fast while my tongue made lazy circles around her clit, then I swapped, moving the dildo in her gently while I sucked her clit like a piece of juicy fruit. Back and forth I alternated as her hips quivered and shook and thrust against me, never quite making up their mind what they should do.

She wasn't as quiet as I had been, and her soft cries echoed off the bathroom walls. My own thighs were clenched together as I rocked my hips in time to the dildo in her cunt, aching to be touched again.

She cried out as I twisted the dildo inside her and nibbled her clit. Whimpered when I withdrew the fake cock and drove it back into her. And then, with a banshee wail, she came against my mouth, her legs tense and quivering, her fist against her mouth as if that would stifle her.

I rode the wave of her orgasm with gentle licks on her clit and the hard, deep thrusting of the dildo in her cunt until she unwound from me and groaned.

I smiled up at her, twisting the dildo inside her so gently before slowly drawing it out of her still-clenching hole.

"Oh. My. God." She panted and shook, fingers clenching

and unclenching.

"Yeah?"

"Amazing."

I grinned at her praise. "Thanks."

She straightened up, trying to compose herself, which was difficult given that she was buck naked except for socks.

"That was incredible."

I started to say she could return the favor, but there was a knock on the bathroom door.

"Damn." She scowled. "I wasn't quite finished with you yet."

A boy after my own heart.

I snatched my dress up and tugged it on. "Later."

We got dressed quickly, her forgoing the wet T-shirt and carrying both it and her shoes in her hand. I didn't bother with the wig—even if I hadn't been drenched in sweat, it wouldn't have been the most comfortable thing to put on.

"You go first," I said, nudging her toward the bathroom door.

"Ladies first," she said, pushing me forward and opening the door before I could say otherwise.

Caroline stood there, grinning like the know-it-all she was. That didn't bother me nearly as much as the twenty-odd costumed people standing behind her and applauding.

I looked at El and she looked at me. I burst out laughing as she said, "Thank you, thank you very much."

Caroline dragged me off to the kitchen, no doubt to get the dirt on my fling with a rock star, but not before El could drag me close and whisper in my ear, "Hell of a performance, doll."

"How do you feel about giving me a private show?" I said over my shoulder.

"For you? That was just an opening act," she said.

Like I said, a boy after my own heart. Blue suede shoes and all.

Flirting into Cami
Tara Alton

Today, in an effort to be more creative, I moved all the lovely
Bettie Page merchandise, such as the key chains, postcards,
wallets, and jewelry, into one central location in the store. I
figured anyone coming into the store to look for items featuring the most beautiful 1950s pinup in the world would
appreciate my initiative. However, Viv, my boss, didn't
appreciate it at all. She said she liked everything in Scarlet
Leather the way it was. Bor-ing. I know you may be thinking:
To the general public, the store doesn't seem boring because
it's a fetish store, featuring everything from leather to PVC
to vintage lingerie, but to me, it was the most boring place in
the world. I hated working here. Nothing ever changed, and I
never made enough money to put a deposit on an apartment,
so I had to rent a room by the week in this dingy, ancient
motel across the street.

Who knows how much longer Viv will put up with me?
Therefore, probably rendering me homeless as well. My list
of workplace sins multiplies by the week. I have already been
reprimanded for wearing the merchandise, which I figured

might help sales because I was modeling it, but Viv says how could we call it new when my skin has been all over it.

Another sore point was that I'm a vegetarian, and sometimes I feel compelled to apologize to the leather for its untimely and painful demise. I tried to steer people to the non-leather items, but leather was our best-seller. You can imagine the conflict.

Now, I had an even bigger problem. If I got caught, I was done for sure. I've been spying on someone in the dressing room. To Viv, the dressing room is a sacred place, the holiest of holies. She said people needed to feel safe while they try on their kinkiest fantasies, and they needed a bond of trust with us.

I agreed with her, but then again, she hadn't seen Neha, this girl from India, who worked at a restaurant around the corner. She came in on her lunch break, and while listening to a CD on her headset, she tried on clothes. Mostly, she chose the same camisole every day. It was baby pink with a zipper down the back. I thought she looked amazing in it, and I loved her boldness and abandon while she danced. No wonder I had become infatuated with her.

I've never had an actual crush on a woman before, but I have had some experiences. I was roommates with a bisexual girl who went to after-hour lesbian clubs, and she took me with her. I experimented, but mostly because my roommate was doing it. In the rear of the clubs, in the dark shadows, I liked making out with tomboyish girls, but I'd never gone past second base.

Another experience was with my yoga instructor a few years back. I nearly had a Tantric sex threesome with her and a fellow student, but I chickened out at the last moment. I made a quick exit and went home to have a soy milk blueberry smoothie instead.

Now I was into this naughty schoolgirl thing. I liked wearing tartan skirts, white blouses, and knee socks while wearing facial piercings. I can't say that it has been working for me. I haven't had sex for months. In an effort to curb my sexual frustration, I've been ripping electrical tape off my skin while I masturbate. I know; I'm a freak. But I'm really into the pain and pleasure at the same time sort of thing.

After Viv gave me a firm reprimand about Bettie Page, she left for lunch. I restored all the merchandise to its original location, apologized to a former cow that was now a leather mask, electrical taped my nipples behind the counter for later, and proceeded to stare at the walls.

And then, Neha came in.

I couldn't believe how gorgeous she was. Her skin was like the color of coffee with cream. Her eyes were like a cat. Her long hair swept over her shoulders like the darkest night.

With no hesitation, she took the baby pink camisole into the dressing room. I sighed, wishing she would give me her own private fashion show, when I realized she had left the dressing room door completely open. Being the quick-change artist of the century, she had already stripped down to her panties and put on the camisole.

Beginning to dance to the music on her headset, Neha glanced over her shoulder at me, shimmying her shoulders to the beat of the music.

I was too stunned to move. Hanging onto the doorjamb, she twitched her hips in a seductive pattern. It was almost as if she was fucking someone. My mouth went dry. Letting go of the door, she beckoned to me with her finger. Like the good sales assistant I was, I took a few hesitant steps her way.

"Do you like me in this?" she asked, very loud, as if she were a little kid wearing a headset who couldn't gauge the level of her voice.

"Very much," I said.

She lowered her headset.

"I'm saving up my tips from the restaurant to buy it," she said, her voice quieter. Now it sounded like honey. "My father says most of my money has to go to college. He would be furious if he knew I wanted to buy this, or if I was even here."

Gracefully, she held up her hair off the nape of her neck and spun around.

"Do you think I look sexy?" she asked.

"Yes."

"Like 'oh baby I want to fuck you' sexy?" she asked.

I nodded.

"So say it," she said.

"Say what?"

She looked at me. I realized what she meant.

"You look 'oh baby I want to fuck you' sexy," I said.

The moment the words left my mouth, I blushed.

"Do you want to fuck me?" she asked.

If she had X-ray vision and looked at my crotch, she probably could have seen the visible proof that I did.

"If you take some of that metal off your face, I'll kiss you," she said.

Hands trembling, I removed my lip and eyebrow ring, but I left my nose stud.

Gracefully, she put her arms around my neck and kissed me. I was startled by the softness of her lips, so smooth. She broke away.

"You taste like an apple," she said.

"I ate a Jolly Rancher before you came in," I said.

"Put this music on," she said, taking out a disc. "We can play."

"Play what?"

"Girl stuff," she said.

"Will there be more kissing involved?" I asked.

She nodded. As I locked the front door, put up the "back in fifteen minutes" sign in the window, and popped the CD in the stereo, I wondered if I should be doing this. Viv would have a kitten if she caught me. The music was Indian Bollywood. Soaring crystal vocals accompanied by an up-tempo beat filled the store.

"Let's be leather girls," she announced.

"I don't do leather," I said.

"Okay. PVC then."

As she went to pick out some outfits, I felt self-conscious getting undressed. I took off my white blouse and tartan skirt, and I looked at myself in the mirror. Now that was a good look: white cotton panties, white socks, nose ring, and the electrical tape on my nipples.

She came back with the most outrageous bright purple PVC hot pants with matching halter top for me. Was this how she saw me? There was no way I could wear my underwear in these. Turning around, I dropped my panties to the floor and tugged on the shorts. I liked the way the PVC hugged my skin, but I wasn't entirely sure how they made my ass look. I started to put on the halter, but she stopped me.

"No. Just wear that," she said. "I like it."

Meanwhile, she took off her own panties. There was no turning around for her, though. For herself, she chose a wet-look PVC and chain thong featuring a stretchy Lycra back and elasticized ends on the chains. Her skin was so smooth. I noticed a spray of freckles on her hip.

"My pink cami doesn't go with my thong," she said, looking in the mirror.

She was right. The styles clashed. Unabashedly, she unzipped her camisole and shrugged it to the floor. So much for its being her favorite thing. Breasts now bare, her nipples erect as little pencil erasers, she reached down and held up a pair of nipple clamps with a chain in between them.

"Now, this goes with my thong," she said, smiling. "Put it on me."

Although I had stocked plenty of these, I had never actually used them. With just a light squeeze, the outsides opened up and I positioned them on her. They were not adjustable. I could tell by her face the pressure was intense, but she sucked in her breath, admiring the almost flowerlike style of the clamps gripping her nipples.

Her fingers strayed over to my breasts. I was wondering what she was about to do when she caught a fingernail under an edge and ripped a piece of tape off me. Yikes. I gasped. The shock nearly knocked me to the wall. It never felt like that when I did it. Nevertheless, I sure did like the tingling afterward. Three more rips and I was exposed, my nipples a nice rosy glow to go with my purple hot pants.

She motioned to me to take off her nipple clamps. Her eyes widened and she held her breath.

"Does it hurt?" I asked.

She let out her breath.

"Like pins and needles," she said with a laugh.

There was a pause. She looked intently at me. I hesitated. Even with all this nipple torture, I realized we still hadn't gone past second base. Did I want to go any further?

Sliding her arms around me again, she embraced me. I felt her body. The bones of her rib cage felt delicate under my fingers, the contours of her body felt downy. I traced her body as if I were tracing my own, intimate, soothing, caressing. Her hands slid down to my ass and she squeezed it hard. She liked me in these hot pants, I realized.

"I want to stick something in you," she said.

Your tongue would be nice, I thought, but I realized she was looking at the display case just outside the dressing door. On the top was a clear Pyrex dildo with blue bumps. It looked more like a work of art than a sex toy.

Lickety split, she grabbed the dildo and a bottle of lube. She crouched in front of me, yanking down my PVC hot pants. She was so frantic I felt like I was being bushwhacked. I tried to protest, but suddenly she grabbed the back of the hot pants from behind and gave it a good yank. I gasped. All my personal business was right in front of her face.

"If you don't get on the floor, I'm going to stick it in you standing up," she said.

I got on the floor.

It was somewhat bizarre with me lying on the dressing room floor, my legs open as if I were at a pelvic exam and her looming over me with the Pyrex. I was supposed to be doing this stuff to her, not the other way around. This certainly wasn't my idea of a seduction, but obviously my pussy had other ideas.

I wanted her to kiss it first, explore it with her tongue, do things to me with her fingers, but she poured some lube on the tip and slid it inside me.

The thickness of Pyrex shocked me. It was so cold and heavy, but it filled me up. The girth of it was almost overwhelming. I couldn't believe how unyieldingly solid it was. Everything slid in and out so easily with the lube. Making love to a woman shouldn't feel like this, I thought. I felt as if I were being fucked by something substantial.

I opened my legs more, becoming lost in the lovely and intense sensations. Closing my eyes, I relished the feeling as she started twisting it, the colorful bumps hitting all the right spots with its extra texture. My knees relaxed. I opened up more, taking in all seven inches. My body started to rock with the thrusts. I slid my hands down between my legs, feeling it going inside me. For a second I panicked, realizing it had no flared base. It felt like it was going to shoot up inside me forever. I grabbed her hand to calm the fluttering in my heart and then we were both fucking me with it.

I was going to come. Right in front of this perfect stranger, I was going to have one of the most intimate moments in the world. With the distorted thinking of a little kid, I thought if I kept my eyes closed, she couldn't see me, but as an adult I knew she could. I opened my eyes. I was shocked. There was no warm and intimate gaze simmering in her eyes. She was looking at me not as a lover, but more as if she was watching something, detached and amused.

A chill shook my body. This wasn't right. Neha wasn't being intimate with me. She was manipulating me as she might a toy. I fought my coming orgasm, but it only made me come that much harder. Little lights popped in my vision, and I felt heat rising from my feet. A tingle rushed up my legs to my thighs to my pelvis to my stomach. Euphoria burst forth and I felt like I was falling. I arched back, letting go of her hand, my orgasm nearly rendering me unconscious for several seconds.

As the last shudder left my body and everything came back into focus, I felt her pull the Pyrex out. I felt pounds lighter and clamped my legs shut.

Suddenly, there was a rattle and then a banging at the front door. Like two schoolgirls nearly caught by their parents, we tugged on our clothes. I shoved the play clothes into the corner and stuck the dildo and lube in a drawer as I came out of the dressing room.

Oh horrors. It was Viv at the front door. The moment I unlocked it, my newly found lover shot past us outside without even a goodbye.

"What is going on?" Viv demanded. "Why was the door locked?"

Quickly, I sought my brain for a lie when I saw Neha almost at the corner with a flash of baby pink in her hand, the zipper flapping in the breeze. She had stolen the camisole, or rather she had fucked me for it, I realized.

Maybe it was the orgasm that cleared my brain, but suddenly the last thing I wanted to do was lose my job, especially because of Neha.

"I just had sex with that girl on the dressing room floor," I said, pointing down the street at her. "And she stole the baby pink cami."

Viv raised an eyebrow and sighed. Affectionately, she patted me on the head as if I were twelve years old, then handed me a box of vibrators the deliveryman must have left on the doorstep.

"You're going to have to come up with something better than that, sweetheart," she said. "You don't even like girls."

Doing the Dressage Queen
Rakelle Valencia

She showed up with sunglasses and an attitude on, and didn't take either of them off. That's how I knew she wanted me.

I'd seen her yesterday, and the day before that. This was the third day of a four-day colt-starting clinic. The woman was immaculately groomed, much as a four-legged, champion show-jumper would be. I pegged her for a Dressage Queen. Her brunette hair was lashed up in a severe bun, obliterating the effect of expensive highlights she'd had painted in. Contempt was smeared across her face as if she had smelled a bad fart. And the lady sauntered around in those skin-tight, stretchy, posh breeches that you could read lips through.

She was making a statement or two with her crumpled, pristine, white slouch socks attempting to rest atop name-brand cross-trainers, and with her starched blouse, prim and proper, peeking from an all-to-purposefully rumpled, brand new, zip-up, hooded sweatshirt. Maybe the classically trained equestrian was dressing down for the likes of a cowboy. Oh, she was making more than one statement, all right. And I was listening to her silent language, but didn't let on. The woman needed to be bent over.

No words would pass between us. That would be the way she would want it. You know, to save face, so that she didn't actually have to speak to the "hired help." She sorely underestimated my abilities. I had never been a two-bit, drifter cowboy, and I'd long ago surpassed being a ranch wrangler. I break colts and lecture about horse language. I'm an equine behaviorist, if you want to get fancy about it. Horse whispering is my trade. So if I can hear the covert language of a majestic, humbled animal, then I can certainly read the overt body language of a spoiled richie.

As the sun waned and the last of the colts had been saddled and mounted for the first time in their lives, then taken from the round pen to be put up for the night, the Dressage Queen hung by the corral gate. Like always, I slapped my coiled lariat against my leather chinks, chasing clouds of dust from the waxed rope before stuffing it into the gear bag. My hand efficiently popped the thigh buckles of my short chaps, then drifted to the center waist-tie slashing above my crotch. I caught her eyes searching me up and down with approval, and a slight plea. Her sporty sunglasses were finally shed after three days, but not her attitude.

I shoved the limp, worn leather chinks, or short chaps, roughly into the bag with the rest of my tools. My day here was done, but the riding wasn't going to end.

I tipped my hat, nodded my head, and hoisted the jingling gear bag over my lean shoulder. She fell in behind me on the walk to my beat-up, rusted dually. I would have offered, but she oozed into her sleek Mercedes.

The hotel wasn't cheap, sturdy furniture and all. The ranch had done right by me. Leaving the door open behind, I dumped my gear on the extra bed and then toe-to-heel, pulled off my boots. The heavy door had slammed and a bolt clicked.

I weaseled out of my Wranglers and boot socks, then turned to pluck one button at a time down the front of my western-yoked work shirt while staring her in the eyes. She seemed unconcerned, feigning boredom. I walked over and sucked her lower lip, at the same time jamming my hand between her legs to where the seam on those stretchy riding pants hid in her crease.

Playing "good girls don't," she halfheartedly tried to pull away. I bit down. Her little, tailored pants grew wet in my palm.

I shed the last of my clothes but the princess made no move to join me in my nudity. She stood and gawked with a holier-than-thou smirk as dust littered the air and dirt polluted the carpeting. But she made no move to leave either.

Undaunted, I unclipped my pocketknife from discarded jeans and flipped open the lock-back blade, the snap of it resounding off hollow-core walls. Her arms crossed in front, not defensively, once again seemingly bored. She stood back on one leg, dropping a hip.

Okay, so I was the naked one, I was the vulnerable-looking one, but I had the knife. I walked my farmer's tan, white-washed hide around back of her and entangled my fingers in that severe bun, loosening strands that went wild to dribble between her shoulders. I breathed into her ear and raked my teeth along the lobe, wanting to whisper for her not to move.

I didn't. She would soon understand, and, after all, this was her game, not mine. I slipped the dull side of my blade from her clit to her anus. She sucked in a breath, standing more erect, and dropped both her hands to cover her pussy. I had her. It was my game now.

Flipping the blade over, with the sharpened point I sliced through those expensive breeches, parting them with an expansive gap. The Dressage Queen reached behind with both her hands, her thin wrists easily captured and subdued in my calloused grip. The knife had done its job. I tugged her a step toward the spare bed, toward my bag so that I could discard the steel blade and retrieve a new tool.

Tripping her forward a few feet, not releasing my hold, I bent her over. The sight of her meaty, rounded ass protruding from the growing slit in her breeches would under different circumstances have made me beg.

My eyes followed the path of a silken, black thong dipping into her smiling crack. I squatted to pull it aside with my teeth. I could smell her. Scrubbed so clean, she had the fragrance of Ivory soap mixed with a new seeping muskiness, even after a day in the sun.

I shoved her over the end of the wooden, polished bureau to sink my face in further. Her pouty, reddened, nether lips pushed at me from below but I attacked her brown, pursed hole. If I hadn't had my other fist filled with a thick, silicone dong, I would have patted those wet, red lips and squeezed their smaller, twin globes of flesh together as I tortured the winking puckered asshole with my tongue. I didn't have enough hands.

From the spit-slicked anus, the head of my rubbery dick sluiced to her sodden snatch in one motion. The slippery sucker found her drenched opening and took it from behind. The sight of my black silicone rod plunging in, only to be withdrawn covered in cream, made my mouth water and my own cunt drool.

I had to do her, then. I had to fuck her like I knew she wanted. But I wasn't harnessed. I slapped the flanged end just above my own slit, holding the dick between split fingers, against my shaven runway strip, and lunged. She moaned and poked her wide ass to my belly. If I were a young boy I would have shot off a load then. I was close now.

Dropping a finger to my clit shaft I clenched at myself, still gripping the dong as I pounded the princess. Again I wished I had more hands. I wanted more fingers. Her asshole winked at me with each thrust, chastising my lack until I loosed the Dressage Queen's wrists and jabbed at its single eye.

The woman shrieked in an unladylike manner. She knocked her head to the wooden top of the bureau and rolled it around with a spittle of drool pooling from her tense, pulled-back lips. Teeth exposed in a snarl like a rabid dog, she clawed and raked my buttocks with her nails, cramming my rangy body to her fleshy asscheeks.

As I pounded her, I was pounding my own clit, straining with an inner force. That, mixed with the sight of my driving dick and the feel of my finger in her butt, shot me off in spasmodic waves of wetness. Not wanting to scream like a girlie-girl, I leaned onto her and bit her meaty side.

She came. Screeching and cussing to put both tomcats and truckers to shame, she came on my dildo and clamped around my finger. Her high-pitched shrill dropped off to silence. One of her hands now dug at the bureau while the other slapped my ass rhythmically until she sucked in a deep breath and began panting.

I was done with that act but I was far from *done*. I climbed off her and abandoned my dick to plop out on its own. Introductions and girlie warm-ups over, I thought I'd get a night out of her highness but first wanted to knock off the dust and grit from the day. I headed for the shower, leaving the satiated, disheveled lump to revive herself.

When I emerged refreshed and clean, the do-me Dressage Queen was gone. Her shredded breeches had been left behind. I assumed she had worn her attitude and the Mercedes home.

Pointed
Skian McGuire

I wedge the Coke bottle between my legs, hard against the crotch of my jeans. Outside, the Connecticut landscape slips by, hardly noticed. The seats around me are empty. I could beat off, probably, grinding against that cold plastic until I got so close to orgasm I could scream. I don't come that easy. I need something inside me, or a vibrator buzzing against the ring in my clit hood like a tiny chainsaw.

I've been reading porn: not a good choice for a four-hour bus ride. The book has one of my own stories in it, but I never had time to look at it until now. I work too much. All my friends say so. Between the day jobs and all the miscellaneous stuff of living, plus whatever sleep I can't get by without, every minute left over is like a nickel to a tightwad. Mostly, I have to choose between living my porn and reading it. Writing porn is like a drug, when my brain is on fire for something I can't have so I have to make it up. I just can't help myself.

It always starts with a picture—something that flashes on the screen of my mind over and over again, film looped around the reels of my imagination, and I might as well be strapped down to a chair with my eyelids wired open. Right now, the picture is your shoes. They are shoes with toes pointed like a mean pair of garden shears, like a raven's beak, like a stingy wedge of pie, and I can't get them out of my head.

The crowded bookstore was loud with conversation and the clatter of folding chairs. I was happy the reading was over, making small talk with the other writers and fans, looking forward to the hot date waiting for me, when you came up behind and put your arm around me. I didn't have to look to know it was you. I hardly missed a beat, just leaned back a little into your touch, feeling your soft warmth, your feathery scarf brushing my arm. I smiled and kept talking. So cool. Until I turned at last, and my self-possession left me at the sight of you.

I get shy. I'm sure you know that, even though you don't know me very well. You may even have been teasing me just a little, the way girls do sometimes, to get me to blush, and I have to look down out of embarrassment and tongue-tied, dry-mouthed panic. I couldn't meet your eyes. I stared at the floor, instead, and there, waiting to shanghai my imagination, were the toes of your pointy, pointy shoes.

An American Van Lines semi rolls slowly by, my eyes following it mindlessly. I know this is ridiculous. I'm not like the foot-fetishists, submissive straight men who go all weak and pathetic at the sight of a woman's shoes. I don't give a rat's ass about shoes, except as I'm a sucker for a well-turned calf and I do appreciate the gift of sex on a plate, when a femme dolls herself up for me with clingy clothes and cleavage and dangerous fuck-me heels. Shoes are things that get strewn somewhere on the way to bed, unless she's the kind of girl who likes to wear high heels while I fuck her from behind, or likes to play porn star, squatting on those strappy stilettos while she sucks my cock, or flings her legs around me while I'm driving it in, and how come the shoes never fall off, anyway? Is there some kind of glue femmes use? I wanna know.

I'm thinking of all the shoes I've ever known as sex objects, trying to find a hook to hang these feelings on, trying to get them out there, get them off me, let me breathe. My own foot-wear was never feminine. As a teenager, I tried to fit in as best I could in bell bottoms and the androgynous Adidas everybody wore, trying not to call attention to my homeliness. Eventually I grew up butch and acquired for myself not only the sturdy shoes guys wear to work, but also the kind that need to be shined. The kind I'd wear to go out with a woman on my arm who has dressed for me as carefully as I have dressed for her, in nice pants and shirt or maybe a suit, and a tie, of course, all the butch splendor I can manage. Men's shoes. Well, boy's shoes. My feet aren't big enough for men's.

But are they sex objects? I think of the way I feel, in my way-too-expensive wingtips, polished to a fare-thee-well, with leather soles that glide across a dance floor. I'm wearing the tuxedo my father was married in, back in 1939, which has fit me perfectly for the twenty years I've owned it—a fact of which I'm more than a little proud. I think of being small enough to learn to waltz by standing on my father's own wingtips, brown workaday shoes he wore to his job as a postal supervisor on the night shift. We're swinging our way around the living room rug in the old apartment in the Bronx, all the walls painted in a light coffee brown, and I'm as giddy as if my father were an amusement park ride, as if his shoes really did have wings. Now I wear his tux, an antique with a button fly, to impress the girls, in my bow tie and stiff white shirt, a stiff dick tucked up in my jockstrap for after the dancing is over and another kind of dance can begin. I weigh the reality of use—how many dry cleanings can an old wool suit sur-vive?—against the pleasure of fucking in it, and throw caution to the wind. Nothing lasts forever; besides, this old tuxedo already has lasted forever. It's a peculiar thing, to have kinky lesbian sex in the same clothes my father was married in, all those years ago, him the handsome young devil in the wedding photo, and me the queer and awkward daughter in her middle age, who only wishes I could be handsome, in my size 6 wing-tips and my fierce and complicated desires. I imagine sitting to put on my fancy shoes, the black serge trousers warm against my arms as I reach, my hard cock pressing against my belly while I tie the laces. I think of the girl, once upon a time, who knelt carefully in her pretty cocktail dress to fix the lace that had come undone without my noticing, my throat full of consternation and surprise and thick with love. In that moment, nothing in the universe existed except that shoe. Those shoes. Are they sex objects? Oh, Holy Mother of God.

The bus rocks and bounces over potholes. It's nice to think intellectual thoughts about butch shoes past and present and not be so conscious of the heat in my crotch, all wrapped up in women's shoes with pathologically unorthopedic toes. It's nice, but impossible. Scurrying for escape from the bright shock of that need like roaches in a suddenly well-lit kitchen, my thoughts rush into corners where they probably shouldn't go. I've always been a top with the girls, and I've been a top most of the time with butches, too. I can be as rough as I please and not be a gentleman. And when I need to let the armor drop, I do it in the haven of another butch's laser-hot regard. She doesn't have to have a lot of props, she doesn't even have to be packing anything in her pants, as long as she's got strong arms and square hands and a pair of Big. Black. Boots.

It makes me sweat, even in the drafty chill of the half-empty Greyhound, roaring its way through the winter countryside. I don't want to think about the woman I called Master, all those years ago, and what I took from her belt and her whip, and took it like a man. I ate pain for her, made her breath come hard with exercise and desire, and when I was good she'd reward me with the taste of her leather while she murmured fond names like *bootlicker* and *cocksucker* and *faggot* in my ear. I'd press my tongue against the instep of her Wellingtons, trying to lick my way through the cowhide to her own soft flesh underneath, trying to imagine the even softer flesh between her legs that I was never allowed to touch. Loving her was dangerous, but I could love her boots. I never realized I had a fetish until a femme pointed it out to me, years later, and sent me links to web pages full of packers and lineman's boots. Even now the taste of shoe polish is an aphrodisiac burned into my brain, but it's a butch thing, as hard and exciting as a steel toe prodding the soaking-wet crotch of my jeans in the instant before she strips them off me. But it's comfortable, too. It doesn't have anything to do with shoes that look like they're just as cruel to the beautiful woman wearing them as they could ever be to me. *Your* shoes.

I feel ignorant and sheepish. A girl would look at those shoes and say, *Oh, they're cute, where did you buy them,* and she'd probably know they're Manolo or whatever just from the sight of that two inches of black leather poking out from under the cuffs of your slacks. Me, I don't know, maybe they're not even shoes, they're boots. *Are they?* comes the whisper in the back of my brain, and the thought makes me even crazier. Makes my mouth water. I've got a bottle full of flat piss-warm Coke rammed into my crotch and I'm twitching like a crack addict, all for those pointy toes.

I've never licked a pair of girls' shoes. In my imagination, we're alone in some city apartment, the stylish furnishings just outside my peripheral vision from where I kneel on the hardwood floor. I'm wearing my 501s and chaps and standard white T-shirt. Daddy clothes, but I'm not the Daddy now. On my feet are the same black engineer boots I always wear, polished to a high gloss and one size too big. You are towering above me in a very, very short black dress; I resist the urge to scooch down to see if I can get a glimpse of your crotch, but you can read what I'm thinking, anyway. Your smile widens; your dark eyes twinkle knowingly. Your hands are on your hips.

"You want to see my pussy, don't you?" you say, your voice teasing, "If you're a good boy, you might get what you want."

My face feels hot. My gaze drops, embarrassed, and I am looking, again, at the pointy toes of your fashionable black leather boots. Boots. Short boots, barely above the ankle. My lips are sandpaper, suddenly, and I have to pry my tongue off the roof of my mouth to try to wet them.

"Are you a good boy?" you ask. You laugh as I stammer an unintelligible reply. You know what I'm staring at, unable to look at your face.

"Oh, you like my boots," you coo, "don't you?" I make a tiny "eep" noise, but you don't laugh. They don't really go with the dress, I know, or with the silk stockings. My inner straight guy obviously has no more taste than his legions of brothers feverishly poring over the Frederick's of Hollywood catalogs they ordered in their wives' names. But it's my fantasy, isn't it?

"You can kiss them, if you want."

I groan and reach for them, doubled over like a supplicant. The boot I cup my trembling hands around is warm and incredibly soft to my work-ravaged fingers. My skin is so rough it catches like Velcro in most girlie-type fabrics; with leather so buttery, I'm almost afraid I'll scratch it. But you murmur an encouraging sound at me, almost inaudible over the pounding of my heart, and I bend my lips to it, and kiss.

The smell of leather is in my nose, soft, so soft, to my dry lips. It's the smell of my Master's boots, her pants, her biker jacket, so long ago, the smell of my own jacket, the left epaulet with its cock ring firmly in place. The tip of my tongue slips out to lap as gentle and tentative as a kitten.

"Yes," you say, "that's right."

I shiver and stretch my tongue as far as it will go to sweep luxuriously across your instep, in my nose the scent of calfskin and polish and your soap and the slight, faint tang of your sweaty foot. I trace the outer edge, leaving a damp line, steering irresistibly toward the tip of your pointy, pointy toe.

Licking boots is like giving head. When I went down on my Master's boots, I licked and sucked and stroked with my tongue, circling the round head of the hard steel toe, laving my way up the shaft, pressing, caressing, cupping the heel in my hands. I wanted her to feel it. I wanted to hear her groan with desire and yank on the back of my T-shirt to haul me up for more direct stimulation—oh, how I dreamed. I wanted to take my bootblack-smeared face and bury it in the hot crotch of her Levi's, nuzzling her, driving her mad, and when she wouldn't take off her pants for me, to be dragged up to face level for one perilously deep kiss.

Such soft leather; such impractical form. I'd thought that setting my mouth to such a feminine bit of apparel would make me think more of eating pussy than sucking cock, but I was wrong. Except for the sweet and sour pleasure of my long-term lover's cunt, snatch-licking in the age of STDs has been stripped of much of its sensual delight and left with the clumsy nuisance of plastic wrap flapping out of hand at exactly the wrong moment. There always seems to be a panicky moment when imaginary headlines flash through my brain, LESBIAN SUFFO-CATES DURING CUNNILINGUS, *Safe sex the culprit, coroner says, story on page 6,* with my partner's imminent orgasm far more important than the grayness of oxygen deprivation creeping around the edges of my vision. I think of plastic wrap faintly bitter with the taste of lube from my own hand, my own spit welling and pooling and dripping on the sheets, and I know: This is not licking pussy. This is sucking cock, and for now, this small, soft, girlishly inutile boot is as much the seat of your power as the big swinging dick of any construction foreman in a hardhat is his. I run my tongue from root to tip, expensive Italian calfskin growing moist from my saliva, the taste of shoe polish and salt and the smell of leather and the heat of you all filling my mouth and nose, and I know for a fact, I am still a cocksucker, a pansy faggot cocksucker, no matter the gender of the top I'm kneeling in front of, no matter what she's wearing.

You are certainly the most feminine of women, always gorgeous, always charming, your considerable power always reined in. You know the power of others' desire for you; you know how to use it. You know your own power, too: that knowing what you want is the first step. You pay attention to details. You persevere. Everything else may be just packaging, but you know: The packaging matters. It seems to be your good fortune that the way you feel most at home in the world, as a feminine woman, is a role you can play superlatively.

I wonder, do you ever fuck it? Fuck gender? Pull on a pair of tight jeans with a strap-on outlined against the worn denim like something out of a Tom of Finland print, your long hair tucked under a leatherman's cap, mirrorshades obscuring the amusement in your eyes? Would you stand wide-legged in engineer boots while some tough butch tried to tongue and gnaw that monster cock out of its denim prison? Would you smile that lovely girlie smile down at her while she tried to swallow that big rod, tried to make you feel every muscle in her throat and tongue, milking it, making the base of it rock against your pubes, so you could feel its belly deep and aching? So you might want to give it to her where it counts, 'cause I can't come like this, rubbing myself against a plastic soda bottle in a half-empty bus dieseling down I-95, with nothing inside me.

I come to myself with a start, suddenly aware that the college kid a few rows back has woken up, and he's staring at me. I hate myself for blushing. I turn to face front, as casual as I can muster, resisting the urge to give him the finger. I shift so both feet are flat on the floor. He can't see the Coke bottle, and what's he looking at anyway, the snot-nosed little freak? I leave it where it is.

My heart is beating fast now, and I can feel its echo pounding in my cunt and burning up my face, 'cause it's not the bottle that's got me here, not the genderfuck cock in my mind, but those shoes, the calfskin hot against my tongue, the pointy toe I lick and prod and thrust my tongue under, trying to get you to pick it up, just a little, just enough to wrap my lips around it and suck. Your foot is small, I know I can take it all in my mouth, never mind the soles that have carried you through the filthy city streets, through garbage and grease and dog shit, never mind. I want it. I am a pervert for sure, a sick fuck who wants to lie belly down on the hardwood floor of your imaginary chic metropolitan flat and cradle that boot in my hands, tipped back on its heel, and suck on it, feel the point of that toe in the back of my throat, praying not to gag.

I imagine I can hear you breathe. I imagine I can hear a soft moan, and I can feel you shift in your seat—you're sitting now, I don't know where that chair came from. I already licked the other shoe, and with one hand I am fondling it like a spent lover when you shift your legs a little wider apart, when you slip down in the chair, when you lean forward abruptly and sit up.

You pull your foot away and step sideways, out of the reach of my mouth. You shake off my hand.

"Ah, ah, ah," you warn. "You are a very good boy, aren't you?" I am breathless and suddenly bashful. I can't pick up my head to look at you. "But that's enough, now," you tell me from high above. "I want something else."

You step around from where I am leaning on my elbows, head bowed. All at once I feel your foot on my back, between my shoulder blades, pushing me flat. I let my arms slide out and press my sweaty cheek against the cool floor. Out of the corner of my eye, I can see you looking down at me, speculating. I shut my eyes tight.

The heel of your shoe is digging in just to the left of my spine. I imagine the horseshoe-shaped dent it will leave, how ever will I explain it to my girlfriend? Just when the pressure becomes painful, you ask, "Is that what you want? Do you want me to trample you?"

I think of a porn shop I visited once, with a corner display geared to that infinitesimally small slice of the straight submissive male foot-worshipper subfetish who want women in really spiky heels to walk all over them. Literally. There were videos and magazines galore, with every cover a photographic variation on dangerous shoes gouging soft naked male flesh. Judging by the cover prices printed in pounds, I guessed it was a particularly British kink. Who knew? I was amazed. But was it me? I imagine your heel pressing into my back. I shrug. You take your foot away.

You nudge me in the ribs with one pointy toe, just hard enough to make me squirm. I'm very ticklish. I hope you don't notice.

"Roll over," you order. As I struggle to comply—I've stiffened up, and even in my fantasy I realize I'm really too old for this—you poke my butt encouragingly.

"Ah," you say in response to the sound I hadn't realized I made, "so that's it." I lie there looking up at you, panting. You smile knowingly. You are very tall. I could probably see up your short dress now, but I'm afraid to. You step between my feet, pushing them open until they are as wide apart as they can go and you are standing between my knees. Casually, idly, you touch my crotch with your toe.

I let out the breath I'd been holding in a rush, half sigh, half moan. Your smile is wider, your eyes are brighter. You rub your pointy toe up and down and around until I am nearly writhing on it. I want to grab your ankle and push your toe in as far as it will go through the thick seams, through the layers of denim and cotton underwear, into my very wet hole.

The bus is slowing, rumbling off the exit ramp. Behind me, there is a rustle as the kid gathers his belongings together, and I yank the Coke bottle from between my legs, startled and guilty. I sneak a look over my shoulder. He isn't paying any attention to me. I stretch and try to get my heart to stop racing, thinking calm thoughts. What I'll do when I get home to my sweetie and the dogs. Have some supper. Put in a load of laundry.

The bus station is not far from the highway; the kid behind me bumps his backpack down the aisle as we hiss to a stop. A few others slowly get to their feet and follow. It's growing dark in the winter afternoon. I wonder how soon I'll be getting off, and I blush ridiculously in the fading light of the nearly empty bus at my own double entendre.

My fantasy comes back to me in the deepening gloom. I imagine you standing over me, the sketchy details of that unknown apartment, the hardwood floor beneath my knees. My eyes track the headlights of oncoming traffic, across the median, but I'm not really seeing them. My hands are cupping the heel of your boot. My tongue tastes the leather. You nudge me and I roll over. Your toe touches my crotch, again, stroking. The Coke bottle is lying on the seat beside me now; I don't need it. Your foot draws back, and in one quick, surprising kick, your toe lands exactly on my clit. Not hard—the sensation is an explosion of pleasure and pain and apprehension, that the next kick will be worse, it will hurt. I want to cover my crotch with my hands, but I don't. You kick again; the blow falls a little lower, cushioned by my swollen labia, enticingly near where I want it, where I want to suck it in. You kick again. Again. My sweaty palms press against the floor. My eyes are closed. Every time you kick, I bark out loud with pain and pleasure and surprise, every time, and steady myself for the next one, until it doesn't come.

"Be a good boy," you tell me. "Take off your pants."

I can hear your voice in my head. Amused but firm. There's heat in it, also, and I know if I could just get close enough, I could smell your arousal. You want this, too.

I hurry to unbutton my pants, lift up, slide them awkwardly down, tugging at the legs to free them and kick them off. The chaps have vanished, and so have the boots. Even in my fantasy, my feet are cold, and I leave my two pairs of socks on, glad when you politely ignore them.

You are standing between my naked legs, pressing them apart, walking tiny deliberate steps as you do so, inching closer to my crotch. I am terribly frightened now that you will kick, but excited, too. I don't know how much it might hurt. I don't know if I want it. Oh, yes, I do. I can't watch.

I am holding myself still, fists clenched at my sides, braced for the blow, when I feel the tip of your toe brush my pubic hair, ever so lightly. I shiver. I imagine your toe dotted with the wetness that has seeped down my luxuriant thatch. You tease me that way for what seems like an eternity, and when I finally squirm, trying to bring about actual contact with my aching, swollen clit, you draw your foot back.

"Ah, ah, ahhh," you say. I open my eyes to see you wagging a finger at me, looking stern. "I want you to stay... absolutely...still."

I try. I can't take my eyes off you now. You go back to teasing, tickling, teasing. I hold my legs so rigid that when your pointy leather toe, already slippery with my juice, finally bumps my clit, I jerk like I've been zapped, and I yell out loud.

You're rubbing against my clit in earnest now, and I'm glad you don't seem to care anymore if I move. The toe of your boot moves back and forth, up and down. I'm rocking against it, bucking my hips, trying to get closer, closer. You stop moving and I do, too, when I realize that, ever so gently, you are pushing against my asshole.

"Is that what you want?" Your head is tilted, curious. Is it? It could be, I think. I've had things as large as your toe and maybe even as large as the ball of your foot in there before. I try to remember how big your feet are. I wonder what lube would do to that nice leather.

You smile and move your foot just a little, and the point of your toe comes to rest at the opening of my cunt. I don't need any lube there, and you know it. For a fleeting instant the thought of latex crosses my mind, and I imagine working a rubber over the toe of your shoe. It has, after all, been treading those dirty city streets, and I don't know if I could relax and enjoy a shoe in my cunt even in fantasy, without at least a nod to hygiene. I wonder if you'd make me do it with my mouth, the way I do with a butch's rubber dick. I wonder if a regular sized condom would be big enough, or would I have to have one of those jumbo ones? I wonder if I should suck your toe like a cock after I put it on. Then I feel your toe pressing against me, forcing its way inside, and I stop thinking. I am nothing but cunt, opening for you, wanting to be filled.

The bus sways and turns, and I rock sideways, blinking in the bright halogen lights of the bus station. I wonder where I am, if I've missed my stop, but no, this is it. There's my girlfriend on the sidewalk, waiting for me. I shake my head, shift in my seat. My crotch is uncomfortably damp. I grope for my briefcase that has fallen to the floor, find the book of porn I'd meant to finish. The lights come up, and I squint as my eyes adjust, getting slowly, stiffly to my feet.

In a few hours I'll be in bed, trying to get the rest I need to get up at three A.M. and start the daily grind all over again, but I don't think I'll be able to sleep right away. There's that film loop, waiting to run again. There I am, too embarrassed to look at your face. There are your pointy, pointy toes.

The Second Hour
L. Shane Conner

I spent the first hour of the party nursing exactly two beers. I wanted to be blind drunk and away from myself, but I couldn't seem to put the stuff down fast enough. I finally made it to my third beer and sat down on one of those flip-a-fuck foldable mattress chairs in a corner. I shouldn't have been tired, especially with the volume of the music. I didn't really even know why I'd come except that I didn't have anything better to do and some girls I met at a club the month before invited me. Moving to a new city's a pain in the ass. I was thinking about looking for something harder to drink when a woman I'd never seen before came right up to me and put one foot down on the chair between my legs. I thought I was imagining it for half a second; then she leaned forward, pressing her weight down through the toe of one high black leather boot directly onto my clit. I stopped breathing for a minute or a day. The party was gone and there was just the light reflecting off this knee-high leather boot and my heart beating in my clit.

Next there was her hand pulling a silver flask from the inside pocket of her leather jacket. She drank, handed it to me, and as I drank she reached forward and tipped the flask up with just her two fingers. It was sweet and strong. I closed my eyes and let it fill my mouth until she pulled it away. Warmth coursed through me, right down to the tip of her boot. I looked up and tried to speak but she caught me with a sharp, open-handed slap, just hard enough to get my attention. My head was light but I could feel the pressure of her boot and the beginning of an even buzz in the base of my brain.

"Get up."

She stepped back and after a short battle with equilibrium and my legs, I stood. I looked at the space between her knees, the hem of her skirt just short of midthigh, and the narrow heels of her boots. She pushed me toward the door, which I opened and held for her.

I followed a step behind her as we walked to her car. It was a small kind of SUV, black, with leather seats. Once we were inside, she kissed me, hard and deep, then she made me kneel on the floor facing the seat and it didn't occur to me to object until I was already on my knees. I heard the glove box open behind me and then there were handcuffs around my wrists. She slid the seat back up and I found I couldn't move. She leaned down and whispered in my ear.

"Either I'm going to take you home and do what I like with you, or you say no and I'll let you out of the car right now."

I wanted her. I kept quiet. She pulled my head toward the dash by the short hairs at the back.

"Give me permission, then. Say yes or it stops now."

I turned my head up toward her and her hand caught my cheek again. It was more than I'd felt in months. I couldn't raise my voice above a whisper and I couldn't move.

"Yes."

She didn't answer and I thought maybe she'd lost interest.

"Please yes."

She blindfolded me then and I felt a kind of relief. If I

couldn't see her anyhow, I didn't have to try to look anymore. I let my weight fall forward onto the seat but she pulled my head back again and pressed what felt like a rubber ball into my mouth. I accepted it like the mouth of the flask earlier. It was another few seconds before I realized it was a gag. As she pulled it tight I could feel my lips spread and my tongue press into the floor of my mouth. She let go and I let my chest rest on the seat again. The car lurched forward.

When the car stopped again I had no idea how much time had passed. For months I hadn't even been able to masturbate successfully, and for however long she'd been driving I'd been closer than anybody's best effort since my last relationship started to go south. The seat slid backward and I went with it. I heard her car door slam shut and for a little while I was alone, then the door next to me swung open.

She dragged me out of the car and I fell on the pavement, somehow not hitting my knees or elbows. I heard the muted sound of what remained of my voice squeeze out around the ball gag and I felt the toe of her boot push in under my face. For the first time since she'd put the gag in place, I wished it wasn't. She helped me roughly to my feet, put some kind of collar around my neck, and took a step away. I felt a tug and realized she'd put me on a leash. I followed her, stumbling blindly on steps, doing my best to keep my feet. I heard a key in a door and heard it swing open. She led me in and, I thought, through a couple of rooms until I found myself face to face with a wall. There was a click and I knew she'd taken the leash off. The handcuffs were next. I wanted to rub my wrists but I stood still, waiting.

She pulled my jacket off and tossed it across the room. Her slow, even, breath made my heart sound loud and fast. She came closer and I could feel the heat of her body through my thin shirt right before she pulled me backward, off balance. I tried to keep my feet, I think just by reflex, but she dropped me easily and smoothly to the floor. She told me to take off my boots and I fumbled, loosening the laces just enough so my socks came half off with my boots. Her voice was low and quiet and, as she directed me to undress completely, I was so focused on listening that I barely noticed what I was doing. The evenly spaced slats of the wood floor were cool under my bare ass but the room was warm. Everything was still. I heard her boots crossing the room and I felt like I was breathing in time with the even clicking of her heels against the floor.

I tried not to move, unsure of where to put my hands, wishing she would touch me again. A dull throb had started in my clit and seemed to radiate out, turning my body into a single pulsing organ. I was sure she was watching me. I heard her boots take a few steps followed by the sound of something scraping across the floor and stopping nearby. I couldn't identify the next several sounds but when I turned my head, trying to capture something more, she put a boot down on my chest just above my breasts and pushed me down. The other boot came to rest just above my pubic bone. She must be sitting down.

I felt more naked than I'd ever felt before. I heard the unmistakable sound of a cigarette lighter sparking to life, and for a moment the light-headed onrush of adrenaline blocked out everything else. I didn't even know why. As the wave of it passed over and out of me I realized she was sitting in a chair smoking, using my body for a foot rest. I became aware of my body then, beginning with the skin her boots rested on. I could feel the exact shape of them and the distribution of her weight. There was a slight draft in the room and it made me more and more aware of the growing wetness between my legs. Once I started to feel that, it held all my attention. I was sure she must see it, must be staring at it.

Suddenly her boots were gone, the chair slid back, she stood. I wanted to move toward her, my body ached to be touched. She made me get onto my hands and knees, walked behind me, and stopped there. I heard a rustling sound followed by a small snap. I felt her gloved hand on the inside of my thigh and I couldn't breathe. I was afraid any movement might make her take her hand away. She slapped at my thigh, forcing me to spread my legs further. The muscles in my lower back tightened and I felt my ass trying to push itself higher. She moved her hand forward across my swollen labia, teasing my clit with a fingertip, letting me feel how slick I was. I felt an involuntary moan trying to escape but I closed down on the gag.

She had me crawl across the floor a little way, then she stopped me and got me up onto a bed, laying me down on my back. My body seemed to sink into the softness of it after the cool hardness of the wood floor. She ran a hand over my breasts and my back arched toward it before I could stop myself. She laughed quietly and pulled her hand away. I tried again to hold as still as possible while she fastened a restraint around my right wrist, then my ankle, and then the other side, stretching me across the bed. All my attention was on whatever part of me she happened to be touching.

She slapped my clit just hard enough to make my whole body jump and I realized how little I could move. My arms and legs tensed. There was a steady hum inside my head. I whimpered around the gag. The muscles around my clit twitched and spasmed. She tapped lightly, teasing. She tickled, she rubbed, she pushed her fingertips between my labia, just barely inside. I tried to thrust my hips toward her and I started to feel my whole body rising off the bed. If I hadn't been gagged I would have pleaded with her. I stopped trying to control the sounds coming from deep in my throat. I stopped trying to struggle and I stopped trying not to. Everything was slick and wet. I could feel her slowly stretching me open wider, pushing my resistance away. Her mouth was on my clit, sucking, nibbling, grazing me with her teeth. I wanted to spread my legs further apart, I wanted to pull her to me. I felt the wave of orgasm begin to sweep through me and then I felt the last piece of resistance give way and she was inside me. I felt the widest part of her hand slip in as I came. My body held her inside and she held me, suspended inside the wave of my orgasm. Nothing else could feel like that. Her whole fist filled me in places I never knew were empty. The universe was reduced to the places her two hands touched. Time was gone, the sunlight was fresh and warm.

Soon my arms and legs were free, the gag and blindfold were gone, and I was curled against her naked breasts. I felt like a child, completely safe. She kissed my forehead and pulled a blanket over me and I slept. In the morning she told me her name.

Fags Like Us
Zane Jackson

We were standing in a small room enclosed by bars, dyke/ trans night in a club more frequently used as a gay men's sex club. He was a big stylish bear of a butch with a gender-queer streak a mile wide and a foot deep. The way he kissed reminded me of the way I've seen gay leatherboys kiss at the Ramrod, the older Daddy leaning up against the bar, pulling the half-naked and quite a bit younger boy up on his toes, to make their mouths meet.

Leathermen kissing is all about tongues meeting, slowly sliding over one another, feeling each other up. Not in the privacy of their mouths but shamelessly stretched out and rubbing over one another in the air between them. Kissing that looks more like cocksucking than kissing.

His tongue worked my tongue over, in a bar backroom sort of way, running the tip of his tongue around the end of my tongue like it was the head of my cock, slow and deliberate.

He was big, a good half a foot taller than me in his big black boots, and I was on my tiptoes, with my back pressed against the wall. I felt little and hungry. He pulled my tongue into his mouth with his teeth, sucking the length of it in and out of his mouth, kissing like fucking, as he worked the underside of my tongue, pressing upward and dragging his teeth across the top. He stopped ever so briefly to lick slowly around the tip before his lips were pressed firmly against mine in the hungriest kiss I've ever been involved in.

We were fully clothed and it felt obscene. Tongues and lips stroking each other like simultaneous blow jobs. Deep soul cock kissing. Kissing that comes as close as I'll ever get to knowing what his mouth would feel like wrapped around the cock I don't have.

Between kisses, under his breath, he told me about the showers downstairs where fags whip out their dicks and piss down each other's pants, where leather Daddies make good boys kneel and drink piss from their cocks. Pressing his knee and thigh into my crotch and taking my chin in his hand, he asked if I might be one of those kinds of boys.

He made me shiver but I looked him right in the eye. Short-cropped black hair, a strong square jaw, and dark brown eyes with a gleam that made my dick hard. I smirked.

"Bring it on, gorgeous."

He laughed out loud and roughly shoved me into the wall with all his weight, digging his fingers into my upper arms hard enough to bruise me and covering my mouth with his, in a kiss that was more like breath control than kissing.

Lightheaded, I struggled against his lips, squirming on his thigh, when he stepped back and abruptly dropped me to the floor. The release was so sudden I laughed out loud from the adrenaline rush of falling to my knees, and when I looked up at him, he had his hands on his hips and there was a slight smile on both our faces.

He stepped slowly out of the way, to give me room to get up. I rose slowly, holding his gaze the entire way up, pausing for some indication of what I should do now that I was on my feet. He gestured toward the hallway, smiling. I did my best brazen femme fag turn-on-my-heels maneuver, making sure to walk out of the room with straight shoulders, so that my shoulders would look as broad as possible, and giving a little strut to show off my narrow hips and boyish ass.

I could feel his eyes on me, and I could feel other eyes on us as we crossed the big open play room. I took the initiative and walked straight to the stairs leading to the basement. I didn't turn to see if he was behind me. I could hear the sound of his heavy boots on the concrete floor.

The basement was darker, with the flicker of candles in iron holders making shadows on the stone walls. It looked like an old wine cellar, except for the shower and a large steel walk-in freezer at the bottom of the stairs. People were fucking in all sorts of nooks and crannies, light flickering on naked bodies, with plenty of onlookers in the darker shadows and back corners.

I barely made it off the last step when I felt his body brush up against my back. I braced myself to be pinned against something, but he just kept slowly walking into me, inching me forward until I was standing chest against the steel freezer door.

His body was warm pressing up against my back and legs, the club was warm, and I was beginning to break a sweat. His arm curled around my throat from behind, and I got ready but he applied no pressure. I waited.

He just held me firmly in the crook of his elbow, while his other hand wandered all over my body, massaging my shoulder, pulling skin and muscle up off my bones, first sliding flathanded across my bare skin and then grabbing handfuls of my flesh and pulling hard. First shoulders, then upper arms, and then forearms. Pain alternating with an almost gentle affection. We were getting to know each other.

His hand came to rest on my ass, fingers curled between my

legs, stroking my asshole with his thumb. I pressed the side of my face into the cold steel door, and pushed my ass back into his hand, moving against him because I was hungry to feel his cock in my mouth, maybe his hand on my dick. He reached around me and cupped his hand over my crotch, massaging my packing dick, and pressing firmly enough to stroke my real dick. I closed my eyes. The side of his face came to rest against my face as he continued to work my dick through my jeans.

"You're my baby boy, aren't you?" he rumbled into my ear.

I could barely breathe.

"Yes, please—"

He turned me around by the shoulders. I kept my eyes turned down. His thick, beefy arms braced against the door on either side of me, and he leaned down and pressed his mouth against mine, kissing me slowly, and repeatedly as if pulling me toward him with each kiss of his mouth.

My boldness was wearing off rapidly. I was beginning to really feel submissive, my hands started getting cold, and my nose started itching, always signs that I'm about to totally go under for someone. He reached down and grabbed me by the front of my jeans, his hand wrapped around my belt, his fist resting against my packing dick, pulling my jeans up into the crack of my ass. I took a deep breath, because I knew we were about to get started.

He turned abruptly and walked away, dragging me roughly by the front of my jeans as I struggled to stay on my feet. I no longer felt my usual cocky coolness at a play party. This boy was at least twice my size and twice as strong, and people turned to watch the big boy drag me across the basement to the shower area.

I had wanted to be a fag before I even knew that girls could grow up to be boys, before I knew I could be a boy. And as the grimy tile floor of the shower room was getting closer and closer, all I could think was that I was finally going to get to kneel for a big butch fag, a big butch fag who was a fag like I am a fag, and that I was going to take whatever he dished out.

He turned and pushed me first into the shower stall, and for a moment we just stood there looking at each other. He reached into his front pants pocket and flicked a condom at me. I didn't catch it, I never do, and it landed on the tile between us. As I was leaning down to pick it up, I heard him start to unbuckle his belt, and the sound made it hard for me to breathe.

I took my time reaching down, embarrassed to look up and catch his eye, trying rather unsuccessfully to play it cool. I love cocksucking so much it makes me painfully shy. I lifted my eyes just enough to see him unzip his pants and adjust himself in his underwear. My face was hot, and I was sure I was blushing furiously.

Standing with his leather pants unzipped and his dick hard and pressing against his boxer briefs, he put one hand on the top of my head and pressed me down to my knees in front of him. He began stroking the back of my head, running his fingers up the buzzed back of my hair. Holding the crown of my head in his hands, he rubbed my face roughly into his crotch.

"I bet you like sucking cock, eh, boy? Little cocksucking faggot."

Sweat was running down my back and pooling at the base of my spine. I could smell him. He smelled hot and wet and strong like sex, his hard dick pressed up against my face. I had to close my eyes for a second when he pulled his boxers down and grasped his cyberskin dick in his hand. When I opened my eyes he was fondling himself, pulling on his dick, and stroking the tip against my closed mouth. He smiled and I closed my eyes again.

"Condom?"

I looked down and the package was still in my hand.

He laughed.

Hands shaking, I ripped open the red foil package and

spread the condom over the tip of his cock, stroking it slowly all the way down to the base. He took a step closer, holding his cock and running his thumb firmly in circles over the slit in the tip. I swallowed hard.

I could tell that he was worked up, and it made my dickhead throb in my pants. Holding his dick in his hand he stroked the head against my closed lips, rubbing the tip across my skin, teasing at first, stroking the side of my face with his other hand. Then slowly but insistently, he pressed the head of his cock against my lips. His face was intent, serious even, with just the slight smirk of someone about to get his dick sucked.

"Open your mouth."

I opened my mouth, and he dragged the tip of his cock against my tongue. He held my chin in his hand. He stroked his dick along my outstretched tongue, repeatedly, deliberately, very much in control of this blow job. I curled the tip of my tongue up against the underside of his cock, very slowly dragging my tongue out to the tip of his cock, feeling hungry for dicksucking and wanting to give him the best blow job of his life.

I drew the head in and out of my mouth, pausing to rub the head against the flat of my tongue, and looked up to catch his eye, asking without asking to be allowed to suck his cock. He removed his hand from my chin, inviting me to take over. I took his dick in my hand, firmly stroking the length of it, to get a feel of him, cupping my hand around his balls and pressing into his body, stroking up the bottom of his balls, and rubbing against his real dick underneath, to get him even more worked up and hard.

I folded my fingers into the edge of his front pocket for better balance and I began to work him. I licked all around the head of his dick, taking my time, pressing my tongue against the piss slit, sucking just the head into my mouth and running my tongue around the ridge, looking up at him. He grunted quietly and I could feel his body move slightly toward me.

He was the quietest top I've ever sucked off, I thought.

His hand was on the back of my head holding me still as he pushed his cock further and further into my mouth. I held tight to the base of his dick with my hand and sucked slowly as I was drawn along the length, taking air in the pause, and then was forced to take his cock back into my mouth almost to the base and slowly pulled down the length, a little faster this time.

His hand on my head prevented me from sucking him as aggressively as I wanted to, reminding me that I wasn't sucking just any cock, but sucking *his* cock. Long, deep-paced strokes, and I could feel his body give toward me, his hands on either side of my head pulling me forward, encouraging me to take as much of his dick in my mouth as I could, and then making me pull back slow. It was cocksucking in slow motion, and we were locked into it.

I could feel my body sway with his strokes, could feel his knees bend slightly as he pulled my head to him, bringing the base of his cock to my lips and pressing my face up against him. I was concentrating on the fact that he was using me to make him come, concentrating on his hard dick in my mouth, his closed eyes and quick breathing. I knew he was feeling how it would be to have me sucking the come out of his balls, as my face pushed the base of the cyberskin dick into his real dick.

His thumbs started to stroke slow circles into my cheeks, and his eyes seemed to close even tighter. I knew he could see my mouth on his cock even with his eyes closed, as he crawled down into that cyberskin dick, making it his own.

I felt like I was going to fall apart with every stroke. Nothing about me was mine anymore. My dick pressing against my jeans, the feel of his cock sliding into and out of my mouth were the only things I was sure of. It wasn't dildosucking for power, gender-fucking for the crowd, a second-best approximation. This was *cock*sucking.

His voice was very quiet.

"I want to come with your mouth wrapped around my dick. I want to come in your mouth."

Shakily I nodded, his cock still in my mouth.

His thumbs slid over my eyelids and pressed gently, instructing me to close my eyes, and I did.

He pulled his dick out of my mouth, grabbed me by both arms, and dragged me across the room still on my knees. I was breathless, frozen in place. Small sounds of clothes moving, weight shifting. I didn't dare open my eyes or move, bad boys get nothing, and I am not a bad boy when it comes to this.

When he reached for me again, it was rough. He yanked my face into his crotch, tilting my chin and face up at a severe angle, and pressing my mouth against his real dick.

He bent over me, his chin resting on the top of my head.

"Are you ready to take my come, boy?"

I could feel his words from the rumble of his voice in his belly, I was so close to him. The energy was electric, my mouth felt like it was on fire, he was the only thing holding me up, and I was so hungry to continue sucking his cock that I would have gladly begged.

I tongued the head of his dick slowly like he taught me, took his dick into my mouth, and sucked it out from his body. Licking the underside with the flat of my tongue in long, slow, even strokes, I could feel the blood filling the head of his cock, the skin stretching and straining, growing harder with every stroke, getting bigger and more erect as I sucked him off.

His breathing got deeper and my heart pounded in my ears.

"Slow, so I can feel it…. Slow is what drags the come up out of my balls…. Come on, boy, do it like I like it."

He was holding my head in a vise grip, rubbing his cock against my tongue. I was being face fucked. Breathing ceased to be important. Sweat ran down my chest. I felt shaky and desperate.

"I know you're going to make me come and shoot all down your throat. You're going to make me come. You're going to make me come."

He shuddered and backed against the wall, legs braced and tight, his whole body stiffening up, locked and rigid. He barely made a noise, just whispered over and over....

"Coming...

   "Coming...

      "Coming...

         "Coming..."

And he let go, warm piss filling my mouth, overflowing my lips and running down my chin. I felt like I was going to break in that moment, I knew it.

The heat was shocking, piss and come from his dick running down my throat, me swallowing just to be able to breathe. I knew I wouldn't be able to take it all as I heard it splash on the tile floor, but I did my best, sucking and drinking and swallowing as much of his stuff as I could. Trying to be his good cocksucking, piss-drinking boy, trying to fight back tears. *This is my place, this is where I belong, I am Daddy's fag boy. I am.*

When he finally let me go, he slid down the wall to the floor in front of me. I was shaking and spent, my ears humming. Our eyes met, and he pulled me to his chest, wrapping his arms all the way around me, and kissed me on the head. We sat for a long time in the corner of the shower room, forehead to forehead, just feeling it.

When we finally got up, he pulled himself together, zipped up his pants, and we turned to walk out, his cyberskin dick shoved into his back pocket. I could only smile. *This is our life.*

Lessons
S. Bear Bergman

She slid her cock out of me slowly, so slowly, then pumped it back in once, hard, to watch me gasp and laugh and grab for it; she knows I can't take that after I've just come but she likes to do it anyhow. It's how she tests to make sure I'm really, thoroughly fucked out, I think. I reached back, grabbed her wrist, and pulled her up and onto my back like so many covers, like I do, snuggling down under her warmth, the weight of her keeping me safe and grounded. She murmured fond and ridiculous things in my ear, calling me *sweet* and *delicious, handsome,* and *beautiful,* licking away the sweat on my neck and sliding a hand under my sweaty chest to hug me a bit. We snuggled and rolled with the afterglow, being silly. I sucked gently on the tips of her fingers, lazing along by my cheeks, kissed the palm of her hand, nuzzled and burrowed into it, lapping like a pup. She giggled. I made a noise, a warm one, low in my throat, something between a growl and a groan, and curled myself against her.

Every time we do this, I like it a little better, and I liked it a whole fuck of a lot to begin with. We don't get a lot of chances, living so far apart and not being Rockefellers, either one of us, but between conferences, relatives, and the occasional frequent flyer ticket, we get just enough to never feel too horribly deprived. Still—this particular meeting had been after an especially long hiatus, and I was glad for the three days, glad for the king-sized bed in the anonymous hotel room on the eighth floor, glad for the weight of her on my back and the way that it never seemed like it had been months since we'd seen each other, even though we don't really talk on the phone much.

We email, though. It's the best part about messing around with writers. The email is so, so good.

Recovering slowly, I disengaged myself long enough to dislodge the head of her dick from a tender spot just above my knee, and tugged on it, experimentally, looking to see if she were ready to take it off, to let me touch her, but also ready to let my touch modulate into a jack-off motion at any minute if she wasn't. She has a harder time with it than I do; I was brought up as a butch by sex–positive, radical perverts who thought that any bullshit about butches not liking to get fucked was so much retrograde nonsense, but she grew up someplace outside of Philly and ten years earlier, where the local lesbo culture was strictly a butch top/femme bottom arrangement, where all the butches were presumed stone until proven guilty, and butch-on-butch pairings were as taboo a thing as could be imagined. Good thing that times change.

I cruised her hard when we first met a couple of years ago at a writers' conference: She made several very smart comments during a panel we were on together, and she had a steel-gray brush cut. Sold. I invited her to have dinner with my friends and me, my dear friends who set me up with ample conversational opportunity to both mention my wife at home and discuss being poly, so this hot thing would know the score. That, plus my outrageous flirting, did the trick, and after dessert I was in her room on my knees, being called a delicious assortment of very dirty things while I struggled to get her buttonfly jeans off and a condom on using only my mouth.

I *love* writers' conferences.

Since then, she's let me talk her out of her boxer briefs and into all kinds of hot and nasty fun, and has even developed quite a liking for getting fucked with my biggest dick, one that makes her crack jokes about getting to be a size queen in her old age. But I always have to wait until she's fucked me at least once, first, like she needs to reground herself in the idea whenever we meet again, as if her gentleman butch sense of the rightness and order of the world can't allow her to experience her own desire until everyone else has been squared away first. Not to suggest that fucking me isn't one of her desires. It seems clear to me at this stage that it is. But.... You know what I mean.

I slide my body up until my mouth is right against her ear. I say, "Oh. Oh, you fucking hot thing, so good to me, I want to make you feel so good, man, I want to do you so right...." I brush my lips against her ear, buck my crotch against her hip, start to move next to her. My hands find her nipples and start to rub, gently, just how she likes. She groans, quietly. I go on: "Mmmm. AJ, I want something. I want something from you, so bad."

She picks her head up and looks at me. She loves when I say what I want, she likes it that I trust her, and that I'm so hot for her. She says low, into my ear, "What's that, hm? Tell me. Tell me what you want, greedy."

Pressing myself against her, selling it with my entire body, lacing my fingers through her hair, I let a rush of hot breath out across her ear, and say, "Please. Please, teach me how to make you come."

She draws back, shocked, looks at my face. She travels with a Magic Wand and uses it, buzzing herself off while I fuck her and having noisy good times about it. But I have a secret hunch about her. I think maybe she's like me, that there's some other, nonelectric way to get the job done, something that requires the exact right touch and a lot of work, something she never confesses because she doesn't want to be that much work, or be that exposed, or make someone else work that hard on her behalf, but which is incredibly satisfying in a totally different way. I've seen the signs. I want to know what it is. I want to do her like that, want to make her come for me without her having to do anything at all. I want her to trust me like that.

I slide closer, out of her gaze, heart pounding, positioning my lips next to her ear again. "Please, AJ. Tell me what to do. I promise I'll do a good job for you. I swear I will. Use me to get yourself off. You deserve it, god, you deserve it."

Her big hands close around two fistfuls of hair, and she drags my head away from hers so she can see my face, mouth slack from panting to catch my breath. I hold her gaze and try to make my eyes communicate exactly what I'm thinking, what she wants to see: Yes, I mean it. Yes, I want this.

She drags my head back, my ear against her mouth, and crushes me tight against her in a hug. I wonder whether she's crying. I didn't mean to make her cry, I wanted to make her come, which is wetness at a totally different *end,* and I'm just about to start apologizing all over myself when she says, "You won't want to do it."

The hell I won't. I'd walk barefoot across a mile of burning sand to watch this butch dry dishes on videotape. "Trust me, I will," I say.

After a long, long pause, during which I have the good sense to keep quiet, she says in my ear, so quietly I can barely hear her: "Lick my asshole."

I'm elated. I groan, "Oh, holy shit, yeah," into her ear, start fumbling the harness off, looking for the plastic wrap, so excited I can't remember not to do five things at once. I knock over the lube, right it, find the plastic, get her out of the harness and flat on her back on the bed with a pillow under her hips before she can start waffling or change her mind. I tear off a piece of wrap, put it aside, and start kissing her, laying my body back along the warm, furry, delicious length of hers, kissing her soft and slow with little nips of my teeth, running my hands down the sides of her body, stroking her strong arms and her wide hips, working my way down her body, so slowly, rolling her nipples between my lips for a long time, sucking them so, so gently and making her push her cunt up to me, licking at her tattoos. I keep my knees between her legs so she can't grind. I want her to be hungry when I finally touch her, want her to want it so much. I want this to last. I want to show her what she's worth—all my attention, all my desire.

Finally, I bend my head and start nuzzling against the crack of her ass, kissing and nipping at her asscheeks, reaching surreptitiously for the Saran Wrap while I squeeze her ass between my hands, pulling her cheeks apart, smoothing the plastic into place, and sliding nose first between her cheeks. Her legs are bent at the knee. I can't believe she's so open to me but I am *not* complaining. I dig in.

I trace my tongue up and down her crack, so gently, full of hot breath. I want her to feel the heat even through the barrier, want her to be able to imagine it isn't there. I start to work my tongue in a little deeper, wriggling it against the sensitive spots, taking long, long licks from just below the opening of her cunt over and past her asshole, licking a fraction harder with each swipe of my tongue. She sighs, shifts her hips, presses against me. Encouraged, I keep on, starting to vary the pressure and depth of each lick, sometimes using the broad flat of my tongue and sometimes just the very tip, as hard as I can make it; I trace around the opening of her asshole, crinkled tightly shut, tracing my tongue along each of the tiny sunburst furrows of skin that radiate out from it, trying to get it to trust me. On one of the licks, I miscalculate and start pressing just a bit too soon, pushing the tip of my tongue right against the hole.

She moans. My cunt starts to do a slow boil, and I redouble my efforts. I kiss, lick, and nuzzle against her asshole, pushing my nose against it playfully, working against it with my tongue, feeling it start to open, starting to smell how much she likes it—when I pick up my head to say this to her, I see the small, slow stream of milky come easing its way out of her cunt and down the crack of her ass. Holy Christ. I put my head back down, and get back to work.

How do I describe this? It becomes the Zen of asslicking, the whole world gets reduced to about three inches of warm, wet flesh and every sound she makes. Her hand comes down and locks itself in my hair, she pulls me closer into her asscrack, tongue first, finally opening up enough for me to insinuate it into her hole and wriggle, just a tiny bit, but it makes her make a noise I'd never heard before, and I suddenly don't care how much my neck hurts or how hard it is to get my tongue into her, I just want her to make that noise again. I start fucking her hole with my tongue, slow and steady, the plastic wrap a mess around my face, and she starts grinding back against me, so hard it hurts my nose, but I am on a mission, now.

Suddenly she lets loose my hair, and I'm not sure what she wants, I start to pick my head up but she growls, "Don't stop, oh, please, don't, please don't stop," and grabs my hand instead, dragging it up and pulling it hard against her clit, which is harder than I have ever felt it, literally standing straight out of the hood like a tiny cock. I work it differently than I normally would, in a two-fingered jack-off motion I learned for transmen with testosterone-enhanced parts, up and down the sides with occasional swipes across the head, and she loves it, starts panting and gasping while I fuck my face further into her now-open, gripping asshole and work her clit at the same time. I can tell she's going to come, soon. I don't change a thing, I keep doing exactly what I'm doing, same speed, same pace, if I'm doing it right I want to keep doing it right, I want to do it right for her, want to make her feel as good as she makes me feel, so I keep my hand steady and blink the sweat out of my eyes and take a deep breath for one more long sally, plunging my tongue back into her ass on the downstroke and pulling it out on the up, letting her buck between the two pleasures, until she yells, "Oh, holy motherfucking god!" and comes with a bellow that even the moderately soundproofed hotel room probably doesn't contain, nearly breaking my neck as she whips her legs together around my face and squeezes them hard, hand clamping down over my hands, writhing on the bed in pleasure and riding what I hope like hell are several strong aftershocks, each one announced with a guttural cry.

Soon, she's still. I tap her on the thigh to remind her that my head is still between her legs and when she opens them, I scramble up, hurrying to cover her naked skin with mine, wrapping her up against me, holding her and whispering, "Thank you. Oh, thank you," into her ear like a mantra, over and over. She looks at me.

"That was...oh. Wow. Em, that was...." She trails off, nuzzles further into the crook of my neck, rubbing her sweaty skin against mine. We breathe together for a minute. I drag the ugly bedspread over us to keep us warm, being careful to hold her tight the whole time, not wanting to break this moment. I can't even believe she trusted me with that. It makes me feel something I can't explain, and while I'm searching for the words, so I can tell her, she picks her head back up, and whispers, so quietly for such a big, confident butch, so shyly, "Did you like it?"

I grin. I take her hand, draw it down to my soaking wet cunt, brushing her fingertips over my hard clit. "What do you think?" I ask, laughing a little into her ear.

She growls hungrily, rolls me over underneath her, and says, "I think you're a little slut, that's what I think."

I nod happily, and spread my legs wider.

Fee Fie Foe Femme
Elaine Miller

All night long she wouldn't let me kiss her because—she said—our lipstick colors clashed.

Checking the address she'd written on a piece of paper, I'd picked her up at her house earlier. Rosalie, the paper said, then her phone number and address. No last name. Dykes don't need last names when we have attributes and ex-lovers to be known by. As a dyke I'm Jez the Goth, or Sharen's-ex Jez, never Jessie Tate. And Rosalie...could be New-in-Town Rosalie, or Rosalie the Beautiful. Maybe if I was into U-Haul rental she could be Jez's Rosalie by the second date.

My heart skipped a beat as she'd appeared in the doorway dressed like an old-time movie starlet, her loose curls bouncing around her sparkling brown eyes. She'd taken my hand, and I'd leaned in for a kiss, which she dodged, laughing impishly. And explained. I was annoyed that she was right about the lipstick clashing. I was wearing my usual vampiric matte blood-red, and hers was something a worker bee would die trying to collect for her queen. Raspberry pink, glittery

under the new-car deep gloss, her lips were startling and perfect jewels against her brown skin.

I took Rosalie the Beautiful to LICK, the only full-time
lezzie bar in town. Once there and seated at a table beside the
dance floor, we lost no time in flirting. She pretended to lose
one of her gold earrings in my cleavage, necessitating that she
trail her fingers around my breasts, trolling for it, while I protested that she had to find it, quick, because I wear only silver
with black clothing. And of course, I only wear black clothing.

But she still wouldn't kiss me. She would dance so close to
me that the lines of her face blurred in our body heat, oh yes.
She would let the slick material of her skirt smooth the way as
she rode my thigh to the beat of the house music. Later in the
evening, she'd let me hold her tight in the dark corners of the
bar, one hand cupping her full breast, my thumb strumming
across her nipple as she squirmed, my other hand tangled in
the hair at the nape of her neck. But every time I tried to kiss
her, throughout the evening, she just laughed and twirled
away, leaving a cloud of girl-scent, a flare of her skirt, and the
teasing word *Lipstick*.

By the end of the night, I was cross-eyed with frustration.
When Rosalie the Beautiful whispered a lewd invitation in my
ear, I simply answered, "Yeah. Let's go to my house," took her
hand, and pulled her out of LICK, past the approving smirks
of my friends. And on the way home she wouldn't kiss me. She
teasingly said that it was all about preserving her shiny, glossy
pink lipstick. Besides, she wouldn't want to distract me from
my driving.

We tumbled in my door as one body with eight limbs,
panting and pulling at each other's clothes all the way to the
bedroom. She didn't seem to want to stop for a tour. We fell
across my bed and I unzipped her dress and, with her whole-
hearted help, peeled off every item of clothing that could get
in my way. I left her the pretty white stockings and garters,

but threw her pinching high-heeled shoes on the floor. I'm a femme too; I know these things.

I hastily shucked off my own clothes, especially my own damned shoes, and they made little black heaps amidst the white piles of Rosalie's clothes.

She looked…well, you can guess how she looked, smooth-skinned and plump-limbed, all curves and soft lines. But you probably haven't imagined with your other senses yet, so close your eyes and imagine the heat of her skin warming the air around us, and her scent like clean sweat from dancing, and just a hint of her sex.

She lay back against the pillows and smiled at me. She didn't say anything, but I just knew that if I leaned forward now she'd let me kiss her and to hell with the lipstick. I didn't try. Instead I pulled a few coils of rope and some bondage cuffs out from the toybox and onto the bed, knowing that with what she already knew of me she wouldn't be at all surprised. Not in the mood for protracted negotiation, I cocked an eyebrow at her in an inquiring gesture.

"Sure," said Rosalie the Beautiful, her eyes outshining her lipstick. "My safeword is 'Untie me now.' "

I tied her flat on her back, her hips held down by a wide belt of ropes crossing back and forth from two of the many eyebolts on either side of the bed. I clipped her hands to the headboard at full extension over her head, allowing her breasts to poke temptingly at the ceiling.

I buckled cuffs around her ankles, and two bigger cuffs a few inches above each knee. I passed a long, slim white rope through the bolts near her hands, and ran it through the rings on the cuffs around her strong, plump, stocking-clad thighs, and as she squeaked in a surprised way, effortlessly pulled her knees high up toward her chest, exposing her sweet, wet cunt. With a quick knot at the ring of the thigh cuffs, I pulled the ropes down to either side of the bed and ran them through two rings there, parting her thighs further. As she began to squirm in earnest, I connected the ends of the ropes to her ankle cuffs and pulled her heels tight to the backs of her thighs, hindering her from kicking or moving her legs.

I stepped back to admire her, and paused, conscious of my own wetness and of my clit pulsing with the beat of my heart. I ached to touch her, and I let that ache build as I looked at her. Warily, she watched me watch her, and relaxed when she saw that, in the symbiosis of being desired, her potent femme's power was intact. Held open like a wanton offering, Rosalie's eyes met mine steadily, proudly. She knew her own beauty; pretty, pretty girl.

"Don't just stand there," she said. "I know you want me."

"Oh yeah, I do. I'm dying to have you," I said. "That's why this is gonna hurt me more than it hurts you."

She looked startled.

I sat for a moment on the bed between her thighs, slowly looking at every intimate detail of her body, finally meeting her eyes. She licked her perfect pink lips in an unconsciously catlike gesture of nervousness.

I leaned forward, letting my long black hair brush her thighs, and made myself comfortable on my belly, my face inches from her exposed cunt. Damn, she smelled good.

I exhaled slowly, open-mouthed, warm breath blowing ever so gently across her flesh.

She squirmed.

"Do it," she muttered.

"Do what?" I breathed

"Go on, taste me."

"Maybe."

She wiggled halfheartedly, but the ropes prevented her from changing position. I moved closer still, my hair swinging once more against her skin, my lips an inch from her clit. I breathed slowly in through my nose, out through my mouth, making the flow of air as warm as possible.

"Fuck," she said, to no one in particular.

"Maybe that's what I'd like to do. Slide my fingers inside you, fuck you," I said, letting each exhaled word play over her clit.

"Yeah, fuck me."

"Maybe," I said.

I noticed the spot I was breathing on seemed to be drying a little from my hot breath, but the very entrance to her cunt was becoming drenched. I lifted up, scooched forward, and dropped a very unladylike wad of spit right at the top of her slit, then added another as I watched the first start to trickle downward.

"Ahh, fuck, what are you...why won't you...? Jez, do something!" she sputtered.

I grinned at her. "Maybe."

I went back to breathing on her, slowly, with all the warmth I could muster. Every so often she tried to shove her cunt in my face, but as she didn't have much slack, it was easy to avoid contact.

I lost myself, as if in meditation, as I pushed each exhale hotly past her clit, thinking nonthoughts about the sweet, musky scent of her cunt and her stifled growling noises. Every so often I added another bit of saliva above her clit, never touching her, but watching her twist and groan at the sudden sensation of wetness.

"There's a puddle under your ass now, not spit but cunt juice," I breathed, whispering to her clit as if it was my secret friend, not mentioning the wetness under my own hips.

"Touch me, you fucker." She started a rhythmic rocking motion, moving as far as the ropes would allow, only an inch or two each way.

I extended my tongue and made it a hard point, letting her make the barest contact between my tongue and her clit. Immediately I felt her reaching for me with her hips, as far as she was able. But I simply held my place, using the faintest possible pressure as her clit brushed my tongue-tip on the upstroke and the downstroke.

After about a few dozen downstrokes, she suddenly sucked in and held her breath, and I leaned back and away from her, watched her pretty face contort in a snarl and the entrance to her cunt twitch hungrily. Nice.

"Why won't you lick me, you evil bitch-bastard?"

"Because I'm worried about mussing my lipstick," I said.

She started cursing, colorfully. Her cursing would have made a pirate's parrot lose feathers. It would have made a biker blush. It made me laugh, out loud and joyful.

I climbed up her body, nestled my hips between her spread thighs, and snuggled in. She gasped as my pubic hair pressed into her cunt after so long without touch, and I smiled down at her.

"Holy, you're so wet, I think I might get a steam burn."

"Fuck you."

"Is that your safeword?"

"No!" And then she started cursing again, as I lifted my body from hers and nuzzled into her tits, getting to know them. They were soft and weighty, full and rounded; the left one was slightly larger, a touching imperfection. Her large, dark nipples pointed straight at the ceiling, and went stiff as I watched.

Not every woman considers her nipples an erogenous zone, so I suckled on one for a second, to test. She gasped and bucked toward me, not away.

"Hey—are these candy?" I exclaimed happily, and dove right in.

I happily lost myself in no time again, moving from nipple to nipple whenever I thought the other might be getting lonely, lightly and experimentally sucking, biting, and licking until I thought I had deciphered the language of her curses and wriggles. What she liked best seemed to be a firm, direct suction at the tip of her nipple, with a slight graze of my teeth every so often. She never quite stopped trying to bring her body in contact with mine, but I stayed up on my elbows, with just my soft belly occasionally picking up wet streaks from her cunt. It wasn't just to tease her; I thought I might embarrass myself by coming if I humped her thigh even for a second.

Finally, I left her wet, chewed, lipstick-stained nipples and ran my tongue in a trail down the curves of her belly, across her garter belt, continuing on in a casual fashion along the length of her cunt. She hissed when I contacted her clit on the way, growled when I dipped inside her, and began to rock against me when I dragged my tongue back, making my tongue flat and soft and dragging it so very slowly up between her labia.

"Oh please," she said when her hard clit just naturally slid into my mouth, my tongue pressing underneath. "Please. That. Do that. Oh...." She sounded sniffly, so I sat up a little to check how she was. Her expression was soft and unfocused, her eyes full of tears. I felt the little spot in my heart grow even warmer with affection for her.

"What do you want, Rosalie the Beautiful?" I asked tenderly, adding my private qualifier to her name for the first time.

She smiled fuzzily at that. "Please touch me, Jez. Lick me. Fuck me. I'm going out of my mind."

"Yeah, I think maybe it's time," I said. And, watching her face, I slid one finger inside her, found she was wet enough, pulled out, and pushed three fingers back in, a little roughly. Her eyes rolled back and her whole body welcomed me in. I slid out and back in again, and her mouth opened soundlessly, her back arched. I did it again, and again, experimenting, trying to learn everything about her in a few short strokes.

I made a guess that she'd like to be fucked hard and fast, in direct contrast to my soft teasing game. Oh yeah. Then I thought maybe adding direct pressure on her G-spot would feel right, and within a second knew I'd guessed correctly. She held nothing back, her body and face telling eloquent stories about her body's responses.

Time enough later, or tomorrow, for my harness and dick. No time, right now, even to reach for the lube. She seemed close to coming already, and I didn't want to tease her for even one moment more.

I moved and took her clit in my mouth again, soon finding the steady side-to-side rhythm that made her cunt clench around my hand. I closed my eyes and put everything I had into pushing her over the edge, lost in her taste and smell, reaching as far as I could inside her with every stroke of my fingers.

Rosalie went rigid, shaking, and her soft cries grew urgent. Her cunt clamped around my fingers, almost squeezing me out, but felt I knew what she needed. I pushed harder inside her.

When I felt her muscles flex and heard the ropes attached to the headboard creak, I concentrated on her clit, flicking it hard with my tongue, once, twice, a third time...and she sucked her breath in and then wailed like a cat. She came in intense, shaking waves, her cunt's deep throbbing squeezing my fingers, and I kept going, fucking her more and more gently until the tension slowly melted out of her muscles, and it was time to stop.

I slid up her bound body, released the buckles on her wrist cuffs, and looked fondly at her. Breathing hard, flushed, and tear-streaked, she was more beautiful to me then than any woman I'd ever seen.

Despite everything we'd done in the last hour, her lipstick was still raspberry-glossy and perfect.

So I kissed her.

Boxer Briefs
Eric(a) Maroney

"I don't like them." Laura's voice breaks the silence as I stand in front of the bedroom mirror modeling my first pair of boxer briefs. I put my back to the mirror, look over my shoulder, and furrow my brow. The gray Hanes stretch across my oval thighs and butt, hugging the curve of my ass.

"I don't know, Laur, they're kind of comfortable."

She looks up at me, running a hand through her chin-length, auburn hair. "They're too *boyish*," she says, raising an eyebrow. "I feel like I'm watching my twelve-year-old cousin."

I met Laura six years ago in a photography class for women, downtown at the New Haven Art Space. Even then I knew the overbearing power of her beauty. She sauntered into the classroom, dodging rows of counters beneath the fluorescent lights of the art hall basement, and slid onto a stool next to me. "Hello," she had said, coolly introducing herself and making little effort to hide the fact that she was looking me up and down, finally allowing her gaze to rest on my rounded breasts.

"I think I look sexy," I say, swaying my hips back and forth, casually flexing what muscles I have in my arms. She is right. I do look like a young boy, but at the same time I can't help manufacturing marvelous fantasies surrounding this new-found sexual dynamic as I stand in front of her, half naked. I close my eyes and picture her on her knees, parting the flap on the front of my Hanes and urging out the peach-colored dildo that could lie tucked inside.

"It's kind of sick, too." Laura looks up at me from where she lounges on the checkered blue-and-green bedspread. Above her, on the olive-drab wall is the black-and-white photograph that she bought for me in San Francisco four years ago: two topless women—their heads shaved—cradling one another. It was the last stop on a road trip that celebrated the culmination of my awkward and unbearable high school years. I lower my eyes and pout, only half pretending.

"I'm sorry, Bradley, I just don't like them," Laura continues, propping herself up on her side and leaning onto her bronzed forearm. The room is chilly and tiny bumps have begun to form on my exposed skin. Outside, the wind thrusts massive tree limbs as if they are twigs snapping beneath someone's tread. Slinking past the fogged windowpane, I sit on the bed by the baseboard and roll the boxer briefs off, revealing my shaved mound. Laura watches as I kick my feet into the air, shimmying into a pair of black bikini-cut panties.

"Better?" My one-word response to being offended.

Laura leans over me, trailing a finger down my muscular belly. "I love the way your body moves, the way your legs frame your vagina, and the way your stomach folds when you bend."

On my back, she towers over me in her favorite cargos and a baby-blue T-shirt that stretches tightly across her breasts. I can see where her erect nipples fight to pierce the cotton of her T-shirt, surrounded by plump mounds of soft but firm flesh. I reach upward to cup my palms around her tits, as she slips her hands under my back, eliminating the space between us. Our faces hover close, so that the tip of my nose tickles hers, and then she dives into me, tracing her tongue around the outline of my lips, parched but now satisfied.

Laura thrusts her tongue into my mouth, her warm breath flavored like the almond coffee she had been sipping, encasing my mouth—now heaving breaths—and locks her lips over mine. I lift my pelvis to meet her thigh, gyrating into her firm muscles as she reaches her hands upward, hooking them around my shoulders and pulling me closer.

I love this motion, this rise and fall of bodies, where I can make-believe I am penetrating her, feeling her from inside as I fill her and run my fingers over her clit.

Laura rolls over and pulls me on top of her. She continues to suck and nibble at my lips as I push my thigh between her legs in an off beat rhythmic pattern. Her breathing shortens—quick sucks of air between kisses and moans. I pull myself off her to unfasten her pants, sliding them down and over her feet. Her cunt lies in the open with a small gleam of cum, waiting to be devoured. I lean into her and close my lips around her pussy, trying to take the whole thing in my mouth at once, stretching from the tip of her asshole to the top of her mound. I flicker my tongue up and over her clit, tracing the sides on the way back down. She squirms and pushes herself closer to my lips.

"Bradley," she moans breathlessly, "come here." She pulls me onto her, forcing my jeans down and off in one swift motion, then positioning my body so that I too am in her mouth while she remains in mine. The scent of her warm, wet cunt urges me to continue burying my face between her lips but now, suddenly, I feel uncomfortable, cold almost. Laura knows I don't like to be naked—even half naked—in the light. Something about the sight of my own pussy, vulnerable and small, puts me on edge. Still sucking at Laura's clit and labia, I try to move myself away from her mouth. The sensation of her lips massaging me feels incredible but I just can't do it, especially after feeling rejected earlier, in my briefs. I slide my lower half away from her and push two fingers deep inside her pussy, now overflowing with wetness.

"Come back, Brad," she calls, reaching for me. I push another finger inside her as I jerk my hand into her again and again. The radiator kicks on, its evasive thunder pouring into the room.

Thursday, I meet Laura for dinner, after carefully plucking my eyebrows and applying just enough makeup so as not to be mistaken for a man.

"And you, sir, would you like to try a new crispy-chicken-super-meal?" the teenage girl says from behind the counter, her face covered in grease and spotted with blackheads.

I pause to think, as her question has interrupted my own thoughts, and watch as she blinks her eyes nervously waiting for my response. "Number one, please," I say, deciding that ignoring the "sir" in her question is the most efficient way to order, "with a Coke and fries."

Laura pushes her tray next to mine as she orders, nudging me down the line. The counter looks as though it's made of imitation wood—probably meant to look rustic, a sad incantation of woodlands. Grabbing a fistful of napkins, I slide into a tiny booth at the back of the dining area, below a plastic mold of Roy Rodgers as a suave-looking cowboy.

"You look beautiful tonight," I mouth, smiling and leaning across the table, taking Laura's palm in mine. She is wearing a pair of slimming black pants and a red V-neck top, just off from work at Smiling Faces Daycare Center. I can smell her lilac-scented perfume from where I sit, as I cross my ankle over my other leg under the table.

I watch as Laura lifts a crumpled napkin to wipe some ketchup from the corner of my mouth; the gleam of a silver bracelet slides to meet her palm.

"Hey, where'd you get the pride bracelet?"

Laura pauses, lifting a chicken nugget to her lips. "Got it from Courin," she finally says.

"Oh," I mutter almost under my breath.

I hate Courin. Okay, I don't hate her, but my feelings toward her border on utter disgust and are close to hatred. Courin and I had the pleasure of attending high school together, where she was one of those soon-to-be-pregnant teenage mother types that everyone seemed to want to walk with in the halls, and I, on the other hand, was lucky if anyone even said hello to me by fifth period. Needless to say, Courin and I never got along. She's hot, though, I'll give her that— dark hair and eyes, with a sweet, puckered mouth that looks like a fresh-cut peach. Oh, and that ass! She has one of those perfect asses that sits real high and round, the kind you want to just dig your nails into.

"I know you don't like her, Bradley," Laura says, rubbing her fingers over my palm, "but, trust me. There is nothing going on between us."

I let out an almost inaudible sigh. I find it hard to believe that the two of them are not at least mildly interested in one another.

"You're too cute when you pout, Baby," she says, leaning over to playfully scratch her fingers in my hair. "I'll make it up to you." The hairs on my arms stand straight up and tickle the pores they originate from, as my breath traps in my chest. Is she coming on to me? Laura and I still have sex, but usually I am the initiator, the beggar at best.

"*Tonight?*" I ask, my voice quivering as I rub fingers through my chaotic short hair. Tonight of all nights is the *worst* possible time Laura could have chosen to come on to me. Beneath my clothes, the dildo is strapped between my legs, tucked tight down the side of my jeans. Tonight is the strap-on's first public appearance. I wear it around the apartment, but only when I'm alone, perhaps reading, lounging on the checkered bedspread in our room. It makes me feel real, authentic maybe, as if that was the way I should have been crafted as I plunged my way out of my mother's womb, a tiny penis flopping between my legs. The pressure of the dildo beneath my jeans is sometimes enough to make me come all by itself. I've never told Laura. She continues her seduction, stroking my leg until she moves up my thigh and discovers it.

"Bradley, what's this?" She draws her hand back to her side of the table, fast.

"What?" I look away and smooth the fronts of my Levis, concentrating on the navy-and-white striped pattern of my polo shirt—anything to avert her gaze.

"*Brad?*" she persists, her eyes fixing onto mine as she leans back against the baby-blue cushioning of the booth. Biting at her lip, she raises an eyebrow and leans forward again. "You're wearing the dick, aren't you?"

I look up at her, but don't want to confirm her statement. I feel like I'm three years old again, aware that I should hide the fact that I have been touching myself, but not sure why.

"This is sick," Laura mouths, hard on the consonants. "What the hell is wrong with you? Do you want to be a man?"

"Of course not, i-it's just fantasy...." I stutter, trying to convince myself.

She gives me a look.

"So is this an everyday thing for you? When were you going to tell me?" Laura crosses her arms and bites at her lip some more.

"No, no," I say, my hand cupped over my mouth muffling my words. "This is the first time." I take the top bun off the chicken sandwich I had ordered and place it on the tray. The large hunk of meat lying there seems less and less appealing.

"Well, why the fuck are you doing it?" She shifts from side to side, ruffling her clothes.

I dig my hands deep into my pockets, not moving as a blond boy nearby sweeps the floor littered with paper straw wrappers and packets of salt. I didn't think wearing the dildo would have been this big a deal. Apparently I was wrong. I look across the table at Laura; even though she is pissed off she seems small, tender almost.

"I-I don't really know how to say this, so you'll understand. I-I, um, I don't want you to take this wrong but, I like girls, Bradley, *girls.*"

"I'm a girl, Laur."

"Well, yeah, but you're not."

She takes my hand and squeezes it. The restaurant is growing cooler as the sun disappears behind balding elms outside the window, and I pull my sleeves down over my hands as Laura pushes the subject further.

"Don't be mad at me." Her hand reaches for mine as her voice snaps me away from the window. She places her other hand in front of my mouth, offering some french fries.

"It's okay," I say, taking the yellow strips of potato from her. Placing the fries on my tongue, I gnaw at their cold, rubbery outside before swallowing. Roy Rogers still grins down at us from the wall. I close my eyes and think of myself as a cowboy, as Roy Rogers even. My tan squared face smiling beneath a wide-brimmed cowboy hat, accompanied by the confident swing of calloused hands. I think of myself as a man, in worn-out leather chaps, riding a stallion, bareback. Something about this isn't right. So I picture myself as a boy.

The next morning, I dress for work, not exactly looking forward to venturing outside the apartment. Beyond the window the sky is a muddle of grays, a Monet in black and white. I slide into a pair of loose-fitting, gray old-man-pants, soft from overuse and years of love, and begin buttoning up a beige collared shirt that looks straight out of the Old West. Peering down at my belly I see my black boxer-briefs riding just above the rim of my pants. "Laura doesn't have to know," I joke aloud to myself while parading in front of the mirror, then head for the door, but as I'm leaving I think. "Why not?" I say aloud. "It's my body and if she has a problem with it...well, whatever." My voice trails off as I pull a black-and-blue beach bag from the bottom drawer of an oak dresser, and then stand up, dumping the contents—two dildos, a harness, and a bottle of lube—onto the bed. I unbutton my slacks again, allowing them to fall around my ankles, and take the black nylon harness from the bed, strapping it over my thighs and ass. I lean over and slip a pale, flaccid cock into the ring of the harness and pull my boxer-briefs and pants over it. The briefs hold the little guy nicely in place, but with enough room to breathe. I grab the other dildo, a hard seven-inch cock, from the bed and put it in my shoulder bag. Walking out the door, I catch my reflection in the full-length mirror, brush my black hair over my forehead with my fingers, and then swing my arms quickly, strutting into the hall. I feel good, I feel right.

"And I'm freeeeeeee, free falling," I sing along to the classic rock station behind the counter at Caffeinated, the shop where I work. The cappuccino machine squeals in the background like a dying squirrel being sucked into a vacuum, whipping the froth that will be heaped on steaming cups of black coffee, well, not black anymore—the latte.

"Can I help you, ma'am?" I say as the noise from the cappuccino machine cuts out. The woman peers at me from behind thick-framed glasses. She has a wiry frame with a long eggplant-colored coat draped over it and a soft burnt-orange scarf wrapped about her neck.

"Can I have, um, *tsa* how do you say *tsa*, just a regular coffee," the woman sucks her tongue between words as two little girls tug at her sleeves.

"Do you want cream?" I ask her, trying not to roll my eyes. I hate it when people are incapable of ordering coffee. Sure, the menu board reads "Café Americano," but if you feel like an ass saying that then just call it coffee. Don't pretend that you don't know what it's called. You wouldn't be here in that case.

"Milk, two percent, and two hot chocolates with whipped cream," the woman orders in a forced but fading British accent.

"Five eighty-five," I tell her, handing over the drinks.

No tip.

Work is actually pretty empty for three in the afternoon. Usually the couches and La-Z-Boy have been claimed by high school kids on their way home, and the tables are frequented by individuals such as the woman who did not tip me. I grab a rag and begin wiping down the counter and the coffee makers. Pink Floyd plays on the radio. I really wish we could listen to another station.

Heading toward the back of the café, I drop the rag on an empty table, planning to continue cleaning on my way back from the bathroom. I push through the beaded curtains and knock on the ladies room door.

"Someone's in here," a voice shouts from within.

I lean my back against the mural-painted wall, waiting. It's a fairly decent rendition of Van Gogh's *Starry Night*. The bathroom door clicks open, and, at the same time I feel someone come up behind me.

"You can't go in there," a shrill voice sounds from behind. I ignore it, stepping forward. "You have to be a girl," the voice continues, and I spin around to meet the lady I had just waited on. "You can't go in there," she instructs, hands on her large hips. "This is the ladies room."

I feel my shoulders slump, a cold twinge shudder from the base of my spine draining the confident mood that had trailed me since this morning. I look down at the small bulge in my pants. It isn't noticeable unless you know it's there, but at that moment I feel like everyone can see me standing, briefs down around my ankles, my flaccid penis hanging there, defeated.

At fourteen, I used to press the tiny lumps of developing breasts back, back into my chest, hoping that if I pushed deep enough they wouldn't resurface. Alone, in my bedroom, I would run my thumbs over my chest, applying pressure, then using my whole palms as a barrier from development the way a sea wall holds the ocean back from destroying land.

"Oh yeah," I nod my head up and down. "Guess what, bitch?" The sound of the words spit out of my mouth as I grab at the rough fabric around my breasts, showing her my chest. Even in the dim light, I see the woman's jaw drop wide open—I could easily fit my entire fist between her teeth.

"So what, Bradley? I thought you wanted to be a boy." Laura retorts later that evening as she leans across the sticker-covered counter. I mop up coffee spills and dropped grounds that have collected in piles over the course of the day. Even when mixed with the dirt and mud from my boots and even after lying on the cold orange tile of the café for eight hours, the assuring aroma of the grounds still permeates the room. They are the silent witnesses to the shit I have endured throughout the day.

"I don't really look like a boy...do I?" I brush some dirt into a pile and bend down to scoop it into a dust pan. Laura looks at me, her big blue eyes searching mine. She runs a hand through her hair and smiles a half smile.

"You are wearing men's pants, aren't you?" She giggles just a little as I try to erase the left-over lines of dirt into the dust pan, finally giving up and scattering the remaining grounds underneath a shelf that holds flavored syrups.

She looks cute tonight, more comfortable even, like the way I remember her when we first met. Laura presses her hands against a sand-blasted pair of baggy jeans, bespattered in black and white paint droplets and covered in tiny holes— probably the places where developer had landed when she used to wear the jeans into the darkroom. I can see her breasts through the top of her black zip-up sweater. The rounded contour of each one pressed together makes my legs tingle.

"Come here." She reaches her arms out and I let myself fall into them, resting my head on her shoulder and smelling her neck—saturated with perfume. I smile, closing my eyes halfway and pushing my body against hers as her hands reach for my shoulders and then push me away just enough that our eyes meet. She reaches her hand down and cups it over the bulge in my pants.

"I thought so," she says, swinging her hand away, "God, Brad, we talked about this, and we are supposed to be lesbians, *lesbians!* If I wanted a man I would date a man." She sighs, "You don't go through all the shit that we go through, the name calling, the lack of civil rights, the degeneration of dignity, just so you can go back to dick."

"But Laura, this is not about conforming. It's about me finding myself." I scratch at my head while stepping back from her, trying not to invade her space. Laura closes her eyes, giving herself a moment to let her anger subside. She climbs onto one of the maroon stools in front of the counter as I slide onto the other one.

Laura lets her head slump into her hands. Her hair fans out around her. "I had this girlfriend, Sarah, when I was in high school. She was my first." Laura's voice is low and I strain to hear her.

"You told me about her," I interrupt.

Laura looks up, distracted by my words. "I didn't tell you everything, asshole." She closes her eyes and then opens them.

"Sorry." The shop has grown cold, and I want to wrap my arms around Laura, want to keep us both warm.

"Sarah was like you. She looked like a guy and, because of it, everywhere that we went people gave her shit. I would hear 'dykes,' or 'lesbos,' gruffly whispered under the breath of middle-aged women, if we walked by them in the isles at Kmart. If we were using a public restroom, no fail, some teen-age prissy would mumble, 'Is that a boy?' And the boys—the boys were the worst. No matter where we went they would stare and sometimes even blatantly challenge her sexuality, 'Hey stud, how about letting your woman come home with a real man?'"

"It won't be like that, Laur," I try to reassure her.

"It *is* like that. I mean, think about what happened to you today. The woman at the bathroom mistook your gender. It's only going to happen more and more, it's only going to get worse."

Or better.

Laura's face is pale, and her forearms are covered in goose bumps.

"I'm sorry," I whisper.

"I love you," she says, "I love you more than anything. It's just...I can't go through that again. I don't like butch girls." Laura pauses. "I'm sorry."

My bottom lip quivers slightly. I bite down to keep it still. "I'm butch, I-I'm more than butch," I say, *and I like it that way,* I think, slipping into silence. I remember being nine, hiding my long hair beneath a baseball hat and staring into a mirror for hours. I thought, even then, that I would have made a much better-looking boy than a girl. I think about the summer that I cried and refused to go swimming in the lake's silky blue-green water, because my father had told me I was too old to go topless like my brothers had always done, too old to allow the cool water to contact my bare chest.

"I know."

"Yeah, you know, and what of it, Laura? I'm not going to change just for you, just because I don't fit your definition of beautiful. I'm not changing for anyone. I like butches, butches are sexy, tranny boys are sexy, and I am sexy." I adjust my shirt and stare at her head-on. Laura lifts her head from her hands again. She glares at me from out of the corner of her eye.

"You think you're sooo righteous, Brad."

I hate it when people call me Brad. It sounds so pretty-boy. I'm more of a Rich or a Derek, a name that says this boy's not afraid to get his hands dirty.

Laura continues, "But you don't even give a fuck about us. You are so wrapped up in your little gender reassignment fantasy... I've been sleeping with Courin." She smiles at this one, proud of the jab she has taken at me.

Silence. I don't know what to say. I just stand there with my mouth open, fishing for air. I had thought maybe she and Courin...but Laura had denied it.

"And she is hot, like a *real* woman should be."

"Fuck you," I say, hitting the light switch and leaving her standing there in the dark. I guess I always knew we weren't going to be together forever, no fairy tale fantasy where we ride off into the sunset. Still, I would have never thought it would end like this.

I can't help but picture Courin's deep brown cunt in Laura's mouth. Laura looking up, her eyes overcome by guttural animalistic fury, a lion tearing a piece of meat from a gazelle's lifeless frame. I think of Courin's cum dripping over Laura's chin, over her lips down her throat, and Laura pushing her tongue deeper into Courin's mound.

I walk behind the coffee shop to a small park that has been deserted for hours and think of my favorite line from Yeats, as leaves fall around me "like faint meteors in the gloom."

The air is that deep purple-black, reminiscent of illustrations in children's books, except for one lamppost casting a circle of light onto a wooden bench. I drag my body over to the bulb, encircled by moths furiously beating their wings against the glass, and collapse onto the bench.

"Fucking bitch." I scuff a pile of dirt with the sole of my boot, my back and thighs still sweating from the argument, the terror of having the dildo discovered. I lean against the uneven back of the bench, unzip the fly of my pants, and jerk the small flaccid penis out of the harness ring, replacing it with the seven-inch peach-colored dildo from my shoulder bag. I shift side to side, shaking one ankle violently.

"How could I have thought she would understand," I mutter aloud to myself while reaching into my bag for the lubricant. I look down at the dildo standing straight in the air like a little soldier ready for orders. "Okay, penis," I smile to myself, "are we ready?," referring collectively to the dick and myself as if we are separate entities, and I guess physically we are.

Pouring a small amount of lube into my palm, I make a ring with my middle finger and thumb, slide it up and down the shaft. "That's right, yeah, who the fuck needs Laura anyway?" and although I know I do need her, I also know I'm going to be okay without her. I squeeze more lube into my hand, this time using all five fingers to pull up on my cock, then to slam down on the base where my clit, now transformed into something larger, quivers beneath. My fingers, cupped around my dick—sticky but loose, from lube and cum—glide along the length of the silicone. It feels real in my hands—warm from friction and stiff but supple. Fingering the vein that runs along the underside of my tremendous cock, I begin breathing air in chunks.

I stretch one leg out, allowing half my body to fall off the edge of the bench while my other leg holds me to the seat, and I continue to pound away at my penis. Cum runs down my thighs the way raindrops chase one another on car windshields. My face tightens, elbows lock, head back. "Fuck," I yell, biting at my bottom lip. "Fuck you, Laura." My fist is clenched around the dick as if it is human, and I try to choke the breath from its body. No, try to release its tension. I try desperately to make it ejaculate thick, milky sperm all over the ground. I reach my other hand beneath the harness and I slip two fingers into my cunt, continuing to hammer my fist up and down my cock—too bad that orgasm depends on contact with the soft baby bird that lies beneath. I massage the outer lips with the tip of my thumb, all the while slithering my palm along seven inches of cock.

I pause, gasping for air. I am almost there, almost there, almost there—my left hand on my massive dick, my other hand thumbing the clit quivering, then pulsating, then spasming beneath. My head rolls back, hitting a tree trunk behind me. I sit silent, in dark night, my legs splayed and cock still standing erect and proud, within the small circle of lamp light overcast by yellow leaves. Everything looks brilliant, glossy. Shadows are edged in gold, the light, the leaves, and me illuminating the otherwise deep black of night. I pull the cock out of its place, stroking the head one last time before putting it in my bag.

The silence of the hour feels heavy. It is here that I feel my boyhood most...here among the air and the leaves and the quiet that I most feel like me.

Eros in Progress
Barrett Bondon

The negotiations had been familiar and not too complicated. It was far from our first scene with others, nor was it our most complex one. We weren't pushing too many safety limits, since Eve's desire was to be fucked for an entire twenty-four-hour period. The dominance would be implied rather than enforced, though some of the play would involve light bondage. We'd take breaks—hell, there would even be a few hours of sleep—but short of her reaching an absolute safeword trigger, we'd be seeing a lot of sweating and friction and orgasms.

One factor we'd thrown in was that she was not to know when the session would start, though I had agreed to keep my ear to the ground so she would not miss any work that couldn't be made up later. I wasn't willing to promise that it would happen on a weekend, as other people's schedules had to be considered. It hadn't been hard to gain the cooperation of several members of my play group and, with a few basic agreements, they were ready to participate. Eve hadn't met any of them, and didn't know them beyond my occasional mention of their play names when I'd tell her about the dungeons I'd been to.

I heard her coming up the back stairs. I stood facing the door as her keys slid into the lock and released the deadbolt. I made one final comfort adjustment to the hard pack I was strapping in my heavy black jeans, and settled my face into a serious expression.

She opened the door and came in without noticing me in the dark kitchen. As her hand moved toward the light switch, I spoke. "Leave it."

I'd startled her, and she stepped toward me. "Stop where you are," I said. "Stop right there."

"Honey, what's...*ooh*." Recognition dawning, she quieted, holding herself very still.

"Put your purse and keys on the counter beside you." She obeyed rapidly, and I could see her gaze flicker over the dining area, looking for anything that might reveal my intentions. "Pay attention, Eve." Her eyes were back on me again. "Take your coat off, and drop it where you stand."

She shucked her lightweight coat, letting it fall from her arms. I sauntered toward her and kicked the coat away from her feet. Stopping right in front of her, I swiftly grabbed her hair and pulled her head back, her neck exposed in a movement I always found erotically inflaming. I pressed my lips to the base of her neck, just above her collarbone, and sucked hard to raise a welt.

"Oww! What are you...."

Pulling her head back further, I clamped my free hand across her mouth and spoke directly into her ear. "I've taken you at your word," I whispered. "I'm gonna be sharing you around over the next twenty-four hours, and I want you to remember who you actually belong to. You can enjoy yourself, if you're able, I don't mind, but do not forget that you are *mine.*" I released her, stepped back, and saw with satisfaction that her pupils were dilating. "Now take off your shoes, but don't forget where they are, because you'll need them later."

She slid out of the moderately heeled sandals she wears for work. Standing still, her hands clasped in front of her, she waited, her shallow breathing the only indication of her nervousness and rising excitement.

"Lift your hem. I want to see which lingerie you're wearing today." She lifted the edge of her blue dress, exposing her panties. I knew she'd have on something hot, she always wore sexy underwear. It was a black thong, with a fancy lace front. I raised my hand for her to stop. I knew what bra she'd be wearing, the matching black underwire a necessary companion to the dress's neckline.

I reached for her breast, stroking back and forth until first one nipple, then the other, gave themselves away, rising hard and firm through the two layers of silky cloth. "Good. I like seeing you aroused. You need to be, if you're gonna enjoy the next twenty-four hours." I could feel her leaning toward me, her need for touch rising as fast as her nipples had.

"All right, now, kneel." Her excitement was visible as she went softly down on her knees in front of me. Kneeling and sucking is perhaps her most favorite position, but I wasn't going to let her have quick gratification. "Give me your hand," I said, and when she offered it, I rubbed it across the front of my jeans, her eyes widening in surprise. I rarely pack hard, but for what I had in mind next, it was necessary. "I suppose..." I said, as if considering the question, "I suppose you would like a taste of butchcock, wouldn't you?"

"Yes, please, yes."

"Hmm. I don't think so, not yet." She frowned. "I have a few other things in mind first. You can't have cock yet, but you will start by licking me through my jeans." Her disappointment was evident, but when I took a handful of hair and pulled her toward the bulge at my crotch, she complied, her tongue stroking over the heavy denim. After a moment, I lifted her from her knees, pushing her ass against the counter and rubbing the hard bulge against her mound. She pushed back, grinding in rhythm.

"Spread your legs," I said, and she settled just a little lower as she separated her legs. I pressed my thigh firmly into her cunt. "Wet already, slut. Ride my thigh. I want my jeans marked by you." Her hips began to undulate as she pressed herself to my thigh, tilting her pelvis back and forth, creating a warming friction as the moisture already soaking her thong began to permeate the jeans. She moaned, enjoying herself, her cunt flowing. I let her go, knowing the motion would not lead to orgasm.

I removed my leg, she reached her hand to her mound. "Ah-ah, not yet, no touching yet."

"Oh baby, please, I'm so wet...."

"Oh really?" I reached my hand between her legs, under her dress, and pressed my cupped palm against her silk-covered cunt. It was swollen and wet, and she would be ready when the time came to fuck. "Turn around and lean over the counter."

Groaning, she did so, and I lifted up her dress, exposing her ass. I love the size and shape of her ass, love to see the thong disappearing between her cheeks. I ran my hand appreciatively over her cool flesh and pushed my bulge against her again, her automatic response being to push back. "Pull your thong down, but don't take it off," I said, "and tilt that ass up a bit more." The thong was soon around her thighs, and she arched her back, offering her ass and cunt in one sweet package. I drew my finger from her clit to her vagina, slipped it briefly in and out, and rested both hands on her hips, again pushing my cock bulge against her, excited by the thought of her cunt marking my fly. Opening the drawer beside her, I gathered the supplies I'd cached there—a bottle of lube and a thin pink dildo, the one best suited for fucking her ass. I held the dildo in her line of sight, delighted at her gasp.

"Now, what I'm gonna do, since I know how you crave having your ass fucked and filled, is I'm gonna fuck you with this, just enough to get you ready for more, and then I'm gonna let your thong help hold this in place for a while." I heard her exhale as she squirmed, and I clicked open the lube, drizzling some on the dildo and some into her asscrack. "There we go, baby, now you back yourself onto this while I hold it still." I positioned the tip at her anus and she pressed back, impaling herself inch by inch.

I started working the tiny shaft in and out as she cried out, "Oh god, that's good. Oh baby, harder, baby, fuck me hard." I complied, freshening the lube, and finally pushed it in to its flared base.

"Hold still, now." She kept moving, so I slapped her ass. "Hold *still*." She complied, collapsing on the countertop. I reached down, keeping one thumb on the dildo, and pulled her thong up. I made sure it passed into her crack, pressing against the base of the dildo. Pulling her dress down, I smoothed my hand over the blue silk, then tapped her ass twice. "C'mere," I said, "I've got one more thing before we really get started." I took her hand, and we walked over to the buffet, where I'd left an object for her. I pointed to it, and her mouth opened wordlessly. "Put it on."

She reached for the collar and, drawing it around her neck, clicked the quick-release snap into place. I reached to adjust it so that one of the D-rings was in front, and gave it just enough of a tug to reinforce the implicit message. "Time for the dress to go," I said. She slipped it off over her head.

"Now," I said, "now you can suck me." She knelt in front of me, reaching for the belt buckle in a practiced response, drawing the thick black leather through the loops, folding it carefully, and setting it between us. I undid the buttons on my jeans as she reached in to claim my cock for her mouth, holding it carefully as I rebuttoned just the top button.

She went full length immediately, moaning and grunting as she worked. Her deep purple nails set off her fingers as she licked and stroked and pumped her way over my cock. I took her head between both hands, fiercely aroused, and began to fuck her mouth, knowing she liked the cock deep enough to choke on, deep enough to nearly block the air flow. I could feel the sensations on my clit building and building, but I wasn't ready for my own orgasm yet, and with the knowledge that I had twenty-three hours of arousal yet to go, I slowed my plunges and then made her stop.

She was winded. Leaving the cock protruding from my jeans, I went to the refrigerator, got a water bottle and took a long drink before handing it to her. She drank gratefully, and the water's reviving effect was visible.

Next I motioned for her to follow me to the dining room. She had refused my previous attempts to take her on the table, but I was leaving her no choice this time. I maneuvered her until she was perched with her cunt at the table's edge. She wasn't resisting now and twined her legs around me. I slipped my fingers between her legs, pushing the thong out of the way, and stroked two fingers in and out of her. Pulling her as close to the table's edge as possible, I put the strength of my arm to use and fucked her until she dug her fingers into my shoulders to anchor her.

I abruptly pulled my fingers out of her and jammed them into her mouth. Adrenaline was coursing through me as I dragged her off the table, turned her roughly, pushing her chest down on the table, and smacked her ass hard. I tugged up on the thong, just above her ass, settling the material further into the crack and increasing the pressure on the dildo filling her there. Reaching for her pussy, I again pushed the material aside and slid the tip of my cock into her. I was holding her down on the table, one hand heavy on her back, my other hand guiding the cock far enough in to be sure it wouldn't easily pop out. I wanted her, would have her, would take her and right damn *now*. My hips began popping against her ass, and she was chanting wordlessly, in rhythm with my surging energy. I thrust hard, all the way in, and she cried out, then began the deep-throated moan that meant she was nearing release. I wasn't ready for her to come yet, so I wrapped a hand in her hair, pulling her head up till it was near enough for me to instruct her. I slowed the fuck just enough that she could pay attention.

"I'm sharing you around today, just like my private whore, just like I know your little slut heart desires. Some bois don't like to think of their woman filled with others' leavings." Pop, another deep thrust, another exclamation from her. "I don't mind it at all, because I'm having you first...." Pop. "...and I'll have you last." Pop. "You'll follow my instructions...." Pop. "...and so will the others." I let go of her hair, resuming my steady deep strokes, and pressed my thumb against the base of the dildo in her ass. "You'll be filled, sometimes every orifice at once...." She moaned, a good moan, a hot wet sound deep in her throat. "...and you will only come with my permission." Pop. "Do you understand?"

"Yes."

I slowed my hips and she lifted her torso, trying to look behind her.

"Do you understand, bitch?"

She groaned. "Yes sir, yes sir. Oh please, fuck me now, please may I come, please sir...."

I grabbed the fleshy part of her shoulders, separated my legs for a base of strength, and pulled her back toward me as I thrust forward. I'd never felt this powerful, this full, this able. "Come *now*," I said, gasping, thrusting deeper and harder, if that was even possible. She screamed, literally screamed, her body trembling and jerking as I rode her to the peak of her orgasm. Collapsing on the table, I slowed my motions to near stillness, then stopped. "I'm pulling out, honey."

She was drenched in sweat, and I pulled carefully out of her cunt, tucking my cock back into my jeans. I draped an afghan over her and guided her to the nearest chair. She sat, her head lolling, and I placed the water bottle in her hands.

We've found a balance, in our power plays, where aftercare can happen between each act in a scene without disrupting the mood and the imbalance of power that makes the sex edgy and hard and fun. I've been grateful for that, because I'm not much good at divorcing myself from the daily reality of our mutual caring enough to treat her like an object each and every moment. Her recovery arc is pretty visible, so when she had nearly finished the water, I could see she was ready.

"That's enough," I said harshly, taking the bottle away from her with a few mouthfuls still sloshing inside. I opened a drawer and took out the bundled leash stored there. "Get over here, now." She stood quietly in front of me, eyes lowered, hands clasped in front of her. I hooked the leash to the collar's biggest D-ring, and the six or eight inches of metal links connecting the clip to the leather jingled as I uncoiled the six-foot length of the leash beneath her lowered eyes.

"Kneel," was the only command I gave, and I knew she'd been anticipating it. "Anytime this leash is on you, you will not speak unless directed to. Do you think you can remember that, bitch?" Smart girl, she nodded, resisting the urge to talk. "Oh, very good. Now get on all fours." She complied rapidly.

From the same buffet drawer that had housed the leash, I brought out her padded wrist cuffs. She lifted her wrists and I Velcroed them in place, then clipped them together, so her hands would essentially have to act as one unit for the time being. Picking up the leash, I led her into the bedroom.

There sat my buddy George on the edge of our bed, naked except for a tight white T-shirt. His hands rested in his lap, not obscuring his dick, which, though soft, was easily three inches in diameter. "Good afternoon," I said with a formality that felt absurd. "You will not talk to this whore. You may only touch her head." George nodded, the rules no surprise for him.

I unclipped the lead from Eve's neck and traced her breasts with a loop of the leather while I instructed her. "Get warm, not hot, water into the basin on the bathroom sink, and bring it in here." She hurried to comply, returning with the shallow bowl in a flash. "Kneel in front of him." She did, and George stood, handing her the thick soft cotton washcloth I had left beside him. "Wash his penis and balls. Make sure they are clean, because they will be in your mouth in a moment."

Eve flashed a look at me, double checking. I nodded. Hands bound, she dropped the cloth in the water, wrung it out, and began carefully swabbing the flaccid six inches hanging in front of her. I laid a hand towel in her lap, and when she finished with George's slowly engorging bio-cock, she used the towel to stroke him dry.

I crouched beside her and clamped her chin in my fingers, making sure she was looking at his dick. "I know you used to fuck men, bitch, so I expect to see you do a thorough job here. Start by sucking his balls before he sits back down." I released her. Balancing herself against his large, muscular thighs, she used the tips of the fingers of one hand to move his penis aside so that her other fingers could lift his scrotum into her open mouth. It was exciting to see her lips in action from this vantage point, and she was following my injunction about enthusiasm. George was watching her work, and after a moment he moved his dick further out of her way. It was starting to take shape, the swelling obvious.

"That's a good start. Now let go, and George, sit down

so she can start with a hand job." George sat, and the transition was seamless, Eve taking his dick between her clipped together hands, starting at the shaft, pumping slowly, running her thumbs along the veins as they began to emerge. His cock was not long, but it was thick. I leaned close to her ear. "You are going to take him in your mouth and suck him off. You ought to enjoy feeling man-dick in your mouth again, all that warm, hard flesh, the veins bulging and the tip jerking when he comes. You, however, will not come. Not yet."

Reaching to the night stand, I took the first condom from the box there, tore open the packet, and handed her the tightly rolled ring of plastic. She positioned it on the tip of his cock where the first small leak of pre-cum was already visible and unrolled it with some difficulty in her restrained condition. Still stroking the length of his swollen member, she closed her eyes briefly, then leaned forward, opening her mouth, taking him in, an appreciative moan emanating from her. George immediately placed his hand on her head, though he didn't force her down yet.

I leaned forward to watch, enjoying the sight of her mouth rippling up and down his sheathed dick, then placed my hand on the small of her back, tracing a line to her butt. She arched her back, making it easy for me to reach the base of the dildo. I pressed it with my finger and she moaned again. I'd wait before really moving it, until George was nearly ready to come and it would be hard for her to avoid her own orgasm. George finally began pushing her head down, his breath more ragged, eyes closed, leaning back on his other arm. I stroked her asscheeks, then stroked her face, feeling the swollen pike of his cock through her flesh as it surrounded him. Her face was flushed, an indication of her enjoyment of my touch even as she cheapened herself sucking him off. I scooted behind her, pulled her thong down, and began to work the slender pink dildo in short bursts. She spread her legs, arching further, and

I knew I could make her come, but that was not part of the plan. George had his hand twisted in her hair, thrusting her down harder and harder, and I stopped moving the dildo as he came with a grunt, pumping hard a few final times into her mouth, then collapsing back on the comforter-covered bed.

Eve pulled her mouth away rapidly, catching her breath, stroking with her fingers until I stopped her. "You have such a nice mouth for whoring around. While you clean him up, I'm going to take the dildo out of your ass." She raised her eyebrows but did not comment, staying in her arched position as I slid it out. That accomplished, she tugged the condom off the newly limp length of penis and reached for the washcloth, following it with the towel. George had recovered enough to prop himself up on his elbow, watching her ministrations. I said, "You may speak to him now."

She knelt back on her heels, eyes lowered. "Thank you, sir, for letting me enjoy your cock."

I nodded at George and he smiled, saying nothing, simply getting up and leaving the room. He started to close the door and I said, "No, leave it open. I want the others to be able to hear." George grinned at that, and Eve flushed to the roots of her hair. "Take this stuff into the bathroom, and clean this dildo up, then go get the plate of cheese and crackers that's in the fridge." Eve took the items, struggling to lift them all with her imposed limitations. I settled back onto the bed, pushing a couple of pillows behind me. Water gushed in the bathroom and it wasn't long before she headed back to the kitchen. I wanted her to eat now, so the food would settle before the heavy-duty fucking started. She didn't know that she'd be sitting out the next act, but I wanted some food in me too, given the stamina I would need.

It was hours later when I went over the restraints one last time, making sure her legs were firmly strapped to the front legs of the chair, her wrist cuff D-rings attached to the short cords tying her hands off to the chair's back legs. Her thong finally off, her bare pussy was dripping a slow accumulation onto the hard chair seat. "We've been at this for a while. I bet you're getting tired. Are you tired, bitch?"

No leash, so she answered. "No sir. I'm fine, sir."

I stroked her hair. "Naw, I can tell you're getting tired. I want to have you rested enough for the group fuck, because we're gonna take you until *I* say we're done, and that may just be more than you can take." Tugging her hair back, I made my point by way of a hard kiss, my tongue opening her mouth wide, thrusting and filling her. Sucking her lower lip between my teeth, I tongued the sensitive inside edge as if it were her clit. The guttural noise from her was no surprise, as her susceptibility to my tonguing wherever it was applied generally reduced her focus to that sensation alone. I took her chin tightly in my free hand, tilting her head back further as I worked her mouth rough and hard, heat rising in me.

An idea came to me, endorphins from fuck-kissing her searing a rapid path through the sleep-deprived tightness in my brain. Releasing her mouth but not the hold on her hair, I nuanced my way to her ear, speaking low and quiet to force her to really listen. "I know how much you like it when I lick you anywhere, but that cunt of yours is a hungry one. At least, when I let you beg for me to do you, that's usually your first choice, isn't it?"

She answered as quietly as I'd asked. "Yes sir."

"I bet you'd like to get eaten right now, wouldn't you?"

"Yes, please sir."

Standing, I crossed my arms, shook my head in the negative. "I still think you need to rest. But you've got me in the mood to eat some pussy. I'm gonna have to do something about that." Eve's eyes went wide when I called down the hall, "Mary!"

A moment later Mary stepped in the room, a short robe barely covering her. I took her hand, pulling her close, kissed her with deliberate attention, then whispered in her ear. A big smile on her face, she said, "That would be great! I can hardly ever get Sue to go down on me and I love a strong butch tongue."

I'm sure I had a smirk on my face when I turned to Eve. Her wish had been for twenty-four hours of sex, and I don't think it occurred to her she wouldn't be an active participant in all of it. Especially if *I* was. I smiled, mean. "Isn't that nice of her?"

She barely whispered, "Yes, sir." I tilted her head back, kissed her hard, and stroked her pussy with my fingers. Very, very wet. "You just relax and watch."

Mary was ready for me on the bed, legs bent at the knees and spread wide, her pussy tilted and open. Taking my time, running my hands over her belly and up her thighs, I calculated how long it would take Eve to make the shift from subject to voyeur. Until now she had been the focus of the entire event. This little interlude would break that up. I was betting that the sidelining would reinforce her submission in a way the restraints could only hint at.

Settling between Mary's legs, I started slow, using long strokes with the broad part of my tongue. Hands on her breasts, Mary settled deeper in the bed as I took just her clit in my mouth, sucking lightly as the tip of my tongue stroked rhythmically. Easing my hand, palm up, past my chin, I slid a couple of fingers in, making short, hard thrusts that brought the "Oh yes" from her at repeated intervals.

I hummed deep and low, working the intersection where her clit now swelled clear of its hood, and was met by trembling, gasping movement that made it hard to keep contact. Planting her feet wide on the bed, Mary bucked upwards, groans rising in pitch as she came.

Eve's eyes were dark, her breathing shallow and rapid, her back curled against the chair's spindles, at the end of the range of motion the ties allowed.

Bill looked at me, and I nodded. His slender cock slid into her slowly. Eve's eyes were closed in concentration as he parted her asscheeks, his pressure steady as he pushed in, bit by bit, massaging and slapping her cheeks. "She's fucking tight, man, this is sweet."

"Just be sure you fuck her hard once you're in."

"Don't worry, man, this tube'll be pounded straight when I'm done."

Dickhead. I walked over to him, took his balls in my hand, shocking him into momentary inaction. "Fuck her hard, but fuck her good."

"Yeah, that's all I meant." I let go of his sac, and as he reached for the lube, he resumed, sliding out a little and then in a little further with each stroke. Moving to where I could see both their dicks, the rubbers stretched tight and slick with lube and Eve, I crossed my arms, feeling my nipples poking through my shirt. Her cunt was soaked, her pussy lips stretched wide around George's hard mass.

Eve rested her head on George's shoulder, her elbows splayed out beside him. "Okay, George," I said, and he began moving his dick where it rested in her cunt. His hips lifted into her, and she sat up a little so she could take him more deeply. I knelt beside George, near his head, and I unbuttoned, pulling my cock out. I'd intended it for Eve, but George surprised me when he reached a hand up, running it along the side of my cock. I looked at him, eyebrows raised, and he opened his mouth wide. My heart thudded pleasurably, blood pumping through me, a sense of mastery, of command, swelling my ego and my cunt. I backed off the bed, standing beside it, and he understood, turning his head, mouth still open wide. Hand on my shaft, I guided it into his mouth, shoving it hard into him. Turned like that, there was only so far I could go, but I felt the practiced suction as he worked me. Eve opened her eyes, unfocused and blurry, as Bill grabbed her hips, beginning to thrust with some vigor. She looked at George, and then at me, smiling. Her breasts were bouncing as both boys picked up the pace.

I motioned to Sue, and pointed to Eve's head. She got up, tightening her straps, and knelt on the other side of George, taking Eve's face in her hand, forcing Eve's mouth onto her butchcock. I reached for Eve's breast, tugging on her nipple. "Fucking slut. Got you filled now. You don't come until we're done." Eve moaned, and Bill started reaming into her, matching George's thrusts, his panting a monotone. George groaned, pumping high and hard into Eve's pussy, his come thrusts taking her unprepared. I pulled my cock out of his mouth, leaving him panting, his hands holding Eve's ribcage as Bill turned abruptly, ramming into her, surely bruising her buttocks. The repetitive "uh uh uh" leaking around Sue's cock made it clear that Eve was in the flow. I knew George's cock, even after he'd shot off, would fill her, giving her a base from which to grow her own orgasm.

Bill hunched over her back, then flung his head back, his hips spasming forward in short, tight bursts, then slowing. He opened his eyes and began to draw his cock from her hole. Once he was out of the way, I motioned for George to pull out as well, and to slide out from under her. Sue shifted, sitting down so Eve could take her cock deep into her mouth. She rested on her elbows, both hands on the cock, and slid as far down as she could take it in. I rubbed my hand over her pussy, her fluid soaking her entire snatch, and eased my cock into her cunt, drifting in with concentration. Grasping her thighs, I moved in steady order, midcock to root, in and out, knowing she liked to always have cock in her, to never think it might slip out. Her body moved as I pushed her toward release, literally pushing her, the butchcock in her mouth a bonus. I could feel my own orgasm nearing, the accumulation of arousal over the nearly twenty-two hours, the swift victory of filling her, of directing her pleasuring, and of taking her now. My inner thighs were wet with my own fluids, the harness and the base of my cock prodding me. I came, using my contractions to push into her, grunting roughly in my throat, trying to focus long enough to tell her, "Come now, bitch, come right now!" She did, collapsing forward, deeper onto Sue's cock as my cock took her full. I lay on top of her.

"Go get cleaned up. You're not quite done yet. Draw yourself a bath. Oh, and keep the collar on."

She nodded, weary, quiet. I rested my palm on her cheek, and she pressed against it, grateful for the contact. George and Bill shook my hand as they left, saying, "Thanks, man" and "See you later." Sue and Mary had waited until they left, then came out of the guest room. Hugs all around, and then they too departed. I took a deep breath, glad to have the apartment back to just the two of us. We weren't done yet, though, and I looked forward, weary as I was, to wrapping this up properly.

Boiling Point
Kyle Walker

Paisley pulled Sallie's sweatshirt over her head, then her long-sleeved thermal shirt, then her undershirt, and finally undid her bra. It took a few minutes.

"You're sure dressed for the weather...in Antarctica," Paisley told her. "This is Boston, not the tundra."

It was December, and Sallie had layered, as she did at home, where winter started early, ended late, and involved a great deal of snow. It was her first winter away from the Midwest, and she felt like a first grader being stripped of her snowsuit.

"You can look good and still stay warm," Paisley said, letting her fingers run from Sallie's cheek, down her neck, and down to her right breast. "I can dress you, if you like. But I'd rather undress you."

Sallie's nipple stood up, and it wasn't from the cold. She got hot whenever she thought of Paisley these days. In high school, back in Schuyler, they'd been best friends, the original odd couple: Sallie Girl Scout and Paisley Bad Girl. If they'd known then what they knew now, Sallie thought, they probably would have been thrown out of school. Beaten up, sent to shrinks, disowned. Schuyler, as a town, was not the safest place to discover you were in love with your best friend.

But Sallie lived in New York now, and Paisley in Boston. They'd found each other again in more amenable circumstances, and were making up for lost time.

Paisley leaned in to kiss Sallie's breast, and Sallie shuddered with pleasure. She started to undo her jeans, tights, long undies, and briefs, thinking that layering might keep you from frostbite, but it certainly didn't help you get warm the best way.

In a moment, Sallie was naked and Paisley still dressed. She wore a blouse made of some shiny material that Sallie thought might be satin, and velvet pants. Paisley rubbed herself against Sallie, and Sallie enveloped her. She loved the feel of the satin and velvet rubbing against her, one gliding across her breasts, the other tickling her thighs.

"Do you want me to take my clothes off?" Paisley whispered.

"You don't have to," Sallie murmured, biting Paisley's earlobe. "It kind of makes it hotter for me to be naked and you wearing clothes."

"That turns you on, huh?" Paisley said between licks and bites of Sallie's neck.

"I'm learning…I'm learning…what I like," she gasped, as Paisley's left hand traveled down to Sallie's pussy, teasing the hairs, as her right hand continued to massage Sallie's breast. "Oh god…yes…there…how did you…find the things that turn you on?"

"How do you get to Carnegie Hall?" Paisley whispered.

"What…."

"Practice, practice, practice!"

After they'd both come, they snuggled in each other's arms

and when Sallie had collected herself enough to form a sentence, she followed up on her earlier question.

"I feel like such a...virgin sometimes," she confessed to Paisley. This was their second weekend together, and she'd only made love with one other woman before that. It was all still mouths and fingers and lots of sucking, and Sallie had the vague idea that there was a lot more that could go on, but wasn't sure either where to go or how to inquire about it.

"Oh, come on..." Paisley teased. "You had sex with what's-his-name, Lonnie, right?" She never remembered Sallie's ex-fiancé's name.

"Larry. It was very...traditional," Sallie said. "Him on top, my legs behind my ears, sometimes we'd do it doggie-style and he'd ask to go in my rear end. I never said yes. He didn't like, you know, licking me...there, but he wanted me to do it to *him* all the time. Everywhere!"

"And you were going to get married to *that?*" Paisley said, rolling her eyes.

"Hey, I didn't, did I?" Sallie reminded her.

"Good for you," Paisley said, playing with Sallie's nipple.

"I did it more on *faith*," Sallie tried to explain. "I didn't leave home to make love to women...but I discovered that I wanted to...and now that I do...I feel like I'm starting all over again." She found herself almost tearful. "What if I'm as pedestrian as a lesbian as I was when I was with Larry? What if he really *was* my speed?"

"Perish the thought!" Paisley declared. "You know what you want: a hot woman. Maybe even a *lot* of hot women."

"All at *once?*" Sallie replied.

"I meant over a period of time, though it's interesting that you instantly thought I meant more than one at a time," Paisley told her. Sallie winced. "I just saw the look on your face. You got all...Moral Majority...on me. Did you get disgusted because the idea is truly not attractive to you, or because you think you're supposed to be appalled?"

"Ummm…" Sallie couldn't begin to answer the question.

"Why didn't you let Larry fuck you in the ass?" she persisted.

"Because he tried one time and it really hurt," she confessed after a pause.

"Well, it probably wasn't because he was that *big*," Paisley told her. "He just didn't know how to do it right. I myself like to get fucked in the butt. Boyfriend Larry probably wasn't the one to introduce you to the pleasures of taking it in the ass."

Sallie was torn between embarrassment at Paisley's language and excitement at how blunt she was. She couldn't imagine saying those words herself.

"Would you like me to…" she began. She couldn't finish.

"Plug me in the ass?" Paisley finished. "You are so cute when you blush. You want to do it, don't you?"

Sallie could only nod. Paisley laughed and got up from the sofa. She retreated to her bedroom and came back in a moment with a dildo in a harness and a videocassette. Paisley tossed the contraption to Sallie and switched on the TV.

"Strap it on, sister!" she ordered as she put the tape in the VCR.

"What're we going to watch?" Sallie asked, frantically trying to figure out how to get into the harness. Did you step in? Put it on backward then turn it around like a bra?

"What do you think? Porn!" Paisley said, as if to a backward child.

"Porn is…bad" Sallie stammered. Larry had tried to get her to watch it with him, but she'd found the women scary, and the boys mostly skeevy. She'd never been turned on by the girls with long nails kissing. It seemed very fake.

"Bad porn *is* bad," Paisley told her, hitting the Play button. "Straight porn doesn't turn me on. I like a fetish flick sometimes, but mostly, I like the men. Here…let me." She got down on her knees and straightened out the harness and pulled the sides tight, giving little tugs and yanks that Sallie felt oddly arousing. "There!"

As Paisley spoke, the blue screen gave way to the title of the video, *In the End Zone,* and immediately there was a locker room with men in football uniforms in various states of undress. Some still had their pads on, others were naked save for their eyeblack, mud, and grass stains.

Sallie looked down at Paisley, who stayed on her knees. Paisley gave her a challenging look, then opened her mouth and started licking and sucking the dildo.

"I've never...seen...gay men...doing it..." Sallie managed to get out.

"It's hot, isn't it?" Paisley said, then got down to serious dildo-sucking.

It *was* hot, Sallie realized, and Paisley going down on her was even hotter. She collapsed backward gently onto the sofa and switched her gaze from Paisley's head bobbing up and down on the dildo to the men in the video, who were soon doing similar things to each other.

Paisley reached up and began to squeeze Sallie's nipples, and of its own accord Sallie's pelvis began to thrust forward. She'd never wished for a penis, but at that moment, she could imagine she had one, could almost feel Paisley's lips on the head of her own cock. Her dick. Her prick. Her rod. She thought the words. She wanted to say them. She saw all the other dicks on the TV, and one guy was lying on a bench in the locker room, another man positioned over him, feeding his cock into the bench guy's mouth. Then another player got between the lying-down guy's legs, and began to tongue his asshole. Sallie wanted to see him put his cock there.

The dildo felt like it was part of her; she wished she could spurt out her come in Paisley's mouth. See it dribbling down her face. *Who am I?* she thought. *Where did this come from?* She felt her rhythm faltering. Paisley looked up and stopped sucking.

"You're allowed to be turned on," she told Sallie. "In fact, it's a crime if you don't admit it. Admit it!"

"Suck me...please," Sallie begged her. In the video, the man who'd been tonguing the other's hole got up and rubbed his cock until it was stiff and shiny. He quickly rolled a condom on it. Then he spread the other man's legs against his chest and drove his cock into the supine guy's ass. There was a long close-up of the hard dick going in, and in and in, and Sallie gave a moan that was almost a sob.

Paisley's hands left Sallie's breasts and she groped on the floor. She came up with a bottle of lube and her own condom. Sallie's breath came in gasps, and she quivered as Paisley put the condom on her dick.

"Stand up!" Paisley ordered. She did, on shaky knees, and Paisley led her around behind the sofa. She leaned over the back of it, facing the TV screen, her ass in the air, and said, "Lube! Lots of lube!" Sallie obliged, and worked the slippery stuff in and around Paisley's asshole, and coated the dildo with it.

"Fuck me...fuck me in the ass, Sallie." Sallie wasn't sure what to do. "Finger! Start with your finger..." Paisley said urgently. Sallie put her forefinger to Paisley's little brown hole, and it slid in easily. Sallie's eyes were glued to the TV, and she found herself thrusting her finger in the same rhythm as the man on the screen was ramming his cock in the other guy's ass. Without being told, she somehow knew to add two, then three fingers. Paisley urged her on with "Fuck...yeah...harder...in me...go in me..." and Sallie knew it was time for the dildo. She pulled her wet fingers from Paisley's relaxed hole, and slowly guided the dildo in.

"What do you want to do?" Paisley grunted. "Tell me!"

"I want to fuck your ass," Sallie cried in a voice she didn't recognize. It was so low and serious. She didn't know she could sound like that. "I want to pound you. Fuck you in the asshole. Now! Hard!"

And she did what she said. She rode Paisley's ass like the men on the screen, shoving her own hard cock into the receptive hole. The man getting fucked screamed he was going to come, and the guy whose cock he'd been sucking rubbed and rubbed it, and suddenly he came on the bench guy's chest and face, spurting and rubbing it in. Then the guy going up his ass pulled out and he came, too, and the two men rubbed their come onto the first guy's body. Then the lying-down guy, smeared with the other two guys' come, came himself with a loud, guttural cry.

Sallie thought she'd come herself, even though there was nothing inside her. The dildo rubbed against her clit. She wanted to come inside Paisley, to ride her until she shrieked with pleasure. Her cock had a rhythm of its own, her hands reached around Paisley and squeezed her nipples. She sank her teeth into Paisley's neck. She put one leg over the back of the sofa, so she could drive even harder and deeper into Paisley. With a sudden lurch and a cry, Paisley came. Sallie felt it in the dildo, then radiating back throughout the rest of her. She thought she might come, too, and reached down behind the harness to stroke her clit, which was ready to explode. She pulled out of Paisley as she rubbed herself, and in a moment, she dropped to her knees in her own orgasm.

Paisley slid down next to her on the floor, and they held each other, both still quivering. Sallie felt her cheeks wet with her own tears. She almost always cried when she had an orgasm. Paisley licked the tears, and it seemed the most intimate gesture she could make. Sallie buried her head in Paisley's chest.

"Thank you," she finally whispered.

"Oh babe, that was...fucking awesome," Paisley murmured back. She did not seem like the glittery, teasing girl who had stood a little ahead, a little above Sallie since they'd known each other. "You could...totally dominate me. Who would've thought..." she trailed off. Sallie held her tighter. Then she felt Paisley pull away a little, and she rolled away so they could both get up. Paisley went to the bathroom, and Sallie slowly unstrapped the harness and pulled on her undershirt. She turned off the video. When Paisley came back, she'd washed her face and run a comb through her hair.

"Are you up for dinner? I'm starved. And maybe a club after? I know a band that's playing at the Middle East tonight...."

"I thought we could, you know...keep going," Sallie said. "That was pretty...spectacular."

"What was?" Paisley asked, challenging.

"When I fucked you in the ass. When you liked it," Sallie said, and the words came smoothly out of her mouth.

"You got in pretty deep," Paisley said, and Sallie couldn't tell whether she meant physically or emotionally. It did seem like both. And for some reason, Paisley was unnerved by it.

"I hope I didn't hurt you..." she began.

"Oh no, it felt real good," Paisley told her. "It felt. *I* felt."

"And that scares you?" Suddenly Sallie was the one asking the questions.

Paisley just shrugged and went into the bedroom.

"Did you bring something other than a parka and mukluks?" she called from the other room. "If I'm taking you places, you have to look nice. I have my reputation to think of."

"What reputation is that?" Sallie called back, thinking it was silly to be in separate rooms after an experience like they'd just shared.

"I'm cool, you know?"

"I know," Sallie told her. "I think I'd rather be hot."

Paisley muttered something in the other room. Sallie

couldn't hear her. "What?"

"I said: you don't have to worry about being hot."

Sallie wasn't sure if that was a compliment. She looked through her things. She didn't feel like putting so many layers back on.

An Incident in Whitechapel
Catherine Lundoff

Max was out late again, her feet stumbling their way over the cobbles in a fog that flowed like water through the streets and alleys. She had been looking for Smiling Jack—the Ripper himself—tonight and every night for the last fortnight. It had been her cousin Annie whom the bastard sent to her grave, and the murder filled her dreams until she could not sleep for the blood, the flash of steel. Annie had been good to her, even when the drink took her; she had deserved better than to die like a butchered hog. Max would have his heart for it, or she would know the reason why.

The gas lamps, scattered as they were, gave the fog a ghostly glow, making it even harder to see down the dark alleyways. It was a prime night for the Ripper and any other hunter who haunted the shadows of Whitechapel. A nearly toothless woman made Max jump as she shouted something from a doorway. Her thick Cockney was blurred by blue ruin until she was nearly impossible to understand. But the grimy finger that she ran over Max's greatcoat spoke for itself.

"What are you doing on the street, mother? Aren't you

worried about Jack? It's no time for that." She brushed the woman's hand away as the whore grinned and pulled a long, wicked-looking butcher's knife from her sash.

"Reckon I'm ready for 'im. You 'im?" She waved the knife menacingly toward Max.

"If I were Jack, mother, you'd be dead now and not chatting me up. Get inside to safety, woman." The old woman snarled at her words, or perhaps just her lack of interest, and vanished into the fog. Max drew a deep breath. If he was out tonight, she was having no luck finding him. Time for home and Isabel, as she'd promised. Her way wound up the darkened street onto the better-lit and more populated thoroughfares.

By the time she reached those more prosperous avenues, the thought of Bel's soft curves lent wings to her feet. The bobby on the corner nodded as she turned the corner for home. "Evenin', Mister Cruthers." Max tipped her hat in response but said nothing. Mr. Cruthers, the knife and scissors grinder, was a quiet man, after all. Kept to himself, just him and the missus living up at the end of the lane and no questions asked. Respectable tradesmen were rare in this part of London, and if Mr. Cruthers seemed a bit odd, well, he was no worse than many.

Max bounded up the wooden steps to her small home and Bel threw herself into her arms the moment she closed the door. "I've been so worried!" The soft country burr reached Max's ears. "Why must you do this? He's sure to kill you, and then what'll become of me?" The blue eyes tilted up reproachfully from Max's shoulder. Max reached up into Bel's mass of red curls and yanked so that her lover's face turned up for a kiss. Bel uttered a small yelp of protest, then returned Max's embrace passionately.

"I made an hot toddy for you. Did you want it now?" Bel's big blue eyes anxiously searched her face. Max nodded, and she trotted off to the kitchen. Bel had been fresh out of the country when she'd been turned out from a fashionable milliner's because she would not oblige the owner's son. She'd been forced to take up whoring then, but the country bloom hadn't been lost to city grime when Max met her.

Her upbringing still showed in her manners and in the way she kept their home. The little house was warm and cozy, filled with the smell of baking bread and the bright warmth of dried flowers. To Max, it was almost as though those desperate, hungry months on the streets had never happened.

Their home had been Max's inheritance, left to her by her father by way of a dowry. Not that any man was good enough for her, except for him of course. She'd wear the scars he had given her to her grave, never forgetting the mixture of joy and pain that filled her when he died of the wasting fever some years back. She swore then that no man, whether husband or lover, would use her like that again.

But if she wanted to live free, she hadn't the looks for what little semblance of freedom whoring might give, even if she had the inclination. There was nothing for it but to take up his clothes and his trade. *Clothes make the man*, she thought as she put up her greatcoat and hat. From a clothing change and her own lack of womanly curves was born Master Maxwell Cruthers, a man who knew how to whet the edge of a blade until it sang a song only he could hear.

Until she met Bel, no one had known her secret, and she'd sworn to herself that she'd never tell a soul. Never mind the lonely nights, the strange looks from the neighbors—she could bear it all. That's how it was before she found she longed for the touch of the blue-eyed whore who worked Tavern Street. She wooed Bel for months, protecting her, feeding her, nursing her when she was sick. Max chuckled to remember the look on Bel's face when she found out that Maxwell wasn't a man. Bel, in turn, had introduced her to the pleasures of the flesh, the way Bel liked them when she trusted someone.

With that thought, the bonny lass herself emerged from the kitchen with the toddy. Max smiled at her, then pulled them both down into the big chair so that Bel sat on her lap. Between sips, she unlaced the top of Bel's nightgown, casually kissing her lover's neck until she heard the gasp she'd been waiting for. All the while, Bel chattered on about the shop where she worked as though nothing was happening. All the while, her small gasps and half-closed eyes told a different story.

The toddy abandoned on the nearby table, Max went to work in earnest unlacing the top of the gown. A few moments' work and she could see the graceful curves of Bel's ample breasts with their hardened nipples. Bel writhed on her lap, trying to reach Max's earlobe with her teeth. Max evaded her and worked a hand up under the heavy nightgown to stroke Bel's soft thighs. Her tongue slowly crept over her lover's exposed neck, tasting, savoring the salty tang of her skin. As if she could not bear such pleasure, Bel gave a desperate twist and stretched for her goal, her teeth closing on Max's lobe.

Max grabbed her long red hair and for the second time that night pulled her face away. "What have I told you about that? You know what happens to bad girls now, don't you?" Bel flushed pink, and favored Max with the slow, lazy grin that had won her heart. "Very well, then." Max's voice took on the proper accents that she affected when she felt like this. "I want you upstairs and presentable by the time I count to twenty. We'll break you of this habit yet, my girl."

With that, she pushed Bel from her lap and the other woman scrambled up the stairs as fast as she could go. Max started counting loudly as she stripped off her jacket and cravat, then marched up to the bedroom to make her own preparations. Stripped to the waist, she advanced briskly toward the hall closet where she kept her tools. A quick glance into the bedroom showed Bel, naked and face down on the bed's faded coverlet, her white skin glowing in the firelight.

The sight roused Max to greater speed as she got prepared. Tonight she had something different in mind. Leather straps in hand, she approached Bel and tied each of her limbs to the bedposts, checking to see that each loop was snug, but not cutting. Bel squirmed with anticipation, prompting Max to smack her bottom so sharply that the print of her hand stood out in red. A strangled yelp greeted the blow and Max smiled in anticipation.

Once Bel's limbs were tied securely, Max went for her favorite tool. The whip had been made by a traveling saddler, one who knew his trade. The handle was all coarse braided strips, the lash of soft and coarse strips bundled together. Its solid feel in her palm made her flush red, her thighs moist with anticipation. Tonight, she'd make Bel sing as she never had before.

She ran the long leather strands up and down Bel's back, over her thighs, even pushing the braided leather inside her briefly. Bel moaned and quivered, red hair tossed back over her shoulders and gold-lashed eyes closed. The wetness between her legs glistened in the light until it was all Max could do not to reach down and taste her. Instead, the whip sang downward and Max grew wet to the music of Bel's groans and yelps. She loved that feeling of power, that sense of fulfilling her lover's every desire. The whip sang downward until Bel's back was streaked with red, but the skin remained unbroken.

Bel writhed into the bed, glistening wetness now coating her thighs. She tugged at the ties on her wrists. "Please… please," she moaned.

"Yes, me love?"

"Put it inside me…please…." Max grinned; she loved this moment, this instant when Bel begs for fulfillment. But she wanted to wait, to prolong the moment a few seconds more. She seized a goose feather from the table and began to run it over Bel's sensitized back, up the inside of her thighs, and over the soles of her feet. Bel shrieked with pent-up frustration and desire.

Max, still dragging the feather over Bel's back, unbuttoned the front of her breeches and dropped them to the floor. Dipping her finger in the bowl of warm lard that she kept near the fire for such occasions, she slid her finger slowly and steadily into Bel's asshole. Her efforts were greeted with Bel's enthusiastic moans and frantic efforts to open her legs even wider. Leaning down, she sank her teeth into Bel's shoulder and bit sharply. She cried out again, and Max grinned as she used her other hand to rub lard onto the wrapped leather that she wore as a false penis.

Balancing herself over Bel's broad thighs, she slid a finger inside her lover's wet slit, then brought it to her lips, savoring the taste and smell. Then, spreading Bel's cheeks, she drove the hard piece of leather into her. Bracing herself with one hand, she wrapped the other in the long red tresses, pulling Bel's head back and arching her neck. Bel's shudders signaled the beginning of her orgasm. "Not yet. Not until I say so," she growled.

Bel tensed, bucking beneath her with the effort of holding back. Max's head spun with desire. "Now!" she yelled. She thrust hard, the leather straps that held the penis rubbing against her until the touch of rough leather and Bel's soft skin took her. She fell, shuddering, onto Bel's quivering back as both collapsed exhausted into the sodden bedclothes.

After some sweet time, Max pulled the piece of wrapped leather from Bel and kissed her gently. Untying the restraints, she held her lover tightly in her arms, listening as Bel's breathing slowed. "Can I taste you tonight?" Bel's large blue eyes had a anxious, pleading look in them.

"How can I say no to that face?" Max responded, smiling. Her fingers found the buckles that held the straps in place, opening with the ease that came from long practice. Bare of its usual covering, her skin tingled in the cool air. Bel's eager tongue slid down her neck, over her collarbone, to her breasts, leaving a trail of goose bumps in its wake. Then she paused, the tip of her tongue caressing Max's nipples until her back arched slightly in pleasure.

"Oh, that's good, my girl," Max groaned. She seldom let Bel pleasure her this way, but tonight it felt right. Bel slid lower, tongue trailing slowly over Max's stomach and thighs until she worked her way to Max's slit. There she paused, tongue lapping faster, rhythmically seeking her lover's release. Max writhed in pleasure for as long as she could bear it, then gently stopped Bel. "Enough, love. Can't calm down enough tonight. Come here." She pulled Bel up close and held her.

They lay quietly for a bit. " 'Tis him you're thinking on, ain't it?" Bel asked apprehensively.

"Aye. How can I not? Who *is* the bastard? Where does he hide himself? How the hell am I going to find him? I want the bleeding sod dead for what he did to Annie! She was good to me when I was but a sprat, better then me whole family, and I'll have vengeance for her, or know why." Bel shook her head, having no answers for this. Max looked down at her. "Think on it girl, it might have been you out on Tavern Street." A cold rage filled her at the thought.

Unspoken questions danced through Max's mind. If she was aroused by her power over Bel, how did Smiling Jack himself feel about the women he murdered? She knew she was no killer, except to avenge those of her own that had been done wrong. She had a brace of pistols for Jack when she found him, and few enough questions then. But sometimes she wondered how thick a line separated her from him.

Not that those questions were enough to stop her quest. The next night and the next, she went out hunting the Ripper. He began to loom large in her mind during the daylight hours as well, a menacing cloaked figure with a bloody great butcher knife, disappearing around every corner and down every alley. The newspapers reported more murders, more speculation, and still she couldn't find the bastard.

When she was home, Bel began to fret over her in a way that Max found irritating. On one occasion, the local bobby even asked Bel some questions about Max, just enough to make it clear that Mr. Cruther's behavior was becoming suspicious. After that, she stayed in for a night or two, long enough for Bel to think all was well.

But blood and knives filled Max's dreams, and more than once she woke screaming from nightmares. It was those dreams more than anything that drove her out into the dark alleys of Whitechapel night after night, fearing sleep. The newspapers all speculated on Jack's identity, and the police net tightened around Whitechapel but still he slipped through, continuing his bloody work. The knowledge drove Max until her eyes stood out from shadowed sockets, glittering with an unhealthy gleam, and her breath wheezed in her lungs from walking in the burning fog at all hours.

Finally the night came when Bel could stand it no longer. Knowing she must do something, she wandered their house looking for something, anything, that would distract Max enough to bring her back. The whip sat neglected along with the ties, and her fingers only stroked it for a few regretful moments. It wouldn't be enough, not this time. But she wouldn't give up yet. Her steps led her to the kitchen where she saw her reflection gleaming dimly at her from across the room. That was it. It had to be.

She took one of the knives from the table and gingerly tested its gleaming edge. The blade was fine enough to split a hair from her head, and she shuddered at its deadly possibilities. Shivering, she rested the gleaming blade against her neck, the exposed skin of her collarbone, letting its cold promise seep into her bones. She imagined it in Max's hands, could almost see her blood gleam on the dark steel.

Hoping she had the courage to endure what she dreamed of, she put it on the table next to their bed. Then there was nothing to do but wait, so she did. When Max finally returned after midnight, bleary-eyed and edgy, Bel was kneeling on the threadbare carpet in the hall, long hair loose around her shoulders and nightgown open at the neck to display her ample bosom. "I did not go to the cobblers today, as you wanted…," Bel began softly.

Max grimaced in fury but forced the words down. She had always feared what might happen if she let her temper go, and tonight the thought made her grind her teeth together. "No, lass. I scarcely know myself tonight. I'd flay you before I knew what I was about."

Bel continued kneeling, her hands unlacing the top of the nightgown further. "And I've not washed the bedding, as you asked." She could feel herself growing damp as she knelt there, shivering with trepidation and chill with Max's eyes fixed on her. They were so strange tonight, those eyes. She hardly recognized them.

With a sudden movement, Max threw her coat and hat aside. She leaned down and ripped the nightgown open to Bel's waist, dragging it over her shoulders. Bel looked up and met her eyes, breasts heaving and mouth slightly open, breath coming in pants. In a snap, Max pulled off her scarf and blindfolded her with it. Then she pulled open her breeches and pulled out the false penis. Grabbing the back of Bel's head, she shoved it into her open mouth. Bel's eager tongue slid over the leather, welcoming it as far down her throat as Max could shove it.

Max shuddered as Bel's eager hands wrapped around her hips, pulling the leather penis further into her mouth. Ah, this felt good! But it wasn't enough, not tonight. Pulling the leather from Bel's mouth, she dragged her swiftly to her feet.

Bel stood trembling while Max tied her hands together with rope from the hallway closet.

"Well, my girl, what are we going to do with you tonight?" Max's left hand twisted Bel's nipple, making her yelp in surprise and pain, and something deeper that sang over Max's skin and into her fevered brain. She pushed Bel hard against the wall, then ripped the nightgown from hem to waist. Her fingers drove savagely inside Bel until she cried out and spread her legs further. Max slammed her hand into her warm, wet welcome until Bel could hardly stand.

"Oh, please...the bed...let me lie down...please...." Max grabbed the rope around her hands and towed her swiftly up the stairs, only just able to make sure she didn't stumble. Pulling Bel into the bedroom, she grabbed the knife and cut off the rest of the gown.

Then it struck her. "What's this doing here, ey?" She touched the flat of the blade to Bel's neck and watched her quiver.

Bel whispered, "Oh please...it's for you. Please...don't stop." Max stroked the blade down Bel's skin, then over her bare nipples, watching them harden in response. By now, Max could smell her own desire and bared her teeth in a savage grin to feel Bel tremble as she ran the knife over her body. She quickly pushed Bel onto her back and then bound her to the bedposts. Her own clothes were hurriedly removed, breath hissing between her teeth in conflicting urges.

This time, there was no pause to admire the curves of Bel's body, to prolong her lover's longing until it was nearly unbearable. She knelt between Bel's thighs with a pantherlike swiftness, her hands trembling with something she hadn't known she could feel. She grabbed the knife's blade, not caring if she cut herself or not, and shoved the long wooden handle into Bel. Bel's back arched as the handle slid in and out, coated thicker each time with her own juices.

Max was dizzy with power and desire. Seizing the candle by the bedside, she held it over Bel's writhing body, carefully tilting it so the hot wax splashed on her belly. Bel screamed softly from the unexpected sensation and pulled back hard on the ties. She shook with a force that almost broke the leather as the knife hilt was once more slammed into her. Putting the candle aside, Max leaned down to sink her teeth into Bel's thigh. She had left the knife handle inside Bel and found she liked the way it looked, dangerous and shining in the candle-light as Bel's muscles clenched around it.

Max straddled her thighs, letting Bel feel how wet she was. Bel tugged futilely at her bonds, trying to get to her. Max began rubbing herself on Bel's softness, letting it caress her own hot flesh as the edge of the blade caressed her skin. Then she slid up to Bel's face, and placed her knees on either side of her head. "Lick me," she commanded, and Bel's eager tongue slid inside her.

Max's back arched as she rode Bel's tongue until she came, hard, filling Bel's mouth with her taste. She climbed off Bel and looked over her lover's body. Small burns marked her thighs in red streaks. The knife handle was still firmly clenched in Bel's cunt, her slick wetness coating it down the blade. Max pulled the knife out and looked at it. Bel groaned and moved her hips as though begging for more. Max ran the tip of the blade lightly over her thighs, pleased with her response.

Undoing the ropes, she flipped Bel onto her stomach and fastened her once again to the bedposts. Going to the closet, she pulled out a flexible cane. Putting the knife aside for the moment, she began to lightly smack Bel's calves and thighs. Bel's moans inspired her and she worked her way up and down her lover's back, striking a little harder each time. "How much can you take tonight, me girl? Can you take all I'm going to do?" Max growled menacingly as she applied the cane.

Bel's shriek after a particularly sharp blow made Max

pause for a moment. Her hand ran slowly up Bel's inner thigh as she writhed and attempted to move closer to Max, to coax her fingers inside her wet warmth. The welts on her back stood out in sharp relief against her white skin, and Max ran her fingers over them, gently tracing them.

She found she wanted more, more power than she had ever exercised over her lover before. The Ripper knew the power of life and death; why shouldn't she? She wanted to see blood on the knife's edge, to know the power of the open cut. She wiped the tears from Bel's wet cheeks and whispered, "Do you trust me, darling? I'm not done yet...." Bel nodded, her eyes still covered by the blindfold. Max could see her stiffen a little, expecting the cane.

Once more the knife was in Max's hands, the cane laid aside. She hesitated a long moment, listening to the call of steel and blood. Slowly and gently, she ran the knife's sharp point over Bel's shoulder, feeling the skin shift beneath it. Then she sank it in, cutting a series of shallow lines on Bel's left shoulder, her hand trembling with the effort it took not to do real harm. Bel screamed as Max drove her other hand into her slit so that she felt the two sensations at once. Bel came hard, pulling Max's hand further inside her as she shook and quaked. Max leaned down and licked the blood carefully from Bel's shoulder before she cut the ropes to set her free.

With an effort at self-control so profound she shook with it, she put the knife back on the table. The tang of Bel's blood still on her lips, she slipped the blindfold from her lover's eyes. She saw Bel's gaze light on the blade, still stained with a drop of her own blood, and Max flinched a little. But she had stopped, not shedding her lover's blood wantonly or brutally. Bel's eyes glowed with something that she had not seen in them before: a strange mixture of lust, terror, and surrender.

It warmed her soul and she pushed her hand inside until she could form a fist inside her lover. Bel clenched, quaking and twisting around her hand, long red hair soaked with sweat. When she stopped shaking, Max pulled her hand gently out and dropped to the soaked sheets beside her lover. Bel shuddered and collapsed on Max's shoulder. Max held her until she fell asleep, then bandaged her shoulder. She blew out the candle and sat thinking in the dark until sleep took her. Tonight, she had called her demons when she chose and dismissed them when their time was done; that was enough for now.

A fortnight later, the papers screamed that there was an end to killings in Whitechapel. The Ripper's reign of terror had ended. What had happened? Had he tired of his game or died in a madhouse? Had he stalked the wrong prey and ended up dead in the Thames or at the end of a longer, sharper blade than one of his own?

No one knew for sure, but Max stopped prowling the streets at night. The strange, feverish light in her eyes was replaced by a newfound calm. True, when Max put up her pistols along with her long nights, Bel thought that there was less lead shot than she remembered. But Max volunteered nothing and Bel did not ask, opting instead to savor her nights on the knife's edge.

My Debut as a Slut
Jean Roberta

"Crystal," said Brock, listening to herself as she studied my alert, cotton-covered breasts. "That's what I want to call you. I want you to be clear and open to me, nothing fancy." She stretched a bare, smoothly muscled arm across the table to reach for my hand. Her grip was hot.

I looked at the biker dyke for whom I had given up an afternoon in the university library. My parents, the historian Abraham Chalkdust and the linguist Anna Parle Chalkdust, had named me Athena before I was even a footnote in their lives. Now I was a thirty-year-old teaching assistant taking a break from my Ph.D. thesis by drinking vile coffee in a fly-specked café because Brock had brought me here. I wondered if she would take me on a bike trip to hell, and how long I would hang on.

I dared to look into her compelling gray eyes. "I don't know how to be a chick named Crystal," I confessed. "Will you show me?" I pulled the brass clip out of my long chestnut hair, hoping this was a start.

Brock grinned wickedly, squeezing my hand. The yellowish

light from a hanging lamp gave her short wood-brown hair a perverse halo. "You know how, baby, you just don't want to admit it," she told me. "You should act like the slut you are when I show you to my friends. It's not your literary theories that'll make an impression. Even when I'm not touching you, pretend I'm squeezing your ass and pinching your nipples whenever you're with me. You like to show off, Crystal. I could see it when I met you at the club."

I had ventured out to the dyke bar for a drink, consciously hoping to meet some compatible Women's Studies majors. Brock had claimed me instead, or I had found what I was really seeking. It was like a serendipitous experience in the library, such as the time my mother's book on eighteenth-century sexual slang fell off its shelf and hit me on the head.

Brock slid close to me in the leatherette booth, pressing a hard thigh against mine. "Put your jacket over your lap, honey," she muttered into my ear. She didn't really seem to care who heard. I focused on my breathing as I carefully covered myself.

Brock's tanned, expressive face looked radiant. "Did I tell you my old buddy Keith is back in town?" she asked conversationally. "He wants to meet you." One of her hands was sliding over my hip, then pulling down the zipper of my pants. Her hot fingers burrowed under my panties on a downward expedition over my quivering belly.

"Brock," I whispered. "We can't do it here."

"Sssh," she replied with a grin. "Do you want everyone in the place to hear you?" Her fingers reached my clit. After a dramatic pause, they teased it like a cat playing with a mouse.

I was in exquisite distress, as usual whenever I was in Brock's company. I felt my wetness gushing over her determined fingers, making it pointless for me to deny the obvious. I clenched my teeth to hold back a moan.

"You're too quiet," she warned me. "If you're not going to

talk to me, make some noise." She pushed in until two of her fingers were knuckle-deep in my cunt. Their insistent stroking pulled my attention back to where she wanted it.

"Keith?" I babbled desperately. "Is that the guy who sells...?" I spread my legs and tilted back to give her more room. A man at the next table seemed to be watching us, but I couldn't afford to look at him.

Brock's fingers sank in as far as they could. "Yep," she remarked, and in a lower voice: "sit forward." I obeyed, and the resulting friction brought me to a crisis point.

"Quiet," said my tormenter in a classic dykey monotone as though talking around a cigarette. "Don't hold back. Go for it, baby." The pressure on her fingers must have been considerable, but she didn't seem to mind.

I gripped the table with one hand while holding my jacket with the other. My urge to ride her fingers had to be suppressed, so I did inner aerobics by squeezing her with my muscles. "Can't do it here," I told her between clenched teeth.

In response, she moved her fingers in spirals, then ran a fingernail in circles over and around my swollen clit. A series of spasms spread outward from there like ripples in my flesh. I covered my panting mouth, trying to pretend I was yawning.

Brock eased her wet fingers out of me, wiping them on my skin with a satisfied air as she pulled them back into public view. I already missed them. "You are so easy," she said, smirking. I felt my face grow hot.

The man at the next table stood up, scraping his chair, and faced us. "Next time, get a room," he snarled down at me in the distinctly Canadian style of a man who minds his own business until some unbearable circumstance forces him to speak. He looked shabbily genteel in a way I recognized, though I was sure we had never met in academic circles. He didn't wait for my answer.

"Crystal," Brock soothed me with her voice. "Let's go."

Outside the café, hot sunlight hit us in the face. I felt prickling sweat all over my body, and wished I could run naked through a fountain. Brock looked at me as though she could read my mind.

"We're going shopping," she told me, approaching her bike at the curb. "You need some new clothes." She threw a leg over the saddle. I slid on behind her, and we were off.

Holding onto Brock's waist with the wind in my hair and a vibrating motor between my legs was such a tease that I was disappointed when the ride ended. She parked the hog in front of the Treasure Chest, a shop that sold Indian cotton clothing, hash pipes, rude bumper stickers, and cheap jewelry. Brock smiled familiarly at the slim brown man behind the counter as she walked in. I followed her, and he gave me a long look. For a moment, I wondered whether I would be offered to him as payment for the merchandise.

Brock found what she wanted. "You wear size eight, don't you, girl?" she asked, sizing up my curves with her eyes. I agreed, she nodded, and she progressed to another rack.

Armed with a scrap of smooth black leather and a red-and-white striped knit top that reminded me of an old-fashioned barber pole, she herded me into a fitting room. "Take everything off," she ordered, then watched with amusement as I did.

I could feel my breasts jiggling with each breath I took. Under Brock's eyes, I was proud of their firm shape; for once, B-cups seemed big enough. She reached for my butt, and spread her fingers to get a firm grasp on each cheek. She pulled, and I took the hint, shamelessly pressing my bare crotch into her denim. Her clear eyes, the color of a late afternoon sky, looked thoughtfully into mine. I saw a flash of pain. "I've never been to college," she reminded me, "but I'm not a fool."

I hoped she could find comfort in my chocolate-brown

eyes. "I know," I told her. "I've never lived on the street, but neither am I."

Brock barked with laughter, then held me and pressed her full lips to mine as if to test my nonacademic skills. Her tongue teased mine and her hips pressed her center seam rhythmically into my opening slit until my breathing showed her what she wanted to know. She pulled away to look at me. "Want me again?" she taunted. "So soon, Crystal?"

"Mhm," I mumbled.

"Good," she said approvingly, casually sliding her sweaty hands down my hips. "Stay ready for me." She handed me the two skimpy items of clothing. "Put these on."

I wriggled into the tight skirt, pulling it up, then tugged the knit cotton down over my head and my bare breasts. My nipples hardened under the touch of clinging fabric as I shook my hair out of my eyes.

Brock held me by the shoulders and made me face my image in the mirror. I licked my lips and tried to suppress the shiver of vanity that ran down my spine. I thought I looked like a hot babe. Judging from Brock's grin, so did she.

"You need lipstick," advised Brock, my fairy godmother. "Cherry red." She ran a salty finger around the edges of my lips. "You don't need stockings, but I want to see you in high-heeled sandals. Nothing flat. Stand on tiptoes." I did, feeling my shoulders pushing up into her palms. I felt like a little girl playing grown-up. "That looks like about four inches," she commented, studying my bare feet. "That'll do. With red polish on your toenails. You'll be wearing your new outfit tomorrow when we go to the woods."

An image of myself as Little Red Riding Hood being grabbed by a drooling wolf jumped into my mind. I reminded myself that fear before the fact wouldn't help me, and that all would be revealed in due course. I knew that in any plot, real or fictional, timing was crucial.

Brock playfully swatted my ass. "Put your shoes back on. We're going to the shoe store." She paid for my outfit as I stuffed my other clothes into a bag. I sauntered out of the store ahead of her, swinging the bag in a girlish style that was new to me.

"We're not riding," she told me on the sidewalk. "It's down the street." She guided me to the shoe store, where she soon found a dangerous pair of strappy black leather heels that she seemed to have willed into being. I found a pair in my size, eased into them, and watched Brock watching my calves as I tottered through the store. Brock approved, told me to keep them on, and paid the smirking salesgirl.

Back on her hog, I clung anxiously to her sweaty back as we whizzed around corners. She took us to my apartment building, parked her hog in my parking spot, and guided me up the stairs ahead of her with a hand on my leather-covered ass.

Inside my apartment, she pulled me close with a gentleness that made me want to cry. She kissed me as though tasting my lips for the first time. At length, she pulled away so she could look questioningly into my eyes.

"You know how important this is to me," she warned me.

"Yes, I know," I assured her. "For me too. I guess I want to find out my limits."

"Greedy bitch," she crooned. "You figured out that you can't live in the library—can't get fucked enough in there."

"You'd be surprised," I said, defending myself. "But anyway, I've never lived only in the library. Even when I was a teenager with a reputation as a nerdy bookworm, I dreamed of being a famous stripper or call girl. I bet you dreamed of being an Amazon warrior."

"More like a magician, babe," she explained. "Or a spy. I found out where to get what I wanted, including slut princesses. There are things you don't know about me." It went without saying. I knew that coming to know another person is a lifetime task, and that we had only started reading each other.

Another thought tickled her mind. "Poor little wannabe whore," she snickered. "I wonder how well you'd really like that life. I could sell you if that's what you want, but we'll have to discuss that later."

I wrapped my arms around her, touching the hollow at the small of her back. She reached behind to take possession of my wrists. I decided to file her latest comment in the back of my mind for future reference. I couldn't keep my hips from moving, as big jolts and little shivers of excitement ran from my tormented nipples to my awakening clit. "Bitch in heat," she stroked me with her voice. "I wasn't planning to do this, but I will. I want you naked and on your knees."

A thin film of sweat covered my skin, and I felt breathless. It didn't take me long to pull off my new clothes and kneel in front of her. I was amazed at my own desire to be what she wanted for as long as I could.

Brock smoothly unzipped her own jeans and pushed them down along with her panties. She stepped out of one denim leg, then the other. Her natural brown bush popped into view, untrimmed and uncovered. Since she usually packed a strap-on when I was with her, I felt honored by the sight and smell of her own center of energy, her holy well. "This is me," she reminded me. "Kiss it, Crystal." She touched herself with two hands, pulling her own lips apart so I could see her fat, rising red clit and her purplish folds that glistened like wet petals.

I approached her first with my nose, breathing in her essence. Her hot flesh moved like a live oyster when I touched it with the tip of my tongue. Her hands held my head lightly but firmly, so I could move just as much as she wanted. "No hands, girl," she prompted me.

My lips and tongue had to be versatile and responsive to her unspoken needs. I licked, nibbled, then thrust my tongue into her salty depths until I felt the strain in its roots. A quiet, satisfying moan came down to me like a blessing. I pulled Brock's clit into my mouth and vibrated it with my tongue. "Ah!" she gasped sharply as her grip tightened on my scalp. I knew she wasn't finished, so I licked her clit insistently between forays into her lush wetness. I could taste her rising tension, then her whole cunt clenched. "Uh!" she gasped. "That's…it." She breathed so loudly that I could feel it in my own lungs. "Damn, Crystal," she praised me, coming down. "You're good."

I closed my eyes, feeling the sweat cooling on my skin. My own pussy ached with the need for release, but I didn't want to stop wanting Brock.

Her strong arms pulled me up, and she held me against her damp shirt. Her small, hard breasts underneath reminded me that she was female like me, but powerful. "Honey," she called to me. "You're mine, but you have to keep working at it." She slid a hand down my back and into the crack between my asscheeks. "You can't come tonight, Crystal," she warned me. "You have to save it for tomorrow." The prospect of coming harder and later appealed to me. I hoped that my lust-fueled dreams would allow me to sleep.

"When I pick you up tomorrow," she reminded me, "you have to call me Mistress." I smiled my consent. She squeezed my shoulders and pinched my butt so that the sting would stay with me for a few heartbeats as a souvenir. She gave me a slow, hot, tormenting kiss before turning away and grunting a farewell. The sound of her boots echoed in the hallway of my building as she descended the old wooden stairs.

I was awakened in the morning by the golden light that poured into my bedroom through my wheat-colored curtains. I sat up and relished being naked in the summer air. My skirt lay on the chair where I had left it, eerily holding the shape of my hips. My halter top clung to the chair back, waiting to hug my breasts. The sight of my simple outfit made my life seem as clear as fresh water.

Brock arrived on schedule, slipping into my building when one of my neighbors opened the security door in the morning. Like a woodsy spy, she announced her presence by whistling outside my apartment door. I opened it to find her looking unusually formal in red pants and a black sleeveless shirt. She carried a cloth jacket in spite of the heat.

I dutifully strapped on my new sandals and tried to follow her gracefully down the stairs. This felt like my first ordeal of the day. Seated behind her on her bike, wearing her jacket as a sign of her ownership, I had no choice but to hang on for dear life. We sped through traffic, out of the city, and onto a dirt road.

Two other bikes, parked in a clearing in the trees, looked like a sign of human culture in the wilderness. Brock slowed to a stop near the vehicles of her tribespeople, to whom I had been offered as a human sacrifice. Looking as if she knew how I felt, Brock offered me her hand to help me land on my feet.

A short fat man who reminded me of one of Robin Hood's merry men called out: "Brock! Is that the slut?" He was stuffed like a sausage into a T-shirt and leather pants. A tall, lanky woman with a long raven ponytail and ripped jeans gave me a knowing smile. I tried not to blush or to stare at the couple who were staring at me.

"This is Crystal," announced Brock with pride. "Master Keith and Mistress Veronica," she told me.

"Is she bi, Brock?" asked the tall woman coolly. She seemed to be the equal of her man. Instead of speaking to me, she touched my hair and ran a finger appraisingly over my lips until I pulled it into my mouth and sucked, wanting to please and to learn her flavor at the same time. Veronica laughed.

Keith watched this scene without cracking a smile. "I'm doing you a big favor, Brock," he reminded her. "It's not like

I need help finding some tail." I realized that I was a form of currency, Brock's payment to her friends, perhaps for some mind-bending substance.

"Keith likes blow jobs, baby," Veronica instructed me. "I hope you're half as good as me." He unbuckled his belt and unzipped his fly without changing his expression.

I panicked; I had not had male meat in my mouth for at least six years, but I still remembered my impulse to gag. I didn't think this man would want to sheath his tool in latex, and I was afraid of what might be living in his fluids.

"You don't want to do it, do you, Crystal?" Brock asked me. I heard a hint of pride in her voice; obviously I was not a man's woman, and I was unlikely to desert her for any sperm-spouting stud. On the other hand, she wanted to show that I could follow orders. I had expected to be tested for physical endurance, but this situation obviously required finesse as well.

"I—" I started unsurely. Keith looked amused, in spite of himself, under a mask of annoyance.

"You could give him a hand job instead," Brock assured me. "Would that be all right?" she asked Keith. His expression made it too clear that he considered this equivalent to the offer of an inferior grade of dope.

"And take a spanking," said Veronica with a smile, "for not using your little mouth." Under the circumstances, that sounded safer to me, even though I suspected that I might regret my choice very soon. A spanking sounded relatively dry and unlikely to make me vomit.

"Yes," I agreed. "Would it please Master Keith to spank me for my lack of skill? I'm not very good at blow jobs." I looked quickly into his eyes to read his temperature before looking as humbly as possible at my uppity shoes.

The man seemed tickled. "Yeah, sure, what the hell," he growled. His eyes were twinkling. "Get your clothes off, girl." He looked around, saw a large rock, and seated himself on it. As I struggled to pull my top off and my skirt down as gracefully as possible, he gave me a meaningful look and patted his thighs.

Veronica watched with amusement. "Hairy bush," she remarked to Brock. "Don't you ever shave it, Brock?"

My Mistress was unfazed by this subtle dig. "I like a woman's hairy bush," she explained. "It's naturally curly, see?" She grabbed a fistful of my pubic hair and tugged it reassuringly.

Keith's eyes on my body didn't give away any secrets as I walked to him and lay my face across his lap. He ran a connoisseur's hand over my bottom, and paused thoughtfully for a moment. His first slap seemed to bounce rather than sting, and I relaxed slightly. "She's a big girl, Keith," sneered Mistress Veronica. "You don't have to baby her."

His hand came down smartly, and the sting rushed into my cunt and thighs. I couldn't keep quiet or hold myself still, but I tried. The earthy smell of the man's sweat was all around me, mixing with the smell of my juices.

Master Keith gave me four businesslike whacks. Then he gave me two more that felt as if they were burning through my skin. The two Mistresses chuckled in appreciation.

When the man shifted his thighs, I realized that he was finished and that I was supposed to stand up. "What, you want more?" he growled down at me.

I mumbled something like "No thank you, Master," as I scrambled off him. My face felt as hot as my behind, which still pulsed in rhythm.

"You should teach your girl to use her mouth, Brock," he remarked. He stood up to pull his pants down, removed them, and handed them to Veronica.

"She knows how, Keith," grinned Mistress Brock. "But she'll pet you nicely with her hands."

Master Keith beckoned me to the thick red cock that rose from a nest of matted hair between his spread thighs. I knelt between them, keeping my heels away from my sore bum, and held onto his knees for balance. Then I gathered up his balls in one hand and began stroking his shaft with the other. Holding a cock gave me a sense of déjà vu, as though I were revisiting the funky small town of my youth.

I stroked him increasingly faster, and his breathing speeded up too. Soon his cream was spurting over my hands as he half-moaned and half-grunted. My Mistress looked amused. I hoped she enjoyed watching me cause her friend or supplier to lose control of himself, even if that was his wish. "Good job, baby," he assured me, but his voice sounded patronizing, and he was looking at his woman. I was being dismissed.

Mistress Brock pulled me up by one arm, looking very pleased. "Wipe your hands, Crystal," she said, smirking. This order confused me, since there was no towel in sight. On impulse, I bent over to wipe my hands on a patch of wild grass. From between my legs, I saw Mistress Veronica arranging her long, pale body on Master Keith's lap as her hair hung over his face.

My Mistress's lips were close to one of my ears. "Don't move," she ordered.

I heard the metallic purr of her zipper, looked at her from between my legs, and panicked. I wasn't sure I could hold my position while being fucked with the big strap-on she was wearing. "Brock—" I protested.

The hard smack of her hand against one of my sensitive buttcheeks took me by surprise, and I wailed. "What do you call me?" she demanded.

"Mistress!" I wondered if I had lost all the credit I had gained with her by following her plans so far. "Please, Mistress!" I added, afraid to say more.

I felt her relenting as she pushed me forward by the hips.

"Brace your hands against this tree trunk, honey," she told me.

I gripped the rough bark, afraid of slipping up in any way. I tried to plant my dangerous shoes as firmly as possible on the uneven ground. I hoped they would provide more leverage than bare feet.

I could hear the combined moans of Master Keith and Mistress Veronica in the distance as my own Mistress held my cunt-lips open and eased her slick tool into me. The cool air in my bush showed me how wet and hot I was, how eager for the comfort she was giving me.

"You can let go, Crystal," she encouraged me. "Don't hold back. The neighbors won't complain about the noise."

I felt something melt inside me as a loud "Ohh!" came out of my mouth to mix with the songs of birds and insects. I pushed back as she thrust into me to the rhythm of her breathing. The rubbing of her thighs against my sore butt almost took my breath away, but it also raised my temperature. My Mistress was working hard to claim me as hers and to bring me to a grand finale. Knowing this made it hard for me to get over the edge.

I was so wet that my Mistress's cock made a slurping sound as it pumped in and out of me, and I could feel the juice sliding down my thighs. My fear of not pleasing her and not being able to find my own release brought tears to my eyes.

"You—stubborn—little brat!" gasped Mistress Brock. I was vastly relieved to hear the affection in her voice. "Okay then," she ordered, "don't come." She reached under me to roll my clit insultingly between hard fingers.

That did it, and my overwrought pussy squeezed and squeezed around the dick it loved. Judging from the sounds she made, my Mistress was getting enough stimulation to come with me.

After she withdrew, she held me for a long time. Eventually, we both remembered the other two.

"Hey, Brock," called Master Keith. "We can't stay. I'll try out your little slut next time. I think she needs my belt." I was aghast at this challenge to my Mistress as well as to me, but she let it pass.

I was allowed to stand up as my Mistress discreetly shook off her tool, then tucked it back into her pants. I watched Master Brock and Mistress Veronica casually pulling their clothes back on. I realized that everyone around me was climbing back into their daytime roles and preparing to go about their business. I was being left behind, left with my still-red behind and wet bush and pink nipples on display for the amusement of the grown-ups who had better things to do than to play with me.

I watched Mistress Veronica sliding her long thighs, one by one, into her ragged pant-legs. When she saw me watching, she laughed aloud. "I'll get to know you better next time, honey," she reminded me. "I like chicks too, but I'm fussy. I hope Brock trains you well."

This time I saw my Mistress's jaw tighten for an instant before she willed herself into a state of calm control. "Don't worry about it, Ronnie," she returned. She strode to my scattered clothes, picked them up, and held them in a tight bundle. I could see that my new outfit meant as much to her as it did to me, but she liked keeping me naked as long as possible.

I sensed that Mistress Brock's friends or associates both looked forward to playing with me on another occasion, but for now it was too obvious whose property I was, and the straight couple didn't want lukewarm leftovers. The glances they both flicked at me showed that I still had value as a form of currency.

Everyone exchanged good-bye hugs as a peace offering. "Brock," muttered Master Keith, apparently as an afterthought. "You want to make money on this one?"

"We'll talk," she promised. Now that prostitution had

come up as a real possibility, I felt relieved that my Mistress seemed reluctant to share me.

The Master and the Mistress mounted their bikes and roared away from us. "Ready for the ride home?" Mistress Brock asked pointedly. She handed me my clothes.

"I hope so," I groaned. I wondered briefly if she would let me walk home instead of bouncing on her hog, but I knew that there was no point in asking. It was too far.

"Try this," she offered, folding her jacket so that I could sit on it. I knew that being her girl would mean having to develop greater physical tolerance, and that this would be good for me. In the meanwhile, though, she was willing to let me toughen up by degrees.

As I climbed on behind her and she kicked her motorcycle into life, I felt that serendipity was still with me. I knew that Brock hadn't had her fill of me for the day, and that we still had many miles to travel together. I had faith that even in the long years of my academic future, I would never regret letting her officially bring me out as a slut named Crystal. That weekend still shines among my memories, even though nothing happened exactly the way I expected. But then, every debut includes some surprises.

Frozen
Andrea Dale

Becca wanted to get a tree on December 1st.

I tried to talk her out of it, but she was having none of that. Her father had a tree farm in the mountains, she said, and when she was a kid she'd always been the one to pick out their family tree. Now, he continued to give her one for free—and she wanted to beat the rush and get the absolute best one possible.

I, on the other hand, wasn't even sure if I'd still be around on the 25th. I went with her because I couldn't resist that adorable uptilted nose and the dimple on her left cheek, but I made no promises otherwise.

It had snowed on and off since early November, and the world was white and eerily silent except for the sound of our boots crunching through the frozen cover. Beneath the tall pines, all lined up stately and proud, the snow cover was thinner, and occasionally I scuffed up enough to see the brown needles and dirt beneath.

"It's not normal," I said for what seemed like the hundredth time. "This white stuff falling from the sky at regular intervals. You should be able to visit winter, and then go home."

Becca laughed and kissed my cheek, her lips warm against the flesh that was reddened by the cold. "Oh, you California girl, you," she said. "How can it be the holidays without snow?"

It was a familiar argument, with no underlying malice or anger. We were just from very different places, and teased each other about it.

A few moments later I realized we'd left the carefully planted rows of trees and had headed on a slight incline, through birches and firs and other trees I couldn't quite identify, all more jumbled together. I pointed out our misdirection.

"Oh, I know," she said. "We never get our own tree from the farm proper. My dad owns acres and acres here, and it's our tradition that we get our tree from farther back."

I bit back a sigh, wistfully imagining a steaming cup of hot chocolate laced with crème de menthe. Shoving my hands in my pockets, I followed Becca deeper into the wintry woods.

It wasn't much of a problem following her, actually, because I could focus on her sweet ass, contained in a pair of tight jeans (with silk long underwear beneath, I happened to know, having been involved in making it difficult for her to keep them on earlier). Right now, there wasn't anything I wanted more than to be in a nice warm bed with her, my hands cupping that tight bottom as I buried my head between her thighs and made her wail as she came. I loved the sweet taste of her slippery folds, like cinnamon, and how they turned so dark when she was aroused, fiery red like the rest of her. Afterward I'd kiss away the orgasmic flush from her delicate breasts, only to be unable to resist taking one of her pert nipples in my mouth, and then we'd be starting all over again....

The trees thinned as we walked, and Becca paused to let me catch up, slipping her hand into mine. The intimacy of the action, despite the layers of knitted wool between our fingers, touched me. We'd been dating for seven months now, living together for two and a half, and yet I was still surprised by the tenderness. I felt guilty, too—after Lindy's death, I didn't think I'd ever open up to anyone like that again.

I hadn't intended to move in with Becca, exactly, but the lease ran out on the apartment I was subletting and Becca had a spare room. Not that I ever slept in it, mind you—we set up the other room as a studio for me and an office for her.

I'd fled California when Lindy died after four years of living and loving together. I immersed myself in grad school in Minneapolis, as different a place as I could find, and that's where I'd met Becca.

We'd started out talking about architecture, and tumbled into bed not long after that. When she was through stunning me with her energy and inventiveness and I'd caught my breath, we went right back to talking...and then right back into screwing again.

I never stopped missing Lindy, but when I was tangled and sweaty with Becca, the pain lessened. She had that effect on me—perhaps because she was so unreserved, so delightfully free.

I made Becca no promises, knowing she deserved more than I could give her. But when I tried to tell her that, Becca would shake her head, brushing her silken red hair across my face, and tell me that our time together was all that mattered.

"We're only given a certain amount of time on this earth," she'd say. "Use every moment wisely, to the greatest extent that you can."

I was afraid Becca would fall in love with me, and I'd have to leave. But right now, I was trying to live in the moment. Even if it was a very chilly one.

We came to a clearing, a circle of trees with the snow untouched in the center.

"So beautiful," Becca breathed. "So pure."

"It *is* pretty," I agreed reluctantly. "Pristine. Like we're the first people to come here."

She kissed me again, this time on the lips, her tongue caressing. Then she pulled back, and I saw a mischievous glint in her eyes.

"Snow angels!" she shouted, her voice startling a cardinal into a flutter of crimson. She grabbed my hand again and dragged me into the center of the clearing. Flinging herself down on her back, she waved her arms and legs frantically.

"Are you having a seizure?" I asked dubiously.

She laughed as she sat up. Carefully she stood and took a big step away from where she'd been lying. I could see the outline of her form in the snow, and suddenly I understood what she'd meant.

"You try it," she said, dusting the snow from her legs.

"I don't know," I said. "Looks cold. And wet. How come snow's never wet in the movies? You see people walking with the snow falling around them, sticking to their heads and shoulders, but when they go inside, they're dry, and there're no puddles on the floor...."

Becca laughed again and pushed me, not quite hard enough to make me fall down. Suddenly catching her playful mood, I nudged her back. She shoved me again, and I started to lose my balance. I grabbed her as I tipped, and she landed atop me, face inches from mine.

Now neither of us was laughing. Becca kissed me until my toes started to tingle (or maybe that was from the cold?). Her mouth was hot, her tongue a frenzy of motion. I was almost forgetting where we were when she jumped up and trotted over to stand beneath one of the trees, a twenty-foot pine with sporadic branches for the first six feet from the ground. She curled her mitten-clad fingers at me, beckoning. I struggled to my feet and followed.

"I didn't want you to get too wet there in the snow," she said. "Turn around." I did, and she brushed me off, her hands particularly clingy around my upper thighs. The kissing and rolling around hadn't made just my toes tingly, I had to admit. The moist warmth growing in my cunt was a nice contrast to the clear, cold day.

Becca finished her ministrations and turned me, walking me a step backward until I was pressed against the tree. "Put your hands up," she said, "and grab hold of that branch above your head." I did, wondering what she had in mind. I felt like a sacrificial virgin. She slipped off her mittens and shoved them in her pocket, then unzipped my down vest.

"Hey!" I protested, reaching down to stop her. She grabbed my hands and pulled them above my head.

"Hold on to the branch," she instructed. "Unless you want me to use that scarf to tie your wrists up there?"

A dull ache spread out from my pussy. We'd talked about trying some light bondage, but hadn't gotten around to it yet, although it intrigued us both. Now, though, wasn't the time I wanted to try. Suddenly I just wanted to do what Becca told me to do.

"Okay, I promise to be good," I whispered. "I'm at your mercy."

Her grin was appreciative and wicked, all at the same time. I knew I was in for it, and boy, was I looking forward to it.

"You're crazy, you know that?" I said as she parted my vest and slid her hands beneath my sweater. "What if someone sees us?"

"Nobody ever comes up here," she said. Her hands moved higher, finding my nipples, already budded hard beneath my own silk turtleneck. My body throbbed. "It's private land."

I didn't make another protest, but she added, "I'm just

trying to help you live in the moment."

To be honest, I couldn't think much past the maddening feel of her fingers massaging my breasts through the slippery soft silk. She pushed my sweater up and suckled one of my nipples through the silk. When she pulled away, my nips contracted harder, reacting to the cold air and the moisture.

I needed to feel her lips on my flesh, with no fabric barrier between.

Becca knelt before me and tugged the undershirt out of my waistband. My stomach contracted against the rush of air. She nuzzled her cold nose into my belly, and I yelped softly. She laughed, her breath warm against my skin. Goose bumps skittered across my flesh, but I didn't want her to stop.

When she stood to reach my nipples, I saw a flash of white in her hand, and before I could register what it was, she pressed the snow to my breast.

I howled in surprise and nearly let go of the branch. My nipple was so hard it hurt, but a moment later her mouth was on it, hot and sucking hard, and my knees would have buckled if I hadn't been holding on. She repeated the process on my other breast, and again on the first, back and forth, back and forth, until heat and cold became a single burning sensation. I was so close to coming, just from the breast play. My cunt was shivering with tiny spasms that weren't quite orgasms, and the moans coming from my mouth were noises I didn't think I'd ever made before.

"Please...."

Becca pulled my jeans and underwear down below my knees, as far as they'd go before getting caught by the tops of my boots. Frigid air blew across my thighs, but my cunt was still scalding.

"Close your eyes." Becca's voice was thick with lust.

I did what she told me to do. I felt her hand stray between my legs and, using the branch for support, I bent my knees to give her access, since I couldn't spread my entangled feet.

She found that I was wet to my inner thighs. Her caress was too light for me to come, but it held the promise of enduring pleasure. Becca's petiteness extended to her hands, and sometimes, if I was wet enough, she could reach completely inside me.

I was wet enough now—I was sure of it. But she toyed with my folds, which I imagined were steaming as they came into contact with the winter air.

"Open your mouth."

I expected Becca to bring her hand to my mouth, to slide in her fingers that would be sweet and pungent and slick with my juices.

Instead something hard passed my lips. Hard and cold and long and thick and shaped like….

My eyes flew open. Becca's green eyes had gone nearly black with excitement, but she managed a tremor of a smile as she slid the icicle back out of my mouth. Her other hand was still between my legs, driving most coherent thoughts from my head.

Still, I knew what she was going to do with that natural, frozen dildo.

My mittened hands clung to the branch above me as she drove it inside of me. It wasn't cold, but burning hot, and oh, so slick, like the glass dildo I'd once owned. I screamed as I clenched and came, bucking my hips as the world whirled in a kaleidoscope of cardinal red and snow white.

I melted.

I slid down the trunk, not caring if my down vest tore against the rough bark. Becca dropped to her knees next to me, helped me raise my hips so she could slide my jeans back up so I wasn't sitting bare-assed in the snow.

"You're so freakin' hot," she said, her voice hoarse, "that you completely melted the icicle. Damn."

I couldn't answer. Couldn't speak. My body started to shake from the sobs I couldn't keep down. I wasn't making any noise, but the tears were on my cheeks, and Becca began kissing them off.

"What's wrong, love?" she asked, her voice now tinged with concern.

I managed to form words. "I let go of the branch."

I know she didn't mean to laugh. For what it's worth, I did know she wasn't laughing at me, and I took no offense. Instead I buried my face in her shoulder, glad she wasn't angry.

"Sweetness, what matters is that you trusted me for that long," she said, rocking me back and forth. "You held on a lot longer than I expected. And there was never, ever any penalty for letting go."

Christmas Eve. I sat on the floor, my back against the sofa, my head tilted back to watch the psychedelic play of blinking colored lights against the ceiling.

Yes, I was still with Becca, about to celebrate with her one of the biggest, most emotional holidays of the year. Fact was, something had snapped in me, that day in the woods. Or, more rightly put, something had thawed.

I still missed Lindy, and loved her dearly. But she was gone. I had to move on.

Becca had showed me how to trust again.

Before we'd left the clearing that day, Becca had pulled a long, bright-red nylon cord out of her pack and wrapped it around the trunk of the tree where we'd just made love. I asked her what she was doing.

"This will tell my dad what tree we want," she said. "He knows where this clearing is; we used to picnic here when I was a kid."

I stared at her, wondering if the lust had fried her brain,

too. "But it's twenty feet tall."

Becca led me to the center of the clearing, near the indentations where we'd lain, and put her arms around me. "Look up," she said, and I did. "The top of the tree is perfect," she said.

And she was right: The top of the tree, especially about seven feet or so, was a flawless conical shape, like a storybook Christmas tree.

"We never take the trees from down below," she said. "We always pick a taller one, and then Dad uses the rest of it for firewood." She grinned mischievously, wriggling her body against mine. "Besides, don't you want that reminder sitting in our living room every day for the rest of the month? I think it'll be...quite inspirational."

She'd been right about that, too. Let's just say we'd been creating our own erotic Twelve Days of Christmas.

Now Becca came into the living room, bearing a tray with milk and sugar cookies. She was wearing a Santa hat, with a button pinned to it that displayed a piece of greenery and the words *Mistletoe: Kiss Below.*

So I did. For a good long time.

The End

Rachel Kramer Bussel

do you see her face
when she's gone
sometimes so bright
your heart just stops

did she answer you
your other half
you know they say
she comes just once

—Sleater-Kinney, "Jenny"

It doesn't help that she looks more beautiful now than ever. Her face glows with a natural tan and the sweetest smile I think I will ever see, her blue eyes shining at me with need and want and love and pain. I want to feel as if we are our own entity, existing in a private universe that nothing and no one else can pierce. That life is all about looking at her, in her, nothing more, nothing less. Without makeup, she is the perfect combination of girl and woman, and she fills me with a need to hold and protect her that leaves me raw and open and more vulnerable than any person should ever be.

I know all the right moves to make, the ways to touch her, the strokes that will make her melt and move and clutch me as if she will need me forever. I know how she wants it. I need to feel as if I'm the only one who can give it to her. I live for those times when she grabs me and looks as deeply inside me as I am inside her.

As she lies there, so small, so seemingly fragile, her doll's body looks like some alluring creature, one that I might break if I handle it improperly. I can easily forget the core of strength and stubbornness she possesses. Spread out in front of me, she is truly the girl of the dreams I never knew I had. I slide my fingers inside her, pushing deep into her core, knowing just where to curve and bend to get to where I want to be. I've never known another woman's body quite like this, navigating her pussy as easily as I trace my fingers over her face, reading her like a well-worn page of a beloved book, instantly, easily.

At this moment, with her hair messy and tangled like an overworked Barbie's, I want to grab it as I've done so many times before, to pull fiercely and then bring her head down into the pillow, to live up to the violent promise of this situation. I almost pull away, because I am not that kind of girl. I'm still getting used to being the girl who wants to hurt someone else, who feels a distinct kind of awe when I hear the sound of my hand slamming down against her ass. I'm still getting used to being the girl who likes giving it rough, who likes to claw and scrape, who sometimes wants to slap her across the face. The girl who got the slightest thrill when she cried the other day while I spanked her.

I see the collar next to the bed glittering brightly. It meant everything when I fastened it around her neck those countless weeks ago, transforming the airport bathroom into our own private sexual sanctuary. Now, it is too bright, too accusatory, a mistake in so many ways. Like the sweetest of forbidden fruit, her neck beckons, so white and exposed, pulsing with veins and life and want. Now when I see her neck, tender and ever-needy, I can barely go near it. The pleasure would be too great. It would be too easy to press a bit too hard, to enjoy it for all the wrong reasons, even though I can feel her angling toward it, begging me to obliterate her for a few blessed seconds. I know what it does to her, and for the first time I don't want to know. That's never been the kind of power I've wanted, even though she'd gladly give it to me, give me almost anything except what I need the most.

I want to slide back to that simple starting point, our bodies blank canvases on which to draw magnificent works of the most special kind of art. Maybe there is still some power left in this bed, something that flows from one of us to the other rather than simply inward, something that binds us together. The ways I thought I knew her have all vanished, lost in a mystery too complex for me to solve. Too many silences and unspoken thoughts war for space between us. She is just as much a stranger to me as she was on our first date, perhaps even more so now, her mind locked away in a box with someone else's keys. Knowing only her body leaves me emptier than if we'd never even met, giving me a hollow victory, a prize I'm forced to return, undeserving and unwanted.

My fingers grant me nothing except access to a disembodied cunt, separated from all reality, the way the old-school feminists described pornography, parceling out body parts at random without context or meaning. I wish I could erase my sense memory of how it feels to fuck her, love her, and know her all at the same time, in the same motions. I am somehow back to square one, vainly hoping, praying, that I can make her happy.

Only this time, we have so much more to do than just fuck, than slide and scream and bite and whisper, than twist and bend and push and probe. The stakes are so much higher that no orgasm will ever be enough, but I try anyway.

No matter how far I reach inside, I cannot crack her. Those eyes are a one-way mirror, reflecting a surface of something I cannot see and probably don't want to. I want to tell her I love her, show her everything inside me, but I open my mouth and just as quickly close it. I can feel her body shaking, the tears and pain rising up like an earthquake's tremors, and I shove harder, grab her neck and push her down, anything to quell the rising tide that will be here soon enough. This may look the same as all those other times, my fingers arching and strok-ing, her eyes shut or staring at me, needy, grabbing me when I touch her in just the right way that is almost—but not quite—too much. But it is nothing like those other times, nothing like anything I've ever done before. It is like touching something totally alien, someone I never even knew, someone not even human. I feel lost as I touch her, my heart so far away I hardly know what to do or how to act. I can see that this is not bridg-ing the gap, but I can't stop myself. I try to pretend that her moans, her wetness, these external signals of desire actually mean she is truly mine. There is no way to make her come and erase the other girl's touch entirely. I am not yet thinking about her and the other girl, wondering how she touches her, not wanting to know but needing to, drawn to that deadly fire with a car-crash allure, though that will all come in time, in those freestanding hours of numbed shock, those lost week-ends when she invades my head and will not leave.

She has written me a letter, as requested, given me exact blueprints for how to fuck her. How to take her up against the wall, how to tie her up, tease her, taunt her, and hold out even when she protests. I want nothing more than to be able to follow these instructions, which by now I don't even need because I know how to trigger her, how to get her to go from laughing to spreading her legs in the briefest of moments. I know exactly how to touch her now, where to stroke and bite and slap to give both of us what we need, but that is no longer enough. I don't have it in me to be that kind of top, to blank out all the rest and fulfill only that viciously visceral urge to pummel, pound, and punish. That urge is too clearly real, too close to the unspoken pain, the words that will come later, the ones right underneath the tears. I know when I hit her what it means. There can be no erotic power exchange when she holds all the real power. I have enough soul left in me to know that sex should not be a mechanical obligation. It should not be the only thing you can do to stay alive, compelled with the force of something so strong you're powerless to resist.

I reach, reach, reach inside her, desperately searching, hoping to wrench us back to wherever we are supposed to be, back to where we were—a week, a month, a lifetime ago. I draw out this process, watch myself as if from afar as my hand slides inside her, as I lube myself up and try to cram all of me into her, make a lasting impression. I have my entire hand inside her, yet I feel more removed from her than I have ever felt. She might as well still be in Florida. She might as well still be a stranger, this might as well still be our first date when I laughed so much because I was so nervous. I'd rather this be any of those nights, even the ones when I was so drunk and afraid, so powerless and unsure; anything would be better than this slow death, this slow withering until we are nothing more than two girls in a room with tears in our eyes and an ocean of questions and scars and hurt between us. I can't predict what will come after this most pregnant of silences, can't know the depths of pain that will puncture me beyond the horrors of my imagination, can't know that I will regret everything I might have, could have, done wrong, or did do wrong.

She turns over on her stomach, face hidden from my

searching eyes, and I fumble to reconnect, to slide into her as if nothing is wrong, as if it's just a matter of finding a comfortable angle. I finally have had enough, cannot keep going with the charade that pressing myself against her will fill all the gaps that still exist between us. But for whatever twisted reasons we need this, this final time. And this is the last time, because nothing is worth feeling so utterly and completely alone while you're fucking your girlfriend before you break up. No power trip or blazing orgasm, no heart-pounding breathless finish, no sadistic impulse or mistaken nostalgia is worth this much pain.

I don't know how to say what I have to, what I'm terrified to, how to ask questions whose answers I know I won't want to hear. There's no book I can read that will teach me how to make her G-spot tell me her secrets, tell me those fantasies and dreams that don't come from her pussy but from her heart. The end, it turns out, is nothing like the beginning. There is no promise of something more, some grand future of possibility, the infinite ways of knowing each other just waiting to be discovered. There is no hope that we can merge, in all the ways love can make you merge, into something so much greater than the sum of our parts. The end is like what they say about death, when your whole life flashes before your eyes. I see moments, fragments—my hand up her skirt on the street, taking her in the doorway of a friend's apartment, so fiercely she can barely sink down to the ground, her on her knees in the bathroom, surprising me as she buries her face into me, no room to protest, grinding the edge of a knife along her back, slapping her tits until they are raw and red—but they seem so far away right now, like a movie, like someone's else's pornographic memories. They don't make me smile, and I don't want them anymore. I want to bury myself in her and never let go, hold on to something that has just fluttered away in the wind, fine as the glittering sparkles she wears on her eyes, miniscule and almost opaque, too minute to ever recapture. But all I can do is back away, as slowly as I can, so slowly that it seems as if I am hardly moving, and before I know it, I, and she—we—are gone, almost as if we never existed.

Trash Talkin'
R. Gay

I met Mia in high school. We were just friends then and I gravitated to her because she had a southern drawl that sounded like she was pouring honey over every word. She was a daddy's girl in the worst way. Her daddy, Old Man Spencer, called Mia his princess and his little lady, and her bedroom looked like one giant confection, all pink and sugary. The best part was a bench for two in front of a huge dressing table with a wide mirror gilded in gold. The top was always covered in hairbrushes and ribbons, bottles of perfume and lotions, and of course, there was her makeup—powders and mascara and eyeshadow in every hue a girl (or stylish boy) could imagine. We spent countless hours painting ourselves like Brooke Shields and Christie Brinkley, our narrow shoulders pressed together, legs crossed, right over left. We were determined to be as stunning as our imaginations would allow, though, looking back, I can admit that we were somewhat deterred by the limitations of late-eighties couture. I fell in love with Mia because she could shape my eyebrows without making me cry and knew the difference between plum and grape.

I was not a daddy's girl—never even knew mine. What I did know was that I was going to get out of Valdosta, Georgia, and hanging on to the tail end of Mia Spencer's star was the fastest way to do that. She took pity on me, I think—a little Puerto Rican girl who came from the proverbial wrong side of the tracks and spoke without thinking, more often than not. My mouth has always gotten me into trouble and it's my mouth that changed things between Mia and me. I was sitting on the edge of my bed, on a Tuesday morning, looking up at Mia who was staring down at me, her eyebrows furrowed, lower lip tucked between her teeth as she held my chin in her hand. I fidgeted and she squeezed my chin harder.

"Sit still, *Mami,* or I won't get this right," she said.

I batted my eyelashes and stilled. She had taken to calling me *Mami* since we moved to New York where we heard Spanglish more than anything else. It made her feel more *urban,* or so she said. Mia started tracing the outline of my lips with a MAC lip pencil, for we only used MAC products—Spice, for contrast. And, I don't know, she was smelling good, wearing a threadbare tank top that I could see right down and a pair of my boxers. Her dirty blonde curls were piled atop her head save for a few stubborn strands that kept falling into her eyes, which, as I said, were staring at me with this intensity. The next thing I know, my hand is wrapped around her wrist and I'm falling back, pulling her with me, and I'm kissing her even though my lips are only half done. I heard the pencil fall to the floor and her breath catch in her throat. I felt my thighs slide apart and press against her sides. And then she planted her left hand against my chest, pushing me away, wiping her lips with her right.

"Jesus, Lettie, why do you always have to go too far?" Mia said. She rolled off the bed and stalked out of the room. I could hear water running in the bathroom and cabinet doors loudly opening and closing.

I stared at the ceiling, rubbing my stomach, and I couldn't help but smile. I was going to turn that girl out. I hated girls like Mia and all their friends who befriend girls like me to reassure themselves that they are part of their very own rainbow coalition. I do my part, of course, adding a little extra *boricua* to my walk and talk—rolling my *r*'s and popping my neck; giving a little extra shimmy to my shake when I'm strolling the block. I paint the picture that they want to see and keep everything else to myself.

Mia and I met in her daddy's peach orchards where my mama worked, when we were both fourteen. For whatever reason, Mama had to bring me to work with her one afternoon. She told me to stay out of the way, so I started wandering through the orchard, eating bruised peaches that had fallen to the ground.

I was about to take a bite of a fresh peach when I heard a sharp little voice say, "What do you think you're doing?"

I looked up, and there was Mia, hands on her hips, chin jutting forward, looking every inch the little princess I would soon learn that she was. "What does it look like I'm doing?" I asked, taking a bigger bite than usual, never looking away. White girls like her did not impress me.

She shrugged, picked up a peach for herself, and we've been friends ever since, going on eleven years now. We came to New York seven years ago to attend Columbia. I majored in business, she majored in art history, and then, because we had nowhere else to go, we stayed, for the shopping, if nothing else. We've done everything together over the years—we even came out together sophomore year, when we grew weary of trying to pretend that the girls we had spending the night in our dorm room were just friends that we shared the same bed with. A lot.

When I think she's calmed down, I go look for Mia, who is lying on the futon mattress in our living room, watching something on television. I sit atop her legs and drag a finger along her bare upper arm. "You mad at me, *querida?*" She loves when I call her *querida* because I told her it was my nickname for her and her alone. Mia doesn't need to know that I've told other women the same thing.

Mia buries her head in the covers and I know I'm forgiven because I also know that I'm doing exactly what she wants. I've been watching her, the way she leaves the bathroom door open just so while she's stepping into the shower, how she walks around the apartment in next to nothing, how she dresses in the outfits she knows I love, how we're more affectionate than any given circumstance warrants—it's all out of a bad high school romance novel. Neither of us has had a girlfriend in over a year, even though the opportunities have been plentiful. I continue to assume we're waiting for each other. I know all about this little dance and so does she. I kiss her cheek, letting my lips linger, then retire to my room to finish getting ready for work.

When Mia calls me in the afternoon, I shake my head when my assistant asks if I'm in. She arches an eyebrow but takes a message anyway. Instead of focusing on a merger of two small bookstore chains, I hike my skirt up over my thighs, twirl my chair around, and brace my feet against the glass window. I spread my legs and stroke my clit hard and fast. I think of Mia and the weight of her body falling against mine. When I come, I'm tired. It's hard work loving and hating someone at the same time.

Mia is meeting me after work for shopping and drinks, so I don't bother washing my hands. When I lean in to kiss her cheek, I want to leave the scent of me on her arm. At 5:30 sharp, she's in the lobby of my building, wearing a dark brown suede sleeveless dress and matching shoes. Her makeup, as usual, is flawless—Film Noir lipstick and Bamboom eye paint, just a touch of Blunt face powder. I would never have thought those shades might work together, but on her they do and I tell her this as we quickly embrace and strategize about the evening's targets. This morning has been forgotten, or so she makes it seem, holding my hand as we head uptown in the back of a cab, her perfectly manicured fingernails lightly grazing over my knuckles in a steady circle. I so appreciate the attention to detail. Meanwhile, the cab reeks of unwashed people, the seat is torn, and the cabbie is taking the wrong route but I'm ignoring all of it, slowly but surely inching closer to Mia until our heads are practically touching. She turns and again our lips brush together.

Before she can turn away, I trace her lips with my thumb, sliding just the tip between her lips. Mia closes her eyes, and I can feel her teeth gently biting my thumb. "Let's stop driving each other crazy," I whisper.

"Were you in the office when I called earlier?"

I nod and slide my thumb from between her teeth, replacing it with the tip of my tongue. I let my hand slide down her dress, over her breasts, to her knees. They're clamped shut, so I tap my fingernails (Naked Tip nail lacquer) against her knees before snaking my fingers between them. The higher my hand reaches, the more her grip loosens. Mia is kissing me back now, breathing in short little bursts. She tastes like wine and cigarettes. I now know that she lied when she said she quit. There is a smudge of my lipstick (Viva Glam III) on her cheek in not quite a lip print. From the corner of my eye I can see the cabbie staring at us and so I cock my head downward for a moment, watching as his eyes cast toward Mia's now-open thighs and her panties pulled aside, my fingers dancing along her pussy lips. By the time we get to where we're going, I only smell her.

The next hour is a flurry of groping between clothing racks and trying on dresses and skirts we won't buy and me putting that extra *boricua* into my strut. I know Mia likes that. Our last stop is at the Boutique Missoni, where the salespeople look positively famished. I am bored by stores like these with their slick floors and slick walls and three outfits for sale, but Mia loves them—again with feeling urban, and her trust fund making it possible. I sit on a plush bench and watch her surveying the inventory. My shoe dangles from my toe and each time I catch her looking at me, I slide my fingers under my nose, and her cheeks redden. She must have discovered modesty while I was at work. Eventually, she waves a gauzy striped blouse and matching skirt and motions toward the dressing room. I follow and once we're inside, I shut the door, loudly, and turn Mia around so that she's facing the wall. She drops her selections to the floor. I pull her skirt up, her panties down, and I kick her legs apart with my left foot.

I nibble the back of her ear, and slide two fingers along the crack of her ass, then along the dark underside toward her cunt, which is hot and wet and quivery as my fingers tease. "Am I going too far?" I ask Mia.

She nods, but pushes her ass toward me. Opening my hand, I slap her ass twice. Mia exhales, and she says, "*Mami,* I like that."

I'm not surprised. Girls such as Mia like it a certain way. Then again, so do girls like me. I slap her ass a third and fourth time, slide my hand over her cheek and back toward her cunt. While she's trying to catch her breath, I slide my fingers inside her where it's tighter than I thought possible. The walls are pulsing, gripping my fingers, and I realize this is an intimate thing I'm doing. Resting my chin against her shoulder, I slide my other hand around front, beneath her dress and up toward her breasts. With a little effort, I work the bra cup out of my way and begin twisting her right nipple between my thumb and my forefinger to the same beat of two fingers sliding in and out of her pussy. She presses herself closer to me still and I can smell the MV2 perfume she's wearing and her shampoo and the scent of tobacco still clinging to her hair. I sink my teeth into the soft tissue of her neck just left of her chin, flicking my tongue as I bite hard and then harder.

There's a moan rumbling at the base of her throat. Mia's lips are pursed shut. She's afraid to let the sound out, afraid to admit that she wants this. "It's okay to let that out, *querida*," I say. "You know you like this shit."

I've thought about a moment like this for a long time. It feels as good as I imagined.

The breath she's been holding hisses from between her lips. She reaches back for me with her right arm, her fingernails digging into my side. Her legs are trembling. So is my arm. She slides the fingers of her left hand through my hair, curling her fingers into a tight fist of pale skin and dark tufts of my hair. Her lips, now slightly swollen, their color smeared, crush against mine in a sloppy kiss that is all tongue and teeth. When she does moan, the sound travels down my throat and into the pit of my chest where it stays. It's fitting.

We stay like that, awkwardly entwined. We're both sweating and sticking to each other. My suit, a skirt and jacket number from Donna Karan's collection last year, feels impossibly heavy. My feet are slipping in my heels. I start to fuck her hard, thrusting my fingers into Mia's cunt until her body allows me no further, holding myself there until she starts to whimper, then retreating, until she whimpers. I call her nasty names in a voice a few notches above a whisper—tell her that she's a slut, a whore, *mi puta* who will do any dirty little thing I tell her to. The only word she keeps saying is *Yes*. It's the only word I want to hear.

She's close to coming because her pussy is thick, wet, slick and four of my fingers have made their way into her and she keeps rolling her head from side to side. I stop talking, fucking her now with silent deliberate thrusts that I hope hurt as good as they feel. I slide my right hand back down her stomach to her clit—small, but hard and swollen and sensitive because I've barely touched it before she is moaning, loud enough for me to know that I can do anything I want. I press against her clit until I can feel the sharp bone beneath, stroking slowly—slow enough that I'm driving myself crazy as well. "Is it my pussy?" I ask her. She says nothing, so I stroke her clit faster, bringing her crazy close to coming, then stop. "Is it my pussy?" I ask again.

"Yes," she says, choking.

"Are you going to give it up again?"

This time she answers much faster. "Yes."

"Good," I say, leaving my fingers inside her as I stroke her clit again in tight fast circles. "Because I'm going to take it when...where...how I want it from now on."

I drag my tongue from her chin up her cheek. I imagine marking her. When Mia comes, I cover her mouth and nose with the hand that was on her clit, feeling her body shudder, feeling her chest constrict, feeling more wetness on my fingers wedged inside her. Slowly, I slide out of her pussy, my fingers instantly cold. She turns around to face me and I slide my fingers deep into her mouth. She swallows them obediently, suckling them clean. I slide my fingers beneath my skirt and into my own wetness, then return those fingers to her mouth. She moans loudly, pulls the taste of me into her, and reaches for me with her lips. Her arms are wrapped around me so tightly I can hardly breathe, and there is a desperation, a hunger in the way we kiss. I imagine what Old Man Spencer would think if he saw his little princess now. When I've had my fill of her, I tell Mia it's time to go home. She tries to get herself together but I shake my head. I want her to walk out of here with her dress wrinkled, her shoes in her hand, her hair tousled, makeup a shitty mess. It's a better look than one might think.

We leave the dressing room with the outfit she was going

to try on in a crumpled heap on the floor. We walk past the famished automatons and into the cool Manhattan night air. Mia hails a cab for us and as we get into the back seat, I can see that she's crying. Mia reaches for my left hand and brings it to her lips for a moment, before holding it in her lap clasped between both of hers. I turn to her and smile, before returning my gaze to the street. I'm still in love with her, but the memory of Mia with the stain of mascara along the arc of her cheekbone will satisfy me for quite some time.

The Trick

D. Alexandria

I picked her because she looked slightly intimidated when I rolled up. I caught her glancing back at her girls, and one made a quick movement with her hand—which I wasn't supposed to notice, but I did—encouraging her to come up to me. Her light brown eyes darted from side to side, making sure that no one was watching as she approached the Hummer. She looked slightly nervous, playing with the hem of her skirt as she walked up to the passenger side window, but forced a sweet smile when our eyes met.

She was fresh. Definitely hadn't been in the game that long. Perfect.

"Wassup?" she asked, her soft voice trying to sound all hard.

"Wassup with you?" I asked back.

Her eyes did the dart dance again, then settled back on me. "You looking for somethin'?"

"I'm looking to hang out." I replied. "You down?"

She was about to nod before her eyes narrowed in suspicion.

"You a chick?"

"Is that a problem?"

She hesitated for only a second, before shaking her head.

I unlocked the door and she quickly slid in, glancing back at her girls, who had already lost themselves in conversation. As soon as she closed the door, I pulled away from the curb, heading toward the highway.

"You a cop?" She asked. " 'Cuz if you are, you have to tell me."

I shook my head, suppressing the urge to laugh at her naïveté. "Nah. You?"

"No." She was still playing with the hem of her skirt.

"How much?"

"Uh. Two hundred."

I just nodded. "A'ight."

"What do you wanna do?"

"Just go relax at a motel and kick it." I said, reaching for the dial on my stereo, turning up the volume, 50 Cent's "Many Men" filling the air. I wasn't in the mood for chitchat. If I wanted chitchat, my ass would have been at the club trying to get into some chickenhead's panties, instead of picking up some trick on a corner.

She got the message and relaxed in the seat, settling for staring out the window as the city blurred by.

I lit a cigarette and tried to lose myself as I headed toward Montel's, a little motel I knew pretty well, that was cheap but clean. Whenever I wanted to just get away for a night or whatever, I'd head over there to clear my head. And tonight I definitely needed to clear my head. I wanted to forget about Lela and her trifling ass. I needed one night to just completely let go, and tomorrow I could go back home and clean house.

This was the first time I ever thought of paying for sex, but I knew that I needed to fuck, and I didn't want to deal with all the unnecessary bullshit that usually went along with it. Normally, if I just wanted a piece of ass, I would go to the club. But that meant having to deal with dancing, chicks wanting you to talk to them and buy them drinks, all so you could spend half the night trying to mack, and you couldn't even guarantee that you'd get laid. And plus, half the time, chicks couldn't understand the concept of a booty call. You fuck, have a good time, then that's it. I don't want to know about your family, how many babies you got, or how much you hate your job even if you have the decency to have one. I don't need to know anything about you except your first name, if you're clean, and if you've got skills with your body. I don't even want to exchange numbers unless you were so damn good I'd consider tapping that ass again. Most chicks ruin booty calls with all that frivolous shit.

I hadn't planned on taking this route, but I knew that a trick would do what she was paid to do. And tonight I just wanted to fuck, not care who was underneath me, and forget about the day-to-day bullshit.

We arrived at Montel's in under fifteen, and I quickly got us a room in the back so we could have privacy. As soon as I entered the room, I went to the bathroom to wash my face. When I came out, she was sitting on the edge of the bed, staring down at her feet.

I sat at the small table in the corner, pulling out my bag and pack of Backwoods to roll a blunt.

"You smoke?" I asked her.

She shrugged. "Sometimes."

I was breaking up the weed, my eyes finally taking her in. I already knew she was a dime from my quick survey from the truck. But under actual lighting I was getting a better look at her.

"Stand up." I said.

She slowly got to her feet facing me. She was light-skinned, reddish-brown hair, standing about five-six without her shoes. Her body was thick but toned with a sweet ass and big tits that I hoped were real. She had a baby face and pouty lips, with the longest lashes I've ever seen. She looked young, and I hoped she was at least eighteen 'cuz I didn't need any extra bullshit tonight. She was wearing a black miniskirt with a red halter top and black platform sandals. Her feet were cute, and I was impressed 'cuz I had an issue about jacked-up feet.

"Clothes off," I ordered.

She was quiet as she pulled off the halter top, tossing it on the floor, and her breasts spilled into view, thankfully hanging normally as real breasts should. Next came the skirt and a pair of red thongs, revealing that she was clean-shaven, something I do appreciate from time to time. She was about to take off the sandals, when I stopped her.

"Nah, leave them on." I was licking the finished blunt, taking my lighter out of my pocket. She was good, remaining quiet and still as I lit up. I took a few hits, just watching her, and I could feel my nipples tightening. She looked good. Real good.

"Come here," I said softly.

She walked toward me and I spread my legs just wide enough so she knew to stand between them. I offered her the blunt, and she took it, taking a couple of hits.

I took the opportunity to touch her breasts, and my clit literally jumped as my hands lifted them, feeling the delicious weight of them. Thank God they were real. And they felt good. She had thick nipples, which were hardening as I gently pinched them.

"What's your name?"

"My friends call me Mocha."

Even I had to smile at that one.

"What's yours?" she asked.

"Right now, I'm Daddy, and you're gonna be a good little whore and do whatever I say, is that understood?"

She trembled slightly and I wasn't sure if it was out of pleasure or fear. But she slowly nodded. I continued playing with her nipples as she smoked. When I thought she was chill, I took the blunt from her, and relaxed in the chair.

"Knees," I said.

Mocha's eyes met mine as she cautiously got down between my legs, and I could already feel myself getting wet. I held her gaze, as I held the blunt between my lips, my hands at my jeans, unbuckling my belt. She finally looked down, her eyes wide with surprise as she watched me unzip my jeans and pull out my dick. I held it firmly in my hand and bent it toward her.

Baby girl knew what to do. And it took every ounce of me not to let loose a gratifying moan as I watched her lower her head, lips parting to take me in. And even though her hands were slightly trembling, she swallowed half my dick with determination on the first try. She pulled back, and I watched her cheeks hollow as she sucked on the head, and it looked so damn fine.

I resumed smoking my blunt as I watched Mocha work my dick. And dammit if she wasn't treating it like it was the real thing. I let go of the base, and her hand replaced mine, holding my dick steady as she gave it a thorough tongue bath, giving me a wonderful view as her pink tongue licked every inch. My mind was flipping to Lela and how she thought this act was fucked up. I couldn't even count how many times I asked her to at least try, but she would just flip me off, telling me that if I had "man wannabe" issues, I could take them somewhere else.

Thanks for the suggestion, baby, I thought.

Mocha's lips had come into play again and she was giving the shaft gentle kisses as she licked. But I had had enough of this prissy shit. I let one hand move to her head, my fingers lacing through her hair until I got a good grip. I roughly pulled her head up until her lips were positioned over the head of my dick. She parted her lips in time as I pushed her head down, forcing it all the way until her mouth met the material of my boxers. I could hear her gagging slightly and her hands were tightly clenching my thighs, but I didn't care. I held her head still for a moment, leisurely smoking, just enjoying the look of my dick buried down her throat as she struggled.

When I was satisfied, I pulled her head up halfway, letting her get some well-deserved air for a few moments, then I pushed her head back down. I did this for a while, getting a good rhythm, my hips lifting from the chair to meet her sucking mouth. I soon let go of her hair, and like a good girl she kept the rhythm, bobbing her head up and down.

"That's it," I crooned, as I puffed. My eyes had lowered to half slits, in this mixed state of being relaxed and sexually worked up. My hips were still lifting to meet her mouth, and Mocha's hands held onto them, gripping me tightly as she literally fucked her own mouth on my dick. Good God, trick knew what she was doing. My hand found its way back to her head, and I pressed her head down on my dick again, my hips thrusting up to bury my dick as far down her throat as possible, and I felt my clit throbbing with a vengeance. Shit was feeling good, but I needed more.

I pulled her head off my dick, pushing her away. "On your back."

When she didn't react fast enough, I lifted my leg, planting my booted foot on her chest and forcing her to sit on the floor before me. I could tell she was unsure of what to do at first, and after a moment's hesitation she allowed my foot to guide her onto her back.

"Fuck yourself," I told her before taking another drag.

Her eyes widened in surprise, but her hand nervously found its way between her legs. Her movements were slightly awkward at first, like she had never masturbated for someone before. But she soon found a rhythm that she liked, because she let out a soft moan. I used my foot to kick her legs wider apart so I could get a better view of what she was doing, and she responded by opening them even wider and I was now looking down at an unblocked view of her pretty pussy. She was already wet, no doubt from sucking my dick, and I had to smile. Real dick or not, the bitch responded.

I continued to smoke, looking down at her. She had her eyes closed, probably trying to imagine I wasn't there as she played with herself. But I *was* here. And I was watching with interest as her fingers gently pulled on her hard clit. It was sweetly large, standing at attention, practically begging for her to toy with it more, and I had an ache to touch it myself. After a while, she became more comfortable, her hips now starting to move. Her free hand lifted to her breast and she was massaging it, softly pinching the nipple, and I had to bite my bottom lip to keep silent. I exhaled smoke as I leaned forward, resting my elbows on my knees to get a closer look at her.

"Get your nipples wet," I told her.

She obeyed quickly, her hand leaving her breast and sliding two fingers into that pouty mouth. Watching her suck her fingers was pure enjoyment and I flashed back to how good she looked sucking my dick. When she felt her fingers were wet enough, she brought them back down to her nipple, and after a few moments of teasing, it hardened even more in response. Her other hand moved, and I watched her lift her legs in the air, as her fingers slid further down to her hole. Blunt forgotten, I hungrily watched her enter herself, and she groaned loudly, her hips lifting to meet her hand. Once she was in, it was all over. I knew I was nowhere in her mind as she fucked herself, steadily thrusting two fingers into her greedy hole. She was panting heavily, her body writhing on the floor, and I could hear the wetness of her pussy as she forced another finger in. She gasped and literally purred, pinching her nipples even harder as she lost herself. She was definitely on fire, the tempting aroma of her pussy filling my nostrils, and surprisingly, I realized she was already close to coming. That fact was my deal breaker and I couldn't hold out anymore.

"Get up," I said as I put the blunt out in the ashtray.

Her eyes flew open and she looked a little dazed, but she quickly got to her feet. I decided to remain dressed and I reached in my pocket for a condom. As I opened it and slid it over my dick, I leaned back in the chair and got comfortable.

I caught the sly smile on her face as she moved toward me, ready to spread her legs to get on, but I held up my hand.

"Turn around."

Doubt flashed in her face, but she slowly turned around, and I was rewarded with a full view of her ass. I placed a hand on her hip to steady her as she straddled my legs. I watched her grab my dick, holding it upright as she slid down. I was strapped big tonight, and it took her a few tries to be able to take all of me in, but when she was finally sitting on my lap, my dick completely buried inside her, she moaned loudly in obvious appreciation. She rocked her hips a few times until she was comfortable, and I leaned further back, watching her start to bounce. I looked down, seeing her juices get the condom so wet that after a few minutes she was able to slide up and down with ease, and I knew I was ready.

When she lifted herself again, my hands found her hips holding her still before she could sink down.

"I wanna fuck your ass."

She tensed, "Now, wait a minute…."

"Am I paying you or not?" I asked her.

She didn't move for a few moments, and I knew she was wrestling with the idea in her head, and I had to wonder if she had ever done it before. She didn't answer me, instead silently rising, my dick popping out of her pussy, and I held it still with one hand.

"Spread your cheeks."

Her hands shook gently as she reached behind her, each hand grabbing a plump asscheek, spreading them apart so I could see her asshole. I bent my dick forward, aiming the head at her hole, and suddenly my mind flashed to Lela. I loved the girl, no doubt, and she was chill in bed, but she was always so fucking quiet and had way too many rules. She was one of those neat fucks, if you know what I mean. Hated to sweat, hated getting down and dirty during a fuck, which I loved to do. During sex, I loved to lose myself, but I couldn't be like that with her. Lela liked sex, she did, but damn...I could only do so much with her. Like this, for instance. She thought that anal sex was degrading to women, and even though I knew a lot of chicks didn't dig it, there were countless things I'd do for her in a heartbeat, but she wouldn't even try the shit once.

Whateva. I didn't have to worry about that shit right now. Right now, I had a bitch who was being paid to accommodate me, and I was definitely going to take advantage.

"Sit down," I told Mocha.

I heard her take a deep breath and she slowly lowered herself, whimpering as the head tried to enter. She was tight, her anal muscles refusing to give, and I had to get a good grip on her waist and push her down. She screamed, and dammit if it didn't sound good to hear it. I pushed her down until she was sitting firmly on my lap, and I held her still. Her entire body was shaking, and her whimpers had grown to loud whines as she tried to adjust. I ignored her, just watching my dick stretch that tight hole, and my clit was practically jumping, wishing it could feel her tightness around it.

I lifted her until only the head was in, then I pushed her back down, feeling the pressure against my clit, and as she cried out again, I groaned. I was urging her to move, but she wasn't reacting fast enough. So I dug my boots into the carpet and just starting lifting her up and down my dick. She reached underneath her, placing hands flat on my thighs for leverage, her body now tense.

"Oh god, oh god, oh god…" she kept saying over and over again. I had to admit, she was taking it well, but her fingers digging into my thighs told me of the pain she was in. And for a moment, I wondered if I should let up. But the stirring in my clit cleared away those thoughts and I forced her down on my dick again.

"How's that feel?" I taunted her. "How's it feel to have all of me in you, bitch?" Right now, she was doing what whores do best. She was a hole for me to fuck, a blank slate that I could pretend was anyone I wished. And right now she was Lela. It was Lela who was being practically skewered on my dick. I thought of every self-centered comment she ever made. Every time she held her hand out asking for money when she hardly did a damn thing around the apartment, as if looking fly was all she needed to do. Every time she turned me down for sex, but expected me to get her off whenever the mood struck her. Right now, she was doing exactly as I wanted her to do.

I reached around Mocha, grabbing both of her beasts and pulling her back, causing her to lose balance and her feet to leave the ground. She was now impaled on my dick. I was now completely in control of her and was fucking her harder and harder, trying to drive my dick as deep into her ass as possible, feeling the base of the dick slam into my clit. I pinched her nipples, twisting them, and she cried out again.

Her grunts were turning to soft pleadings, begging for me to come. Hearing the distress in her voice inflamed me, and I felt the familiar stirrings in my clit. I felt tremors starting to spread throughout my hips, up my back, down my legs, and as they traveled through my body I punctuated each delicious new feeling with a slam into her flailing frame. Mocha was trying to hold onto me, but I felt myself start to leave her as the stirrings expanded and grew and finally exploded. The traveling tremors ignited, setting my flesh on fire, and I let out a growl as I came, my body still moving, my dick still punching her.

When my body finally calmed down, I slapped her hip, urging her off my lap. She moved cautiously, her legs obviously shaking as she fell forward, collapsing on the bed. I got to my feet and went to the bathroom to toss the condom and clean up. When I reentered the room, I made my way to the table and reached for my smokes.

Mocha watched me from the bed, as I lit my cigarette, slipping my jacket on.

"Where are you going?" she asked as she sat up.

"I'm going home," I said, pulling some bills from my money clip. I handed her two-fifty. "That's for the night and for a taxi back to wherever you want to go. The room's paid for, so if you want to stay, you got until checkout at ten. You can smoke the rest of the blunt in the ashtray."

I took a drag, giving her a once-over, feeling my body stir again, remembering how good she felt on me. But I just gave her a wink before I left the room.

It was time to toss Lela out of the house.

Fairgrounds
Peggy Munson

"All's fair in love and whores," said Daddy Billy, spooning me after sex.

"Then all's fair at the fairgrounds tomorrow," I retorted, kissing him on the nose.

I had barely grown out of my colt legs—my wobbly girlish knees that always spread for Daddy Billy—when the carnival grew in spindly metal limbs into a buzzing drove that overtook the Mason County fairgrounds. Things had been rocky between us for a while, but this was the kind of flawless summer day that people nearly trample with enthusiasm. We acted like new lovers. Daddy Billy roused me early with kisses. "Freak Day's here!" he shrilled. He was already clothed. I'd started sleeping naked because Daddy liked to slip beneath the sheets at night. "I need my favorite midnight snack," he'd say, as he was waking me with gropes and sticking fingers into me.

At the carnival, the sun hung with its fake sticky orange of flypaper sap as we wove through kids with droopy snow-cones. I was horny and listless, as I always was when Daddy

Billy wasn't fucking me. But he was distracted by another yawning circumference—for once, not a lipsticked one. He lobbed Ping Pong balls at little fishbowls, trying to win a prize I didn't even want. He seemed unconcerned that my thighs might melt together in the heat; but his certain confidence, even against the sun, made me wet. I corkscrewed my hair, shifting on grass ironed flat by weeks of footfalls. "Be good so Daddy doesn't sell you to the carnival," he said, grinning big. If I wasn't going to ride him, I wanted to ride the rides. I had a pocket full of tickets and a jeweled sky asleep on cumulus, just waiting for my eager hands. I tried to pull away but Daddy Billy tugged my wrist. "This is not one of those postmodern Canadian sideshows," he warned. "With adorable, tumbling twins. The inbreeding here makes them ugly and mean. So stay close to Daddy and stay away from the octopus man."

For the past three weeks, the octopus man had been my nemesis. I was the sole rider who was screaming on the night of an electrical storm, when he wouldn't stop the ride and let me down. With a lizard hobble, and skin more inked than a letterpress, the octopus man was a surly sadist with an oiled machine. "His octopus is his flail," Daddy teased. And that night of the storm, he commanded the throttle and laughed as the lightning unzipped the sooty dark. He flailed me with my fear. He was not as nice as Daddy Billy was, though Daddy had been known to laugh when I screamed. Daddy had been known to do a lot of things.

Daddy Billy—also known as Reverend Billy, Outlaw Billy, and, on rare occasions, Billy Boi—had taught me how it felt to call a lover "Daddy," and then infused the word with sultry power. His naughty drills had turned me from a full-grown woman into an adolescent nymphomaniac. He taught me need that built like summer heat on asphalt. I wanted him explosively. While real girls at the fairgrounds showed their wifely 4-H projects—hand-sewn outfits and fruit pies—I only had a singular ambition: to be the docking station for his giant silicone cock. I sucked my straw to court attention. I rubbed up against him so he'd feel my gumdrop nipple pressing into his sleeve. I watched his last Ping Pong ball skip around the fishbowl rim and fall. "Harumph," he growled. I loved his Grant Wood–painted brow and every other part of him that hardened at the sight of me.

Daddy gravitated toward the Fun House, where not a single patron queued. The carnie gestured forward like a prison guard. He knew what Daddy was up to, and he didn't approve. Nonetheless, he ogled Daddy's hand cupped around my ass, and the ashy cap of his cigarette dribbled like cum. He saw that we were perverts playing games, and he didn't like that we were civilian freaks instead of rubes. Daddy steered my ass into the spooky dark, then seized my hand in the distorting mirror room. What the mirrors didn't distort, Daddy would pervert. "Today, we're on a date," said Daddy Billy. "But it's secret, because Daddies aren't supposed to date little girls. So let's pretend we're both teenagers. Do you know what teenagers do in the Fun House?"

"Do they tongue kiss?" I asked eagerly.

"They kiss, but in a different way." He grabbed me and pulled me to his body near the wavy mirror. His lips barely grazed my lips and then they pressed against me hard, flash-flooding my groin. The kiss was elasticized by the wobbly glass, and then grew wide and tall as Daddy pawed the soft white of my bra. He pinched my nipple, under my shirt, and said gruffly, "Your nipples make Daddy Billy grow long, like our faces in the mirror. Do you want to feel the way Daddy is growing long?" Daddy guided my hand to his jeans and let me feel the dick tunneling down his pantleg. I wanted to put the full length in my mouth. My lips took on its shape automatically, with robotic memory.

"No," chided Daddy. "You'll get that later." He shoved one hand under the waistband of my cutoffs and slid a coarse finger into me. "Mmm. Daddy likes it when you're dripping like a little slut," he said. He kept two fingers on my nipple and twisted it to see if I could hold my scream. "Good little pet," he said. We walked through the rolling barrel and traversed the shaking floor, then spilled into a labyrinthine configuration of mirrors, where Daddy lined me up in front of a replica of me.

"In the carnival," said Daddy-as-benevolent-dictator, "awful things go on. You need to learn to run if anyone tries to do such things to you, so I must demonstrate." He slid his hand down the front of my cutoffs. "See how you have a twin?" asked Daddy, gesturing to my image. "In the carnival, if girls have twins, they're made to fondle each other while dirty carnies watch. Did you know that, sweet girl?"

"No," I said. "But that is wrong."

"Of course. Of *course* it is," said Daddy sternly. "But let's pretend today that I'm your Daddy and you have a twin and we are carnies. Aren't you curious about your twin? Don't you wonder what it's like to have the perfect narcissistic fuck? She's just like you."

He forced my hand up to the mirror, to touch my reflection twin's breasts. He watched me stroke her cool, planed face. He kept one hand on his cock as I made a circle on her nipple, then slid my fingers down. My left hand burrowed past the silver button of my cutoffs and down into my drenched white panties. My twin gawked. Her eyes were scared rabbits fleeing a mad scientist's lab. I bent down to kiss and pin her there, a specimen of need.

Behind me, Daddy Billy rubbed against my ass. He wanted his cock inside me so bad. I felt the way that it was homing desperately, yet ramming up against the home sweet home of comfortable clothes. He flattened me against the mirror. I left a trace of lipstick and of steam. Daddy embossed me with cock from behind. His need was hurting me. I wanted so much to let him in. He put my arms up so my tits pancaked against the glass. He bit my neck and groaned and fought to push his cock through tiresome threads. But suddenly, we heard footsteps approaching. Daddy hitched his belt and pulled away. The twin retreated as we walked away from her. She backed away like she was running off to join the carnival.

The sun had morphed into a disapproving eye. My pussy ached for Daddy's cock, but we could not find any private shaded spots. Daddy stopped to buy me funnel cakes so I'd get powdered sugar on my hands and then he licked it off while passersby clucked meddling tongues. "I need it, Daddy, please," I whispered in his ear. He got distracted and stopped to try to cop some plush by throwing rings at a grid of Coke bottles. I saw the octopus man skulking by but the crowd was cheering wildly as Daddy got a ringer. "We've got a sharpie!" the carnie yelled, pulling down a giant blue bear with his shepherd's crook. Daddy told me I could put the bear between my legs at night when I was waiting up for him. He said the bear was wicked just like me and liked rubbing up against the Coke bottles while carnies slept. He asked if I would like to feel the Coke bottle inside his pants. I grinned and said, "Yes, Daddy, please." I loved it when he let me know my waiting time was up. He led me back behind the line of game booths where the narrow alley filled with aromatic funnel cake exhaust.

He eased the ragged edge of cutoffs to the side and rammed two fingers into me and made me smell the way my pussy was burnt sugar. Then he gave a furtive look around and opened up his belt buckle and asked me if I wanted to feel his Coke bottle, and I said yes. He took my hand and slid it between denim and his boxers. "I don't think that is a bottle," I said skeptically, but when I tried to pull away he grabbed my wrist.

"I think it is," he said. "If Daddy Billy says it is. Now if you put your fingers in a ring and rub them up and down the bottle, you might win another prize."

"You're trying to trick me like a dirty carnie," I said indignantly. "I know that it's your thing and not a bottle. I'm not some dumb white carnie trash." I hitched my tube top higher and I tightened up the knot that held my gingham shirt above my belly stud.

"Well," Daddy said, "close your eyes and put your fingers in a ring and I will show you that it is. Have you heard of soda jerks? You are the pretty girl your Daddy needs to jerk his soda." Daddy Billy took my hand and rubbed it up and down his thing. He had the special Japanese flex-dick on, the one that felt like skin. "Oh honey, you are such a good girl when you do that and you're going to get a *very* special prize," he groaned. I felt his fingers prying up the edge of my cutoffs. He moved my panties over quickly and he rammed the bottle into me. His hips were pushing me against a pole.

"Not here," I said, and tried to push him off, though inside I was squeezing, holding him, and oh, he felt so good. "You're lying. It's a trick."

"I have to fuck you, baby girl. You know you make my cock ache."

He wrapped his arm around the pole and pinned me there and snarled into my ear. "You're such a dirty girl," he said. "To wear these slutty cutoff jeans, so loose that anyone can find a way inside you. What's Daddy supposed to do but pop your cherry with his soda pop?" I closed my eyes and, just to humor him, pretended I believed he had a bottle, not a dick. He fucked me hard against the pole to make me feel the temper of the glass. I wondered what would happen if the bottle shattered in me and I had a bunch of fragments cutting me and liquid spilled inside me until my blood was carbonated. Behind my eyes, I saw a screen of bubbly blood, the little comic bubbles emptied of their words. What if Daddy's shards would never leave, and hurt me every time he pulled away because they wanted wholeness back? And what if I became a mirror maze inside so nobody could tell which me I was, and whether I was inside me or out? He seemed to want to shatter us.

Out of the corner of my eye, I saw a tapestry of moving clothes. Daddy had a way of making raunchy things look innocent, and though I worried, we did not get caught. "You feel so sweet," I whispered in his ear. He moved his cock so gracefully. I thought of standing really still and spreading out my legs so wide that nothing would shatter and there would be no bottlenecking in the throughways of my heart.

"That's right," said Daddy. "Spread your legs so wide for Daddy. Let me in."

I didn't tell him how I felt like glass each time I called him "Daddy." A luminous cocoon that's twirled around a pole into a fire until it takes the shape of something else, until its roundness grows and all of its blue beauty comes to light. I couldn't tell him what it was to be a Daddy's Girl, the way I burned in screaming fires to take the shape of what I had become.

But some distortion from the Fun House cast a spell on me. As good as Daddy felt to me, I was so hollow afterward, like something scraped out with a knife. Maybe the pulsing lights and sounds and sugar shock had made me yearn. I watched the roller coaster ratchet up a hill and thought, some day, the ride must end. It's Newton and the apple. Up goes down.

I realized that I was waiting for a ticket. Some way out. But I did not know why.

"Hey, you," the octopus man called out. I was half-tranced with afterglow. I had been watching people rock atop the Ferris wheel, and playing with green rattling beads around my wrist. He cupped a cigarette and slithered out of nowhere, leagues from where he should have been. "I have been trying to corner you all day," he said. I'd heard about the carnies who taught girls to barter blow jobs for a ride. I braced myself and licked my lips. Daddy had strolled off to find a Port-a-Potty and I couldn't see him in the crowd. "I know who you are," he said. "You rode the octopus that night when it was storming. Thursday, right?"

"You wouldn't let me down," I answered curtly.

"Sorry," he said, lighting up his smoke. "But I was high from cotton candy syrup. I was so high the moon was telling puns, and then the storm rolled in."

"I could have been electrocuted! All the other rides stopped long before you let me down." I crossed my arms around my belly, so he couldn't catch a glimpse of skin. I'd noticed that his eyes were drifting over me. One eye was edged with brine; the other one was clear. I licked my lips again, in case I had to lubricate a scream.

"I know, and that's why I have found you now. One time, when I was younger, I was struck by lightning and I died. That's why I thought I should apologize," he said. His whole face frowned into a toady droop.

"You died?" I asked. I wondered if I smelled to him like I'd been fucked. My hands were fragrant as a caramelizing pan. He had an octopuslike quality. His flesh looked pliable, like he could cram himself into a tiny space, or camouflage his freakishness to blend in with a school of sharks that might have otherwise devoured him.

"I died and was resuscitated. When I touch things now, I give a shock," he said. He grabbed my arm and jolted me. He also had a quality of suction. I felt drawn to him and couldn't pull away. "So, miss lone rider, tell me, is that person you are with a guy or a girl?" he asked.

"What do you think?" I said. I felt uneasy. Daddy Billy often passed as male. But secretly, he wore a sports bra cinching both his breasts, and underneath his dick he had an opening we never talked about. He hadn't taken T and had no plans of doing surgery. I loved his body's complex history.

"I think if that's your Daddy and he takes advantage of a little girl like you, perhaps you should run off and join the carnival." The octopus man blew smoke in little puffs. I coughed. Had he been eavesdropping? "I told you that I know you, who you are," he said and tapped his chest. "Aversion therapy will not cure a girl like you," he said, and touched my arm again so that I felt a shock. "You're quite the conduit. I saw the way you made your friend light up."

His old tobacco teeth were grinning in a yellow rind.

"You're one of us," he said. "You are a freak. So come tonight at midnight, when the carnival is closed. The carnies meet to ride the rides. Stop by the gate and bring your friend. We'll let you in." He sidled off and ducked behind a tent flap, winking with his wayward eye. "Come one, come all," he said and swept the air. "Before we strike the tents and watch the grand illusion fall." I saw that Daddy had his fists clenched as he ambled up.

"I told you not to talk to carnie folk," he said, and slapped me on the butt. "Don't make me put an apple in your mouth and have you crawl ass-first into the Future Farmers of America display. Remember, you are *Daddy's* little pig today." He kissed my cheek and led me off to play.

Daddy was right. I was a little pig who never had her fill of thrills. By that night, I felt as hollow as a whistle made of rotted trees. Maybe the tall, dismembered Ferris wheel began to get to me. When we approached, it was a giant piece of star anise but had no seats from which to kick the stars. The other lights were dimmed to dissuade townsfolk, so rides revolved with minimal illumination. Some carnies worked to strike the game booths down, but others twirled batons of fire, or gave a balding friend a cotton candy hairdo. Everything was shadowy, giving an eerie sense of dissolution. I'd changed into a frilly summer dress, and Daddy wore some pants that bulged out to signify he was a dude. I felt so sexy hanging on his arm. "Come on, you two," the octopus man yelled, and beckoned us with grinning warmth. "I'll stop you at the top and you can hang out there and watch the stars. There's nothing like it."

His girlfriend, Cherry, dangled on his arm. "Frank's right," she said. "Be brave—don't be an octopussy." Cherry stroked a tattoo of a tiny snake behind her ear. Her belly fat filled out the fabric of her dress to make foothills beneath her giant boobs. The octopus man—Frank, she'd said—clamped down the bar of our seat and pulled the throttle back. He watched us spin a bunch of times, then slowly stopped the ride so we were poised on top. The wind was rocking us and then it stopped.

The pod was weighted so we hung half upside down and couldn't look behind us, only up. We hung from spider silk; it felt that weightless. The sky was going to suck the blood right out of me. Then Daddy grabbed me with a clammy hand. I looked and saw the beads of sweat, the way his breath had changed to panic speed. Daddy was terrified. He didn't like to lose control. I pointed to the sky and told him Orion's belt was strapping us in place. "But your belt has to go," I said. "So that you can relax." He nodded gratefully.

I slid the leather from the clasp. I worked my mouth around his cock. "Oh, baby girl," he said, and grabbed my hair. I wanted him to feel that he was in a hammock of my care. Instead, he leaned back and he thought of barber's chairs and sexy women brushing tiny hairs away, or La-Z-Boys and daily blow jobs from a loyal wife. "I saw a shooting star just now," he said, as he continued thrusting in my mouth. "I filled my balls with shooting stars and now you're going to swallow them." I bobbed my head so that he'd know I understood. I took him deep into my throat. "Oh yes," he said. "Eat up the universe from me."

He fed me meteors. "You are the best," I said, and hugged him when his dick was done. I meant it. I was dazzled then.

The moon had turned into a magnifying glass, and it was burning out our insect eyes each time we wandered into light, so we sought shelter in the carnie tent. "It's time for dirty Truth or Dare," said Frank. "Are you two in the game?" At this point, we felt warm, embraced, and Daddy sat beside me with his palm on my knee.

"We're in," he said.

They made me drink enough to numb an elephant, and that's when things got raunchy. On a dare, Frank's girl began to do a sexy dance on me. She hiked her juicy gorgeous leg up on my shoulder. She took my hand and rubbed it up and down her wisp of underwear. Her pussy smelled like dandelion wine and winding wind that grabs at any cloying flower. I rubbed along her pussy lips with the beer bottle. I bent down and I blew a hollow sound into the bottle, then held it like a tuning fork against her clit. She made the oddest little dolphin chirps, then moaned. She looked at me and said, "Now you. Lie back, so I can test how breakable you are."

I looked at Daddy and I shrugged. I rested back against the folding chair and Cherry straddled me. She pried my legs apart and yanked my panties off. I loved how big and rough and soft she was. My folding chair began to tilt. That's when I accidentally backed into the velvet drape that sectioned off the tent, and saw the startled boi behind the velvet shield. The boi was sitting in a wheelchair and his biceps flexed when he rolled back the wheels reflexively. He had an octopus tattoo on his left arm. "J. Monarch Young!" she scolded him. "What are you doing there?" The boi looked sheepish and she shook her head. She said to me, "That's Young. He is the son of

Frank. He's paraplegic from a test ride fall. He is a naughty little voyeur too."

Young coughed and shyly said, "Hello."

"You ready for the bottle, dear?" she asked me gently. Young's eyes were tracing me. "To join the carnival, you swallow either fire or glass," she said.

"I swallow glass," I said, and grinned at her. I felt the coolness and the ridges of the bottle's mouth, and tried to open up my hole for her. I wasn't just performing so that Daddy could get off. I was performing for the boi. I knew his eyes were riveted on where he wished he'd put a message in a bottle just for me. As people hooted from the side, I glimpsed the boi's gray eyes. I saw the tension in his skull beneath his perfect crew cut and I wanted to find handholds of his bones. "I think you've had your christening," said Cherry, pulling out the glass. "You're shatterproof and bulletproof. I toast you with my eighty proof." She raised the whiskey bottle and she drank a slug. "As carnies used to say, 'You've got some snap in your garter, sweetheart.' "

Seeing the boi gave me a flutter in my belly, so I thought I'd better wander off to ride some rides alone. I half-hoped—fantasized—that Young would find me sectioned off from Daddy Billy but I doubted that he would. I closed my eyes and felt the Tilt-O-Whirl lift up my dress, and then I wandered further out to the periphery of human noise. The cornfields came right up to where the fairgrounds ended and I strolled up to the edge to stare at them. At night, they stood as still as antelope that know they're being watched. I loved how soft the grass got when it had been broken down. I felt a little dizzy so I lay on the tamped green. It was as soft as puppy fur and then I felt the infamous stealth wind that comes at such a tiny height and underscores the breathy and affected speech that's slung above. I was enjoying how the Great Plains wind felt tickling at my nipples when I heard their stomping feet. The two guys chortled devilishly. I lifted up my head. I saw the two of them, and Daddy said, "I've finally sold you to the carnival." He smirked.

"You've *what?*" I asked. I sat up and I brushed the dirt out of my hair.

"I've sold you to the dirty carnie folk," he said. His face was smug.

Frank gestured with his sucking arms. "I bought you from your Daddy for *one* night. To do it with my kid. We made a deal."

I'd promised Daddy, late some nights when he was fucking me, that I would always be his whore. He said these words a lot: *You're Daddy's slut, his whore, his prostitute, his fuck-hole, tricky little trick.* I loved it when he talked to me like that. One time, I dressed up and he dropped me off beside the river where the fags turned tricks. I waited on a bench in ripped-up stockings and a miniskirt and fetish shoes until he came and lured me into the car and gave me twenty bucks to suck his cock. It was so hot the way he forced it down my throat that day, as if he didn't care how much I gagged. We made a lot of promises and deals when we made love. We used a fake fiducial language but I never thought he'd pimp me out for *real.*

"Just one night," goaded Frank. His voice was pitchy, not quite on its tracks.

"How old's your kid?" I asked.

"The kid is nineteen, never had a girl. The kid's shy ever since the accident and not-so-certain gender situation."

He could not say it: *My kid's queer. He wants to make it with a little pervert girl like you.* Frank only had his suction, and he used it to derail me with his voice. "Please?" he begged. "The thing is, Young had picked you out this afternoon. He saw you overturning rubber ducks to win some shoddy trinket and—quite honestly—I never seen his eyes light up like that."

"I can't," I answered. "It's not right." I backed away but was fenced in.

So Daddy Billy turned to Frank and said, "I'll handle her," and herded me against the fence. He rubbed his bulge against my pubic bone. He made me quiver, gasp. He knew my weaknesses. He took his hand—which he had outfitted with one warm leather glove—and held my neck beneath my chin. He traced my jawbone with his thumb. "Won't you be Daddy's perfect whore?" he asked me sweetly. "Daddy was so nice and took you to the carnival." In truth, I thought that Young was beautiful but knew I'd better protest some, or Daddy would be jealous later. I knew that Daddy thought a brother in a wheelchair wouldn't be a threat. This knowledge made me realize the one thing that unnerved me about Daddy Billy: Daddy felt a power over everything he saw as weak, and I could not be sure I wasn't cast in the same caste.

I let my voice get soft, coquettish. "I guess so, Daddy, if it's what you want." I loved to please him anyway.

"Good girl," he said to me, then, "Sold!" he yelled to Frank. They put a blindfold on me and they made me walk in front of them. I had a vague awareness that the plank I walked was pivotal for me. I felt the warmth of light and heard the buzzing insects as we neared Young's tent. "I'll come back when you've sanded down the kid," I heard Frank say. The tent flapped shut behind me and I listened to Young's breathing, and his wheels creak as he came my way. He traced my knucklebones with fingertips. He pulled me toward his chair.

"Sit on my lap," he said. "Tell me what pity story they gave you so that you'd stay."

When I sat down on him, still blindfolded, I felt what he was packing in his pants. "How did you—?" I asked.

"Idle hands make idle minds, but nimble hands shape ideal packaging," he said. "They told you that I've never done it, right?"

"I find that hard to fathom."

"I've never done it, not the way I want." He wrapped his arms around me and he kissed my neck. "My life consists of dictatorial wheels and all I want to do is reinvent the wheel with this, my dick." I reached down and I put my hand around his bulge. I turned and started kissing him, his salty mouth. I ran my hands over his muscular arms. He slipped the blindfold off my eyes so I could see his grinning face. I touched his bristly crew cut. I stroked the bluish bands of his tattoo. He cupped my hair and pulled me to his lips and gave me an exquisite kiss. "I saw you at the carnival today," he said. "I knew you wanted to be watched." I stood up and walked around his chair.

"I did," I said. "I do." And then I started playing with his buttons and his belt loops, lifting up my leg and pulling back my dress so he could see the vacant place where underwear was ripped away. I touched my close-cropped pubes and stroked one finger on my pussy and then traced it where his barely-mustache grazed his upper lip.

"Smell me," I said. He inhaled deeply, then he grabbed for me. I pulled away and kneeled down so that he could see into the V of cleavage. I pulled his belt out of its latch and started undoing the buttons of his pants. And then I freed it—his enormous cock. "It's huge," I laughed. "Most people who are virgins don't go out and buy Paul Bunyan's dick."

"The carnival believes in grandiosity," he said. I licked the massive head and took his huge cock in my mouth. I swear I felt the ground drop down beneath me, like it did on the centrifugal force ride. I wanted his cock deep, to choke on it, to show the boi his cock was magical. He moaned a little bit. "Now will you ride me?" he asked, timidly. "Will you ride on my chair?"

"I'd love to ride you, Young."

I backed on top of him and slid my pussy down his cock.

The head went in, and then I let my weight down so his cock was unilaterally inclined to fuck. "Oh god," I said, "you feel amazing." He wrapped both his arms around me and began to kiss my earlobes and my hair. His fingers started pulling up my dress until he had it at my shoulders. He grabbed my boobs and held me by them so I squeezed against his chest. I rocked back on his cock. Then cleverly, he moved the wheelchair back and forth. "Just ride me, baby," said the boi. With one hand on the wheel, he rocked us in erratic jolts, so that the cock was fucking me—and he was fucking me—despite the fact that he could not move anything below his waist. His other hand was sliding down my soft bare skin and reaching for my clit. He licked his middle finger and he started circling my clit. "You take a lot of cock for such a little girl," he said. And then he fiddled with my clit until he made me come.

"Don't move," he said, as I was gasping from how sweet his fingers felt. He pulled my dress back down. He took his coat and placed it on my lap. "I'm going to wheel you through the carnival while I am still inside you. I've always wanted to do that."

His cock was threading me onto its shaft. His wheelchair did a loop around the grounds. The rides were whirling round. The carnies waved at us, and, when I said hello to them, teased, "Are you a ventriloquist now, Young?" They didn't know that he was fucking me right then, and acted like I was a wooden dummy and he was a star. I ground my pussy down on him and looked back so that I could see his grinning face. He took me to the edge of things, where rides had already been disassembled. The fantasy was breaking down, and Young was suddenly symbolic of my blooming need for change. I wanted something sweet and virginal. I put a blanket down and scooped him from his chair. For hours, we cuddled and we lay inside a circle of the flattened grass, as if the axles of a carousel had broken and we had fallen under the hooves of a wooden horse stampede. I'd been undone by him.

"You look so sacrificial in those savaged clothes," J. Monarch Young exclaimed. "What will you do when all these mechanical illusions drive away?"

"I will go home to Daddy and my real life. Why do you ask?" I touched his face.

"Because my cock wants more of you. I think you want it too."

For just a moment, I felt something rising from the beaten fairgrounds, a construction not of steel or fantasy but heart. Young braided grass into a ring. I broke off little sticks and made a tiny raft. "Look at the waist-high fields out there," Young said. "I always thought their layout looked like squares on calendars. And yet, you shouldn't have to feel boxed in."

"What if I do?" I asked. "The Fun House has to end."

"Well, sure, but think of the alternatives. Perhaps you need a carnival that doesn't end, with a defector from a land of freaks," he said, and looked at me so earnestly. "I'll stay and be your Tilt-O-Whirl. I'll give you tickets. You can ride on me all day."

The crickets turned their legs into string instruments just then. Something so usual seemed capable of reinvention. I realized why people ran away to join the carnival, and then ran back again: to make the axis turn. "All's fair in love and fairground whores," I said, and took Young's hand and led it to my ragged hem and slid it in.

About the Authors

D. ALEXANDRIA, a Gemini child and a Jamaican descendant, hails from Boston. A self-proclaimed "Boughetto Princess," she will be the constant thorn in the right wing's "perfect world." A regular contributor to Kuma2.net (pseudonym *Glitter*) and *Queer Ramblings*, she is working on her first novel and a collection of black lesbian erotica.

TARA ALTON's erotica has appeared in *The Mammoth Book of Best New Erotica, Best Women's Erotica, Guilty Pleasures*, Cleansheets.com, and Scarletletters.com. She lives in the Midwest and writes erotica because that is what's in her head and it needs to come out. Check out her website at www.taraalton.com.

CHERYL B. is a writer who has performed her work throughout the United States and internationally. Her writing has appeared in numerous anthologies, literary journals, and magazines. She has received fellowships from the New York Foundation for the Arts and the Virginia Center for the

Creative Arts. A native New Yorker, she lives in Brooklyn and online at www.cherylb.com.

S. BEAR BERGMAN is a theater artist, writer, book reviewer, and pornographer; touring hir award-winning show *Ex Post Papa* around the country to colleges, universities, and theater festivals, including the National Gay and Lesbian Theater Festival and the National Transgender Theater Festival. Ze has been heard and published in a variety of places, lives on the web at www.sbearbergman.com, and makes a home in Northampton, Massachusetts, where ze is the very lucky hus-bear of a magnificent femme.

BARRETT BONDON has two surprisingly well-behaved cats and a beautiful girlfriend. She is working on novels that will be ready for publication as soon as a compelling deadline can be found. Though she is inordinately proud of growing award-winning vegetables (don't get her started on the cut-throat competition in the "cabbage" class), her actual goal is to write lesbian fiction that someone like William Wyler could have directed for the big screen.

RACHEL KRAMER BUSSEL (www.rachelkramerbussel.com) serves as senior editor at *Penthouse Variations*. Her books include *The Lesbian Sex Book*, *Up All Night: Adventures in Lesbian Sex*, *Glamour Girls: Femme/Femme Erotica*, *Naughty Spanking Stories from A to Z*, and *A Spanking Good Time*. Her writing has been published in more than forty anthologies, including *Best American Erotica 2004* and *Best Lesbian Erotica 2001* and *2004,* as well as *AVN, Bust,* Cleansheets.com, *Curve, Diva, Girlfriends, On Our Backs,* Oxygen.com, and *The Village Voice.*

L. SHANE CONNER is a thirty-year-old lesbian living in the heartland. She followed her lover of over three years to Cleveland just a few short months ago. She's never had any fiction published unless you count her high school literary magazine, but, after a late-night drunken discussion with several of the better influences in her life, she decided to try writing erotica. After several attempts, she selected their favorite story and, for the time being, hers.

SHANNON CUMMINGS was almost kicked out of her mid-western elementary school for chronic masturbation. Since then, she has been writing and performing as an alternative to keeping her hands in her pants. Despite her name, she now passes as a shy, prudish dyke in the San Francisco Bay area.

ANDREA DALE lives in Southern California within scent of the ocean. Her stories have appeared in *Dyke the Halls*, *Sacred Exchange*, and *Erotic History*. Under the name Sophie Mouette she and a lover have cowritten stories for *Best Women's Erotica*, *Erotic Women*, and *Erotic Mythology*. In other incarnations, she is a published writer of fantasy and romance.

SCARLETT FRENCH feels very lucky. Originally from beautiful Aotearoa, New Zealand, she has chosen to settle in London for now, where she works a job she actually likes, lives with her partner and an irascible marmalade cat, and indulges her love of increasingly ridiculous shoes. She has written poetry for seventeen years, but recently discovered the joy of writing erotica. She is a rabid feminist, social theorist, and chocolate connoisseur.

R. GAY is a trash talker in her own right. Her writing can be found in *Best Lesbian Erotica 2002* and *2003*, *Best American Erotica 2004*, *The Mammoth Book of New Erotica* volumes 3 and 4, and many others. She is also in love with her best friend, only with a happier ending.

ZANE JACKSON is a queer, genderfluid switch who loves female-bodied boys and the cyberskin dicks that come with them. A gender dissident, a survivor of queer domestic abuse, and an outspoken activist for genderqueer visibility, Z writes about people who live, love, and fuck outside the gender mainstream. Z lives with his big boy partner in Lesbianville, USA.

TERESA LAMAI lives in the Pacific Northwest, where she finds inspiration in the area's vibrant artistic communities. She started writing fiction a year ago, and it's swiftly become a full-blown obsession. In her other life, she's worked in refugee advocacy throughout North America and abroad. Her work can be found in *Best Women's Erotica 2005* and online at both Cleansheets.com and the Erotica Readers and Writers Association website.

CATHERINE LUNDOFF lives in Minneapolis with her terrific girlfriend and tests software when not writing or teaching. Her writings have appeared in a number of anthologies, including *The Mammoth Book of Best New Erotica*, *The Big Book of Hot Women's Erotica 2004*, *Erotic Travel Tales II*, *Shameless*, *Below the Belt*, *Zaftig*, *Best Lesbian Erotica 1999* and *2001*, *Electric*, and *Electric 2*.

ERIC(A) MARONEY writes poetry, fiction, and erotica. S/he has studied erotic fiction at New York University with Jamie Callan and in Cambridge, Massachusetts, with Amie Evans. S/he is an undergraduate in the Southern Connecticut State

University Honors College and spends much of her time screwing with the binary gender system and being pissed off about the corruption in the U.S. government. This is her first published story.

SKIAN MCGUIRE is a working-class Quaker leatherdyke who lives in the wilds of western Massachusetts with her dog pack, a collection of motorcycles, and her partner of twenty-two years. Her work has appeared in *On Our Backs, Best Bisexual Erotica 2, Best Lesbian Erotica, HLFQ,* and a variety of webzines, not to mention the *On Our Backs* anthology and *The Big Book of Erotic Ghost Stories.*

ANDREA MILLER hails from Canada's East Coast, but at the moment she is teaching English at a university in Mexico. Her smut has appeared in *Hot and Bothered 4, Best Lesbian Erotica 2004, Best Women's Erotica 2005, Working Hard,* and *Velvet Heat.* When not thinking about sex, she likes to cook and practice yoga.

ELAINE MILLER is a Vancouver leatherdyke who spends her time playing, learning, educating, performing, and writing. Her work has appeared in *Skin Deep II, Brazen Femme, Best Lesbian Erotica 1998* and *2001, Best of Best Lesbian Erotica, On Our Backs, Paramour, Anything That Moves, The No SafeWord Anthology,* and quite a few tawdry porn sites. She has a regular column in both the *Xtra West* newspaper and *Desire,* a new Canadian lesbian magazine.

PEGGY MUNSON has published in every edition of *Best Lesbian Erotica* since 1998, as well as *Best of Best Lesbian Erotica.* Her work can also be found in *Best American Poetry 2003, Lodestar Quarterly, Blithe House Quarterly, On Our Backs, Genderqueer, Best Bisexual Erotica 2, Tough*

Girls, Sinister Wisdom, Margin: Exploring Modern Magical Realism, and other collections. Visit www.peggymunson.com for news on her latest publications and projects.

MADELEINE OH is a transplanted Brit, retired teacher, and grandmother now living in Ohio with her husband of thirty-four years. She has published erotic short fiction, novels, and novellas in the United States, United Kingdom, and Australia. Visit her website at www.madeleineoh.com.

JACK PERILOUS is a New York–based journalist whose work has appeared in *Best Lesbian Erotica 2003, Glamour Girls: Femme/Femme Erotica, The Time Out New York Guide to Bars and Clubs,* and *The Rough Guide to New York City,* among other titles. She writes for the gay and lesbian press, and contributes regularly to *The Village Voice, Girlfriends, Curve, Lambda Book Report, On Our Backs, POZ,* and *Heeb.* Her otherwise evil grandma, whom she suspects strongly of lesbianism and perhaps incest, gave her the rocking horse, and her kind parents knocked first.

RENEE RIVERA is a member of the San Francisco–based group Dirty Ink, a collective of dyke writers who come together around their passion for language, voice, and sex. She has read in the National Queer Arts Festival and has been heard on *Outright Radio,* a syndicated PRI show on queer life.

JEAN ROBERTA teaches English at a university in the Canadian heartland, sings alto in the local queer choir, and writes in several genres. Her erotic stories have appeared in several editions of *Best Lesbian Erotica* (2000, 2001, 2004) and *Best Women's Erotica* (2000, 2003, 2005), as well as numerous other places. Her reviews and opinion pieces appear regularly on several websites, including her column "In My Jeans" on Bluefood.cc. She looks younger than her years, but does not survive on the blood of virgins.

RAKELLE VALENCIA loses control when smelling fine leather and feeling supple hide. Though riding and roping call to her, she has written short stories for *Best Lesbian Erotica 2004*, *Ride 'Em Cowboy*, *On Our Backs*, and Sextoytales.com. With Sacchi Green, she will coedit the anthology *Rode Hard, Put Away Wet: Lesbian Cowboy Erotica*, to be published by Suspect Thoughts Press in 2005.

KYLE WALKER's work has appeared in *Best Lesbian Erotica 2003* and *2004*, as well as *A Woman's Touch* and *Friction 7*. "Boiling Point," like her previous appearances in *Best Lesbian Erotica*, is a chapter from a novel in progress, *What People Want*.

KRISTINA WRIGHT lives in Virginia with her husband, Jay, and a menagerie of pets. She is published in a variety of genres, and her erotic fiction has appeared in numerous anthologies, including *Best Women's Erotica*, *Best Lesbian Erotica 2002* and *2004*, *Ripe Fruit: Well-Seasoned Erotica*, and *Bedroom Eyes: Tales of Lesbians in the Boudoir*, as well as online at Goodvibes.com and Scarletletters.com. Visit her website (www.kristinawright.com) for more about her and her writing.

About the Editors

TRISTAN TAORMINO is the award-winning author of three books: *True Lust: Adventures in Sex, Porn and Perversion; Down and Dirty Sex Secrets;* and *The Ultimate Guide to Anal Sex for Women.* She is director, producer and star of two videos based on her book, *Tristan Taormino's Ultimate Guide to Anal Sex for Women 1* & *2,* which are distributed by Evil Angel Video. She is a columnist for *The Village Voice* and *Taboo Magazine.* She has been featured in over three-hundred publications including the *New York Times, Redbook, Glamour, Cosmopolitan, Playboy, Penthouse, Entertainment Weekly, Vibe,* and *Men's Health.* She has appeared on CNN, *The Ricki Lake Show,* NBC's *The Other Half,* MTV, HBO's *Real Sex, The Howard Stern Show,* The Discovery Channel, Oxygen, and *Loveline.* She teaches sexuality workshops around the country and her official website is www.puckerup.com.

FELICE NEWMAN is the author of *The Whole Lesbian Sex Book: A Passionate Guide for All of Us* (Cleis Press). She is the resident sex expert on ClassicDykes.com. As publisher of Cleis Press since 1980, she has developed and edited books on sexuality and gender by Annie Sprinkle, Joan Nestle, Violet Blue, Patrick Califia, Carol Queen, Loren Cameron, and Tristan Taormino. A writer and sex educator, she lives in the San Francisco Bay area.